DEBBIE MACOMBER

A Second Glance

Debbie Macomber
2 Tim 1:7

mira

mira™

Recycling programs for this product may not exist in your area.

ISBN-13: 978-0-7783-0942-0

A Second Glance

Copyright © 2020 by Harlequin Books S.A.

Shadow Chasing
First published in 1986. This edition published in 2020.
Copyright © 1986 by Debbie Macomber

Yesterday Once More
First published in 1986. This edition published in 2020.
Copyright © 1986 by Debbie Macomber

This edition published by arrangement with Harlequin Books S.A.

For questions and comments about the quality of this book, please contact us at CustomerService@Harlequin.com.

Mira
22 Adelaide St. West, 40th Floor
Toronto, Ontario M5H 4E3, Canada
www.Harlequin.com

Printed in U.S.A.

Also available from Debbie Macomber and MIRA

CONTENTS

SHADOW CHASING

One

"You're kidding." Carla Walker glanced at her friend suspiciously. "What did they put in that margarita, anyway? Sodium pentothal?"

Nancy Listten's dark eyes brightened, but her attention didn't waver from the mariachi band that played softly in the background.

"I'm serious," Nancy replied. "This happens every vacation. We now have seven glorious days in Mazatlán. What do you want to bet that we don't find a man to flirt with until day six?"

"That's because it takes awhile to scout out who's available," Carla argued, taking a sip of her drink. The granules of salt from the edge of the glass felt gritty on the inside of her bottom lip. But she enjoyed the feel and the taste.

"Exactly my point."

Nancy took off her glasses and placed them inside her purse. That action said a lot. Her friend meant every word. She was dead serious.

"We spend at least two days trying to figure out who's married and who isn't."

"Your idea isn't going to help," Carla insisted. "The next two men who walk in here could be married."

"But imagine how much time it'll save if we *ask*. And"—Nancy inhaled a deep breath—"have you noticed how picky we are? We always act like our choices are going to improve if given enough time. We've simply got to realize that there're no better candidates than whoever walks through that door tonight."

"I don't know…" Carla hesitated, wondering if there was something wrong with her drink, too. Nancy's idea was beginning to make sense. "What if they speak Spanish?" That was a stupid question, and the look Nancy gave her said as much. They each had a phrase book, and Carla had watched enough *Sesame Street* when baby-sitting her nieces to pick up the basics of the language. She groaned inwardly. She'd begun this vacation with such high hopes. Seven glorious days in one of the most popular vacation spots in the world. Men galore. Tanned, gorgeous men. And she was going to end up introducing herself in *Sesame Street* Spanish to the next guy who walked through the door. Even worse, the idea was growing more appealing by the minute. Nancy was right. For two years they'd ruined their vacations looking for Mr. Perfect. Not only hadn't they ever found him, but as their time had grown shorter, their standards had lowered. The men they'd found marginal on day one looked like rare finds by day six. And on day seven, frustrated and discouraged, they'd flown back to Seattle, having wasted their entire vacation.

"I think we should establish some sort of criteria, don't you?"

Carla nodded. "Unencumbered."

"That goes without saying." Nancy gave her a classroom glare that Carla had seen often enough to recognize. "They should walk in here alone. And be under thirty-five." Nancy's eyes sought Carla. "Anything else?"

"I, for one, happen to be a little more particular than you."

"All right, add what you want."

"I think they should order a margarita."

"Carla! We could be here all night if we did that."

"We're in Mazatlán; everyone orders margaritas," Carla countered. Well, a tourist would and that was what she wanted. No serious stuff, just a nice holiday romance.

"Okay," Nancy agreed.

Their eyes focused on the two entrances. Waiting.

"Have you noticed how all the cocktail lounges are beginning to look like furniture showrooms?" Carla commented, just to have something to say. Her hands felt damp as she stuidied the entry to the nightclub.

"Shh…someone's coming."

A middle-aged couple walked through the door.

They both relaxed. "We'd better decide who goes first."

"You," Carla returned instantly. "It was your idea."

"All right," she agreed, and straightened, nervously folding her hands on her lap.

Carla pulled up the spaghetti strap of her summer dress. Normally, a redhead couldn't wear pink, but this shade, the color of camellias, complemented the unusual color of her hair.

"Here comes a single man."

Two pairs of intense eyes followed the lumbering gait of a dark-haired Latin-American who entered the lounge and took the closest available love seat.

"He's in a cast," Nancy observed in a high-pitched whisper.

"Don't panic," Carla said in a reassuring tone. "He doesn't look like the type to order a margarita."

Nancy opened her purse and put on her glasses. "Not bad-looking, though."

"Yes, I suppose so," Carla agreed, although she thought he looked too much like a movie star, smooth and suave to suit her. His toothy smile looked bright enough to blind someone in broad daylight. For Nancy's sake, she hoped the guy was into wine. "You can back out if you want," Carla said, almost wishing Nancy would. The whole idea was crazy.

"Not on your life."

"The guy's in a cast up to his hip. I'd say he was encumbered, wouldn't you?"

"No," Nancy replied smoothly. "You're doing it again."

"Doing what?"

"You know."

"All right, I'll shut up. If you want to be stuck with a guy who leaves a funny trail in the sand, that's fine with me."

"Look," Nancy whispered, "your fellow's arrived."

Quickly, Carla's attention focused on the lounge entrance at the other side of the room. She recognized him immediately as someone from the same flight as theirs. Not that she'd found him particularly interesting at the time. He'd sat across the aisle from Nancy and read a book during the entire trip.

"Hey, he was on the plane with us," Nancy pointed out.

"I know," Carla answered evenly, trying to disguise her disappointment. Secretly, she'd been hoping for someone compelling and forcefully masculine. She should have known better.

Both girls sat in rigid silence as their eyes followed the

young cocktail waitress, who delivered two margaritas, one to looker, and one to the bookworm.

"You ready?" Nancy whispered.

"What are we going to say?" Carla's hand tightened around her purse.

Nancy gave another of those glares normally reserved for her pupils. "Good grief, Carla, we're mature women. We know what to say."

Carla shook her head. "Mature women wouldn't do something like this."

They stood together, condemned prisoners marching to the hangman's noose. "How do I look?" Nancy asked with a weak smile.

"Like you're about to throw up."

Her friend briefly closed her eyes. "That's the way I feel."

Carla hesitated.

"Come on," Nancy hissed. "We aren't backing out now."

Carla couldn't believe that calm, level-headed, left-brained Nancy would actually suggest something like this. It was completely out of character. Carla was the impulsive one—creative, imaginative, right-brained. That was why they were such good friends: their personalities comple-mented each other perfectly. Right-brained, left-brained, Carla mused. That was the problem. Each of them had only half a brain.

She studied the man from the plane. He wasn't anyone she would normally have sought out. For a light romance, she wanted someone more dynamic. This guy was decidedly—she searched for the right word—undashing. He was tall, she remembered, which was lucky. At five nine she didn't look up to many men. And he was on the lanky side. Almost reedy. He wore horn-rimmed glasses, which gave him a serious look. His sandy hair, parted on the side, fell carelessly across his wide brow. His tan was rich, but Carla mused that he didn't look like the type to use a tanning machine or lie lazily in the sun. He probably worked outdoors—maybe he was a mailman.

He glanced at her and smiled. Carla nearly tripped on the plush carpet. His eyes were fantastic. A deep gray like the overcast winter clouds with the sun beaming through. A brilliant silver shade that she had never seen. Her spirits brightened; the man's eyes, at least, were encouragingly attractive.

"Hello," she said as she stood in front of his deep cushioned chair. "I'm Carla Walker." She extended her hand. Might as well be forthright about this.

He stood, dwarfing her by a good four inches, and shook hands. "Philip Garrison."

He looked like a Philip. "We were on the same flight, weren't we?"

He pushed his glasses up the bridge of his nose with his index finger. The action reminded her of Clark Kent. But Carla wasn't kidding herself—Philip Garrison was no Superman.

"I believe we were," he said with a smile that was surprisingly compelling. "Would you like to sit down?"

"Yes, thank you." Carla took the chair beside him. Hoping to give an impression of nonchalance, she crossed her shapely legs. "Are you from Seattle?"

"Spokane."

"On vacation?"

His smile deepened. "In a way. My parents have a condominium here that needs a few repairs."

Carla smiled absently into her drink. So he was a carpenter. The occupation suited him, she decided. He was deceptively lean and muscular. And he had a subtle, understated appeal, something she found refreshing.

"Would you like another margarita?" he asked as he glanced at her empty glass.

"Yes. Thank you."

He raised his hand to get the waitress's attention. The lovely olive-skinned girl acknowledged his gesture and indicated that she would be there in a moment. Service here was notoriously slow, but right now Carla didn't mind. She looked around for Nancy and discovered that her friend was chatting easily and seemed to be enjoying herself. At the moment, this crazy scheme appeared to be working beautifully.

"Is this your first visit to Mazatlán?" Philip asked, and took a sip of his drink.

Carla noted the way the tip of his tongue eased the salt from the bottom of his lip. She dropped her gaze, finding his action disturbingly provocative. "Yes, my first time in Mexico, actually. To be honest, I didn't expect it to be this beautiful."

The waitress arrived, and Carla handed the girl her empty glass. She had noticed that the waitresses spoke only minimal English. Although her Spanish wasn't terrific, the urge to impress Philip with her knowledge of the language overpowered her good sense, so, proudly, without the hint of a foreign accent, Carla asked for another drink.

The waitress frowned and glanced at Philip, who was obviously trying to contain his laughter. He delivered a crisp request to the girl in Spanish, who nodded and smiled before turning away.

"What's so humorous?" Carla could feel herself blushing.

Philip composed himself quickly. "You just told the waitress that Big Bird wants a drink of water."

Carla closed her eyes and did her best to laugh, but the sound was weak and revealing. She would never watch *Sesame Street* again, she vowed, no matter how desperate she was to entertain her two nieces.

"How long will you be staying?" he asked pleasantly, deftly changing the subject.

"A week. My roommate, Nancy, and I are on a discount vacation package for teachers."

"You teach preschool?"

It was a logical assumption. "No, I'm a surgical assistant."

One thick brow arched with surprise. "You don't look much older than a student yourself."

"I'm twenty-five." And old enough to know better than to make a fool of myself like this, she added silently.

Their drinks arrived, and Carla restrained the urge to gulp hers down and ease the parched feeling in her throat. Gradually she relaxed as they spoke about the flight and the weather.

After a half hour of exchanging pleasantries, Philip asked her if she was available to join him for dinner. The invitation pleased her. Since her faux pas with the waitress, she'd imagined he'd wanted to be rid of her as quickly as he could manage to do so without appearing impolite.

"Yes, I'd like to have dinner with you." To her surprise, Carla discovered it was the truth.

He took her to a restaurant named El Marinero. The view of the harbor was excellent, as was the shrimp dinner. Philip spoke to the waiter in Spanish, then quietly translated for Carla. It was a thoughtful gesture. She would have felt excluded otherwise. Not once did he try to overwhelm her with his wit and charm. He was who he was, quiet and a little reserved, and apparently he saw no need to change because he'd been approached by her.

"I can't believe I ate that much," Carla groaned as they left the restaurant. The air was still sultry but much cooler than when they'd arrived.

"Would you like to walk along the beach? It'll be less crowded outside the hotel."

"I'd love to." Her blue eyes looked fondly into his. "But can we? I mean, it's all privately owned, isn't it?"

"Not in Mexico. The beaches are for everyone."

"How nice," Carla murmured, thinking she was beginning to like Philip more with every passing minute.

They rode back to the hotel in an open-air vehicle that resembled a golf cart—a hot-rod golf cart. The driver weaved his way in and out of lanes with complete disregard for pedestrians and traffic signals.

Philip took her by the hand and led her through the lobby, around the huge swimming pool in back of the hotel and to the stairs that descended to the beach. The strip of white sand stretched as far as the eye could see. So did the array of hotels.

"I don't suppose you've been in the ocean yet."

"No time," Carla confessed. "The first thing Nancy and I did was take a shower." The heat that had greeted them on their arrival had been suffocating. They'd stepped from the air-conditioned plane into one-hundred-degree weather. By the time they'd arrived at the hotel room, their clothes had been damp from the humidity and clinging. "I couldn't believe that death trap of a shuttle bus actually made it all the way to the hotel."

Philip grinned in amusement. "I think the same thing every time I visit."

"Do you come often?" Carla asked as they sat in the

sand and removed their shoes. Philip rolled up the tan pant legs to his knees.

"Once or twice a year."

He stood and tucked her hand into the crook of his arm.

"I think there's something I should tell you," Carla said as an ocean wave gently lapped up to her bare feet. The warm water was another surprise.

"You mean that you don't usually pick up men in bars," Philip said with a chuckle. "I already knew that."

"You did?" Carla was astonished.

"What made you do it this time?"

Carla kicked idly at the sand with her big toe. "You aren't going to like hearing this," she mumbled.

"Try me."

She took a deep breath, then exhaled slowly. "It happens every vacation. Nancy and I spend the entire time waiting to meet someone. This time we decided that instead of wasting our vacation, we'd take the initiative ourself. To make the decision easy we decided we could find someone on the first day. One problem is that we're too picky so we decided to be a bit more spontaneous. You came in alone. You're under thirty-five, and you ordered a margarita."

The pleasant sound of his laughter blended with a crashing wave that pounded the beach. "I almost asked for a beer."

"I'm glad you didn't." The words were automatic and sincere. It surprised Carla how much she meant them.

The sun became a huge red ball that slowly descended to meet a blue horizon. Carla couldn't remember ever seeing anything more spectacular. She glanced at Philip to see if he was also enjoying the beauty of their surroundings. He wasn't the chatty sort, she realized, which was fine—

she could do enough talking for them both. His laugh was free and easy, and the sound of it warmed her.

"What were you reading so intently on the plane?" Carla asked, curious to know more about him.

"The latest book by Ann Rule, she's—"

"I know who she is," Carla interrupted. The talented Seattle author was a policewoman turned reporter turned writer. Ann's books specialized in true crime cases. Her novel on serial murderer Ted Bundy was a national best-seller. "My father worked with Ann before she took up writing," Carla explained. "She's from Seattle."

"I read that on the cover flap. What does your father do?"

Carla swallowed uncomfortably. "He's a cop," she murmured, not looking at Philip.

"You sound like it bothers you."

"It does," Carla replied vigorously. "Half the boys in high school wouldn't ask me out. They were afraid I'd tell my father if they tried anything, and then he'd go after them."

"Your father would arrest them for making a pass?" Philip sounded incredulous.

"Not that." She tossed him a defiant look. It was obvious that Philip, like everyone else in her life, didn't understand. "It's too hard to explain."

"Try me."

Carla felt a tightening in her stomach. Although she'd held these feelings deep inside since childhood, she had never verbalized them. She wasn't sure she was capable of expressing them now. "A good example of what I'm saying happened when I was about ten. Our family went to a friend's wedding reception. Everyone had been drinking, and an uncle had given some of the teens spiked punch.

The minute Dad walked in the room the temperature dropped fifteen degrees."

"Were they afraid he was going to make a scene?"

"I don't know. But I do recall how uncomfortable everyone was."

"Including you?"

She hesitated. "Yes."

"But that's not all, is it?" he asked gently.

"No," she admitted. "It was far more than that. I can count on one hand the number of Christmases Dad spent home. It was the same thing every holiday. And we were lucky if he was there for our birthdays. It got so that I'd dread it every time the phone rang, because I knew he was always on call. It was his job."

"I don't blame you for resenting that."

Once started, Carla discovered she couldn't stop. "He worked with the scum of the earth: pimps, prostitutes, muggers, murderers, drunks and derelicts. Then there were the sick people, dying people, dead people, wife beaters and child abusers. Sometimes he'd come home at night and…" She stopped, realizing that everything had come out in one huge rush. When she'd caught her breath, Carla continued. "I'm sorry, I didn't mean to unload on you like this."

"You didn't," Philip said, and casually draped his hand over her shoulder. "You've never told your father any of this, have you?"

"No. What was the use? Dad loves his work." Philip's hand cupped her shoulder. He was comforting her, and in a strange way Carla appreciated it. Never before had she voiced these thoughts, and the fierce intensity of her feelings had surprised her.

By unspoken agreement, they turned back toward the

hotel. The sky had grown dark now, and the lights from the long row of hotels dimly lit the beach. Other couples were walking along the sandy shores. A few flirted with the cresting ocean waves.

"Philip." Carla stopped and turned toward him. "Thank you," she whispered.

"What for?"

Their eyes met in the moonlight, and Carla was trapped in the silvery glow of his gaze. Those beautiful, warm gray eyes held her as effectively as the arms that had slipped around her waist and brought her into his embrace.

"I may never drink anything but margaritas again." His whisper was husky, but he didn't make a move to do anything more than hold her. His arms pressed her gently as he rubbed his chin across the top of her head. A mist-filled breeze off the ocean had ruined her carefully styled hair; now it fell in tight ringlets around her oval face.

Her hair was another thing that endeared her to Philip. Not once had he mentioned its color. Men invariably teased her about it, asking if her temper matched the color of her hair. The only time it did was when someone made tiresome remarks about it. Not red and not blond, the shade fell somewhere in between. Red oak, her mother claimed, like her grandmother's. Like russet potatoes, her brother suggested. The color of her hair and her fair complexion had been the bane of Carla's existence.

"Would you like to go for a swim?" Philip asked, dropping his arms and taking her hand. They continued walking toward the hotel.

"In the ocean?" She'd have to get her suit.

"No, the current's too dangerous. I meant the pool."

The hotel's swimming pool was the most luxurious Carla had ever seen. A picture of the massive pool area at the hotel had been the determining factor in their decision to book their holidays at the El Cid. Blue, watery channels stretched all around the hotel, with bridges joining one section to another.

"I'd love to go swimming," Carla replied enthusiastically. They reached the short flight of stairs that led to the hotel from the beach. "Give me ten minutes to change and I'll meet you back here."

"Ten minutes?" Philip arched one brow. Carla had noticed him do that a couple of times during the evening. It seemed to be Philip's way of expressing mild surprise.

"Ten minutes—easy," Carla confirmed confidently. She knew exactly which corner of her suitcase held her swimsuit. It wouldn't take her more than five minutes to change, so she figured she'd easily have five minutes to spare. But what she hadn't counted on was that Nancy had neatly stored their suitcases under the beds. Carla spent a frantic five minutes tearing their room apart, certain that they'd been robbed. Finally, she found it. She should have remembered her friend's penchant for neatness.

Fifteen minutes later, a chagrined look pinching her face, Carla met Philip at poolside.

Pointedly, he glanced at his watch.

"I couldn't help it," she told him breathlessly, and offered a sketchy explanation as she placed her towel on a chaise longue. The pool was empty, which surprised Carla until she removed her wristwatch and noted that it was after midnight.

She tugged the elastic of the forest-green maillot over her thigh and tested the water by dipping one foot into the pool. Warm. Almost too warm.

"Are you one of those women who gets wet by degrees?"

Philip asked as he took off his glasses and tossed them on his towel.

"Not me." She walked to his side, stretched out her arms and dived in. Her slim body sliced into the water. Philip joined her almost immediately, and together they swam the width of the pool.

"Do you want to race?" he called out.

"No," Carla answered with a giggle.

"Why not?"

"Because I was on my college swim team, and I'm fast. Men can't stand to lose."

"Is that a fact?"

"It's true."

"I'm not like most men."

Carla had noticed that. But this was turning out to be a promising relationship, and she didn't want to ruin it. Floating lackadaisically on her back, she paddled rhythmically with her hands at her side. Carla decided to ignore the challenge in his voice.

Philip joined her, floating on his back as well. "If you don't want to race, what would you like to do?"

"Kiss underwater." She laughed at the surprised look on his face as he struggled to a standing position. Philip looked different without his glasses, almost handsome. But not quite.

He stood completely still in the shoulder-deep water. "I'm not that kind of man."

He was so serious that it took Carla a moment to realize he was kidding.

"I'm not easy, you know," she said, flirting. "You have to catch me first." They were acting like adolescents, and Carla loved it. With Philip she could be herself. There wasn't any need to put on sophisticated airs.

Laughing, she twisted and dived underwater, surfacing several feet away from him. He came after her, and Carla took off with all the energy she'd expend for an important race. Using her most powerful strokes, she surged ahead. When his hand groped for her foot, she kicked frantically and managed to escape. That he'd caught up with her so quickly was hard to believe.

She was even more amazed when his solid stroke matched hers and he gripped her waist and pulled her to the side of the pool.

"You're as slippery as an eel."

"You're good," she countered. "Who taught you to swim like that?"

"My mother." They were hidden under the shadow of a bridge that crossed a narrow section of the pool.

Carla slipped her arms around his neck. She wanted him to kiss her. She could tell he was attracted to her; she'd seen it in his eyes when they were on the beach. That look had prompted her flippant challenge about kissing underwater.

He pushed the wet strands of hair from her face. The silver light in his eyes darkened. He moved closer, but Carla assumed it was because he couldn't see her clearly without his glasses. She liked his eyes. They were so expressive. She liked the way they darkened when he was serious and how they sparkled when he was teasing. Tiny lines fanned out from the edges, and Carla recognized that this man laughed and enjoyed life. Her feelings for him were intensifying every minute they were together.

His hand rested on either side of her face, pressing her against the side of the pool. "I'm going to kiss you," he whispered. He released one hand and encircled her waist to pull her gently but firmly toward him.

Slowly, lengthening each moment, each breath, he lowered his mouth to hers. Carla felt herself relax, felt her body, her heart, opening to him. Wanting to touch him, needing to, she ran her hand along the side of his face, twisting her head so that when he found her lips their mouths slanted across each other's. The kiss was gentle and soft, gradually building in intensity until Carla melted against him.

Philip let go of the side of the pool, and they sank just below the surface. Their legs entwined, and Carla opened her mouth to him. His tongue sought hers, forcing her mouth to open farther under its exploring pressure. Carla felt as if she were drowning, but the sensation was exquisite.

They broke the surface of the water together and drew in deep, shaky breaths. Her body remained tucked in his embrace. His chest pressed against the softness of her breasts, and a crazy dizziness overcame her.

The pressure of his embrace backed her against the side of the pool, and he kissed her again. Carla gloried in the wonderful, inexplicable sensations that overwhelmed her.

Their breathing was ragged when Philip buried his face in the side of her neck.

"My word," she murmured breathlessly, "who taught you to kiss like that?"

Philip responded with a weak laugh. "Carla." Philip hesitated and wiped the moisture from his eyes. "I wish I could see you better."

"I'm glad you can't," she replied happily. "You might get a swelled head if you could see how much I like you."

"Carla." His voice grew strong, serious.

"What's wrong?" She placed a hand on each of his shoulders, liking the feel of her body floating against his.

"There's something you should know."

"What?" He was so serious that her heart throbbed. She didn't want anything to ruin this. If he told her he was married she wasn't sure what she'd do.

"Carla, I'm a policeman for the city of Spokane."

Two

Carla woke just as the sun crested the horizon and bathed the beach in a flashy glow of color. Nancy had been asleep by the time Carla had returned last night, which was just as well. She hadn't felt much like talking.

Philip Garrison had taught her a valuable lesson. She should have trusted her instincts. From her first look at Philip, she'd felt he wasn't her type. At the time, she hadn't realized how true that was. True, his kisses had been... She couldn't find a word to describe them. Pleasant, she mused. All right, very pleasant. But that certainly wasn't enough to overcome *what* he was.

Drat. Drat. Drat... She'd liked him. In fact she'd liked him a lot. He was sensitive, sympathetic, compassionate, kind, caring... Carla placed the pillow over her head to drown out her thoughts. She wouldn't allow herself to think about him again. This crazy idea of Nancy's had been ridiculous from the beginning. She'd put the episode behind her and get on with her vacation.

Throwing back the covers of her bed, she stood and stretched. Nancy grumbled and curled into a tight ball. Typical of Nancy, who hated mornings.

"What time is it?" she demanded in a growling whisper.

"Early, the sun just came up."

"Sun!" Nancy's eyes popped open. "I forgot to set the alarm."

Carla smiled as she sat in the middle of the single bed and ran a brush through her hair to tame the wild array of red curls. "Don't worry about the time. We're on vacation, remember?"

With an uncharacteristically hurried movement, Nancy threw back the sheets. "But I promised to meet Eduardo on the beach at dawn," she cried out. "Oh, good grief, how could I have been so stupid?"

For Nancy to forget anything was surprising by itself. But to have her friend show this much enthusiasm in the morning was astonishing.

"I take it you and… Eduardo hit it off?"

Nancy's head bobbed energetically. "What about you?"

"Not so lucky," Carla returned with a wistful sigh.

Nancy's most attractive summer dress slid over her hips as she turned her back to Carla in an unspoken request for her to do up the zipper. "What went wrong?"

"You don't have time to hear," Carla said with forced cheerfulness.

"He looked nice."

Nice was only the beginning, Carla thought. "Looks are often deceiving." That much was true. Who would have imagined that Philip Garrison would turn out to be so appealing? "If I'm not mistaken, I'd say you and Eduardo got along famously."

"He's fabulous. I can't remember a night I've enjoyed more." Nancy paused, and a dreamy look replaced the hurried frown that had marred her smooth features.

"His cast doesn't bother you?" Carla couldn't help asking.

"Good grief, no. I hardly thought about it."

That was saying something.

"He's taking me on an all-day tour of Mazatlán. You don't mind, do you?"

"Mind? Me? Of course not." Carla's mouth formed a tight smile. Now she'd be forced to spend the entire day alone. "Have a good time," she managed without a hint of sarcasm. No need to ruin Nancy's fun.

"Thanks, I will." Always practical, Nancy grabbed a hat to protect her from the sun, tucked her credit cards in a secret flap in her purse and was out the door in a rush.

Carla flopped back on her bed and stared at the shadows on the ceiling. This vacation was rapidly turning into a disaster. Day two and already she wished she were back in Seattle.

After an unhurried shower, Carla decided to head for the pool. With her skin color, she wasn't able to stay out in the sun long, and morning was generally the best time for her to sunbathe.

The pool area was filling up with early sun worshippers, and Carla chose a chaise longue near the deep end. That way she could dive in and cool off whenever necessary. This afternoon she'd do some shopping at the Mazatlán Arts and Crafts Center. She'd heard about the center almost immediately after her arrival. With twenty-eight shops to explore, she was certain to find souvenirs for her family. But even shopping had lost its appeal, especially since she'd be doing it alone. If she was lucky, she might meet someone at the pool—preferably someone male and handsome. She spread her towel out as a cushion for the longue and lay on her stomach, facing the pool. With her arms crossed she pressed her cheeks against her forearm. Boring, she admitted regretfully. Day two and she was bored to death. The turquoise bikini she wore was modest, especially when compared to the daring suit on the luscious, curvy creature across the pool from her. Carla guessed that if she had a body like that, she might be tempted to wear the same thing. She'd heard of string bikinis, but this one was hardly more than threads. The woman was attracting the attention of almost everyone at poolside. When Philip moved into her line of vision, Carla's eyes widened. He smiled, and his gray eyes twinkled. It didn't bother her that his smile wasn't directed at her. For all the attention he'd given her, he obviously hadn't noticed that she was across the pool from him.

Carla chose to ignore him, but her heart leaped just seeing him again. He wasn't muscular or strikingly masculine, but he was compelling in a way she couldn't describe. If she hadn't spent yesterday with him, she wouldn't have given him a second look today. But she'd felt the lean hardness of him against her in the water. She'd tasted the sweetness of his kiss. She'd experienced the gentle comfort of his arms. Her eyes refused to move from him, and when he looked her way, she shook herself from her musings and lowered her cheek against her arm, pretending not to see him.

Her heart was racing and that angered her. One look from Philip was no reason for her pulse to quicken. Although Carla refused to pay attention to him, she could feel Philip's gaze on her. She smiled as she imagined the satisfaction in his gaze, the look of admiration that would dominate those smoky-gray eyes of his. How she loved his expressive eyes! Unable to resist, she raised her head a fraction to catch a glimpse of his approval. To her dismay, Carla discovered that Philip wasn't studying her at all. His concentration was centered on the daring blond beauty at the other side of the pool.

Carla expected the woman to treat Philip like a pesky intruder. But she didn't—in fact, she seemed to encourage his attentions. Grudgingly, Carla admitted there *was* a certain attraction to Philip, and an aura of quiet confidence that was...well, masculine. His sandy hair had a tendency to curl at the ends, she observed, and most men would have styled it into submission. But not Philip; professionally groomed hair wouldn't be on his list of priorities.

After several minutes of what appeared to be light conversation, Philip dived into the pool and did a number of laps. Carla couldn't help admiring the way his bronze body sliced through the water. Anyone would. A rush of pink colored her cheeks as she recalled their antics last night. Yes, Philip Garrison was indeed gifted.

When Philip came out of the pool, he maneuvered himself so that he "accidentally" dripped water on his scantily clad acquaintance. The luscious blonde sat up to hand him a towel and laughed lightly when more drops of water splashed on her bare midriff.

Forcefully, Carla directed her gaze elsewhere. For a full five minutes she refused to allow herself to turn their way. When curiosity got the better of her, she casually glanced toward Philip and the other woman, who were an unlikely match. To her dismay she found that they were laughing and enjoying a cocktail. One side of Carla's mouth curved up sarcastically. One would assume a dedicated police officer would know better than to consume alcohol at such an early hour.

Pretending that the sun was burning her tender skin, Carla made a show of standing and draping a light terry-cloth wrap over her shoulders. She tucked her towel and tanning lotion in the oversized bag and walked down the cement stairs that led to the beach.

The beach wasn't nearly as crowded as the pool area. Carla had just settled in the sandy mattress when she was approached by a vendor carrying a black case. He knelt in front of her and opened the lid to display a large number of silver earrings, bracelets and rings. She smiled and shook her head. But the man persisted, telling her in poor English that he would sell jewelry to her at a very good price.

Politely but firmly, Carla shook her head.

Still the man insisted, holding out a lovely silver-and-turquoise ring for her to inspect. His eyes pleaded with her, and Carla couldn't refuse. The ring was pretty.

Someone spoke in Spanish from behind her. It didn't take Carla two seconds to realize it was Philip. His words were heavy with authority, although he hadn't raised his voice. Resenting his intrusion, she tossed him an angry look.

"Do you like the ring?" He directed his comment to her.

"Well, it's more than I wanted to spend—"

She wasn't allowed to finish. Philip said something to the vendor, who nodded resignedly, took back the ring and turned away.

"That wasn't necessary, you know," she told him stiffly.

"Perhaps not, but you could buy the same ring in the hotel gift shop for less than what he was asking." Philip spread out his towel a respectable distance from her. "Do you mind?" he asked before he sat down.

"It's a public beach," she returned coolly, recognizing it wouldn't do any good to object. "Just leave enough space between us so no one will assume we're together." She suspected that Philip would only follow her if she got up and moved. "What happened with Miss String Bikini?" Carla had hoped to resist any hint of acid in her query.

Philip chuckled. "Unfortunately, Miss is a Mrs., and hubby looked like the jealous type."

Now it was Carla's turn to laugh. She was sorry to have missed the scene of Philip meeting the irate husband. "I'll admit, though, she had quite a body."

"Passable," Philip admitted dryly as his eyes swept over the beach.

Passable! Carla's mind echoed, wondering what he considered terrific.

"Where's your roommate?" he asked breezily.

"With... Eduardo. They seem to have hit it off quite well."

"We did, too, as I recall. I wonder what it would take to get you to agree to have lunch with me."

"Forget it, Garrison," Carla said forcefully.

"You know what a good time we could have," he prodded softly.

"I'm not interested," Carla replied without looking at him. She felt a twinge of regret at how callous she sounded, and recalled how cold she'd been to him after he'd told her his occupation. She wouldn't have been so unfeeling, she suspected, if she hadn't previously expressed her resentment about her father being a policeman. Later, unable to sleep, she decided she was glad she'd told him. It had saved an unnecessary explanation. As it was, she'd pushed herself from his arms and swum to the opposite side of the pool. "It was a pleasure meeting you, Philip Garrison," she'd said tersely while toweling dry. "But I have one strict code regarding the men I date."

"I think I can guess what that is," he'd replied with a control that was frightening. "You realize I didn't have to tell you. We could have had a pleasant vacation together without you ever being the wiser."

"Perhaps." Carla hadn't been in any mood to reason. "But you saved us both a lot of trouble." With the damp towel draped over her neck, she'd hurried back to her room. Not until she'd changed out of her swimsuit had Carla realized how miserable she was. Disappointed in herself and disappointed in Philip. He might as well have admitted to being married; he was as off-limits as if he had a wife and ten children.

"Nice-looking brunette to your left," Philip pointed out, breaking her train of thought.

"It doesn't look like she's sporting a jealous husband, either," Carla said jokingly.

Philip's laugh was good-natured. "I'll use my practiced routine on her. Care to watch me in action?"

"I'd love it," Carla answered with open delight. "At least with you out of the picture some handsome tourist can make a play for me."

"Good luck," he called as he stood and loped lazily down the beach.

Handsome tourist; Carla almost laughed. At the rate things were going, the only men she'd be fighting off would be persistent vendors.

Carla watched with growing interest as Philip carelessly tossed his towel on the beach close to the girl and ran into the rolling surf. She'd remember to ask him later about swimming in the ocean. Last night he'd told her the tide was too dangerous, yet he was diving headlong into it without a second's hesitation.

After a few minutes, which he apparently thought suitable for a favorable impression, he stood, wiped the water from his face and walked out of the ocean. He squinted and

rubbed his eyes, giving the impression the water was sting-
ing. The way he groped for his towel made Carla laugh
outright. Again by an apparent accident, he flicked sand
on the tanning beauty. The girl sat up and brushed the offending particles from her well-oiled body. Philip fell to
his knees, and although Carla couldn't hear what he was
saying, she was sure it was some practiced apology. Soon
the two of them were talking and laughing. Spreading
out his long body, he lay beside the brown-haired beauty.
His technique, tried and true, had worked well. Rolling
his head, Philip caught Carla's gaze and winked when she
gestured with two fingers, giving the okay sign.

For the first time in recent memory, Carla wished that
she were as good at acting as Philip. For a moment she
toyed with the idea of following his lead and blatantly approaching a man. Carla's devil-may-care system should
work as well on the beach as in the cocktail lounge. But a
quick survey of the area didn't turn up a single male she
cared to flirt with. There wasn't anyone she particularly
wanted to meet. Maybe Nancy was right, maybe she had
become much too picky lately.

Ten minutes later, Carla stood, brushed the sand from
her skin and picked up her things. After lunch she'd do
some shopping.

Philip gave her a brief wave, which she returned. At
least one of them had been successful. At least one of them
was having a good time.

The oppressive afternoon heat eventually brought Carla
back into the air-conditioned cocktail lounge. Sipping a
pina colada, she surveyed the growing crowd of tourists.
A couple of times men had asked if they could buy her
a drink, but she'd declined. Men who used tanning machines, wore gold chains around their necks and left their

shirts open to their navels didn't interest Carla. Her spirits were low, and she hated to think she'd be fighting this
depression the entire week. If she wasn't careful, she'd get
locked in a state of self-pity.

The room was filling up rapidly, and when Philip entered Carla pretended an inordinate amount of interest in
her drink.

"Hi." He sauntered to her side. "Do you mind if I join
you, or will I be distracting any potential margarita drink-
ers?"

"By all means join me," she said with a poor attempt
at a smile. "I don't exactly seem to be drawing a crowd.
How about you? I expected you to stroll in here with Miss
September."

He cleared his throat and took the plush seat beside her.
"That didn't work out."

"Was there a Mr. September?"

"No." Philip cleared his throat a second time. "Things
didn't work out, that's all."

"Philip," she moaned impatiently, "come on, tell me what
happened. You can't leave me in suspense like this." Something perverse inside her wanted to know about Philip's
latest rejection. Maybe she needed to salve her pride at his
expense, which was childish, Carla thought, but shared
misery beats the solo kind.

He ignored her while he raised his hand to attract the
waitress's attention. "What's that you're drinking?"

"Pina colada," Carla answered quickly. "Out with it,
Garrison. Details, I want details."

The waitress came to take his order. Carla had lost the
desire to impress him with her vast knowledge of the Spanish language. As it was, the waitress eyed her warily, as if
she were afraid Carla were a *loco gringo*.

"No margarita tonight?" His eyes mocked hers as a smile touched the corners of his mouth.

"Don't change the subject."

"I'll tell you over dinner." He raised both thick brows suggestively.

"Do you think bribing me is going to work?"

He smiled faintly, rather tenderly, at her. "I was hoping it would."

This was the best offer she'd had all day. And she wasn't about to refuse. "All right, as long as we understand one another."

"Of course we do," he replied formally. "You don't want to date cops, and with good reason."

"With a very good reason," she repeated emphatically.

The waitress delivered their drinks and brought a plate with two tacos, or what Carla assumed were tacos. She'd noticed that a sign outside the lounge stated that anyone buying a drink between four and five would receive a free taco. But this fried corn tortilla that had been filled with meat and rolled didn't resemble anything she'd call a taco. No lettuce, no cheese, no tomato.

One nibble confirmed that it didn't taste anything like one, either. "What's in this?"

Philip eyed her doubtfully. "Are you sure you want to know?"

"Of course I do."

He shrugged. "Turtle."

Carla closed her eyes and swallowed. "Turtle," she repeated. "It tastes more like week-old tuna fish to me."

"You don't have to eat it if you don't want."

She set it back on the plate. "It's something to tell my friends about, but it's nothing I'd recommend."

"It'll grow on you," Philip commented.

"I certainly hope not," Carla said with a grimace. "Have you ever examined the skin on those things?"

Suddenly, they were both laughing as if she'd said the most uproariously funny thing in the world. "Come on." His hand reached for hers. "Let's get out of here before they throw us out." He laid several bills beside their uneaten turtle tacos. Together, hand in hand, they practically ran out of the cocktail lounge.

Not until they were in a golf cart/taxi did Carla ask where they were headed.

"Senor Frog's," Philip shouted, the wind whipping his voice past her.

"No." She waved her hand dramatically. "Not if they serve what I think they do."

"Not to worry." Philip placed an arm around her shoulder and spoke close to her ear. "This is a famous tourist trap. The food's good, but the place is wild. You'll love it."

And just as he'd promised, Carla did love it. After almost an hour's delay, they were ushered through the restaurant doors only to be led to a cocktail lounge. The music and boisterous singing were so loud that Carla couldn't hear herself speak when she leaned over to ask Philip something. He bent closer but finally gestured that they'd have to talk afterward outside.

Two hours later, well fed and singing softly, Carla and Philip left the restaurant with their arms wrapped around each other.

"That was wild."

"I knew you'd like it," Philip said, smiling tenderly at her.

"But there's a method to your madness."

"How's that?"

"With all the noise, you weren't able to tell me about Miss September."

"All right, if you must know."

"I must," she replied firmly. "I hope you realize I baked in the hot sun while I waited to see how you did. Honestly, Philip, your approach could have been a little more original."

The look he gave told her that he was offended. "I thought my technique was one of a kind."

Carla looked at the darkening sky and rolled her eyes, but refrained from comment. "I'm surprised that you didn't go up to her and ask if you'd met someplace before."

Philip shifted his weight onto the other foot. "To be honest, that occurred to me, too."

Laughing, Carla slipped her arm through his. "You, my dear Philip, are refreshingly unimaginative."

He made a funny little noise that sounded as if he was clearing his throat. He seemed to be studying the cracks in the sidewalk on which they were strolling. He didn't appear to have any clear direction.

"Now, will you spill the beans about Miss September? I'm dying to know what happened."

He was quiet for a few moments. "You prefer not to date policemen, and I have a thing about flight attendants."

Most men had a "thing" about flight attendants, too, but it wasn't to avoid them. It wasn't one of her more brilliant deductions to guess that Philip had once loved a flight attendant and been hurt. "Do you want to tell me about her? I make a great wailing wall," she murmured sympathetically.

"Not if I can avoid it." He looked at her and smiled. "Tell me about your afternoon. Any success?"

"No one," she said dejectedly, and shook her head for

emphasis. "Unless you count guys in gold chains who enjoy revealing their chest hair."

"Some women like those kind of men."

"Not me."

Philip hesitated, then asked, "I wonder if I could interest you in a short-term, no-obligation, strictly regulated, but guaranteed fun relationship."

Carla's mouth curved wryly. She'd had a better time with Philip tonight than the entire day she'd spent alone. Her mind was flashing a bright neon "NO" in bold red letters. If she had any sense whatsoever, she'd shake her head and decline without another word.

"Well?" he urged.

"I don't know," she answered truthfully. Five days, what could possibly happen in five days? She'd come to Mexico looking for a good time. She knew who Philip was and, more important, *what* he was.

The silence lengthened. "I think I should make one thing clear. I have no intention of treating you like a sister."

He could have lied. But again, he'd chosen to be straight with her. She appreciated that.

"I don't want anything more than these five days. Once we leave Mazatlán it's over."

"Agreed," he said, and a finger tenderly traced the outline of her jaw.

A tingling sensation burned across her face, and she closed her eyes against its potency. She'd be safe. She'd walked into this with her eyes wide open. He lived in Spokane. She lived in Seattle. A light flirtation was what she'd had in mind in the first place. Knowing what he was should make it all the easier to walk away next Saturday. But it hadn't lessened the attraction she felt for him—and that appeared to be growing every minute.

"I...haven't agreed yet." Her pride demanded one last stand.

"But you will," Philip said confidently.

"How can you be so sure?" Carla returned, piqued by his attitude.

"Well, for one thing, you're looking at me with 'kiss me' eyes."

Embarrassed, Carla shot her gaze to the ground. "That's not true," she denied hotly, and was ready to argue further, but Philip cut her off.

"Do you agree or not?" He held out his hand for her to shake.

"I have a feeling I'm going to regret this," she said, and placed her hand in his.

Philip didn't argue. But when his arm closed around her shoulders, she didn't object. She liked the idea of being linked with this man, even if it was only for a few days.

"How about a ride on an araña?" he suggested, his mouth disturbingly close to her ear.

"I don't know what you're suggesting, Philip Garrison, but that doesn't sound like something nice girls do."

His laughter filled the night. "That's a two-wheeled, horse-drawn cab."

"Sounds romantic." Knowing Philip, Carla was willing to bet he'd instruct the driver to take the long way back to the hotel through scented, shady boulevards. She was in the mood for a few stolen kisses, and so was Philip, gauging by his look.

"If we can't find one, we can always jog back to the hotel," he said seriously.

"With a name like Walker you expect me to run?"

"What's the matter with running? I thought you'd be into physical fitness."

She laughed softly. "I swim, and that's the entire reper-
toire of my athletic abilities."

"You mean you weren't in track? With those long legs
of yours, I'd think you'd be a natural."

"So did my high school coach—until the first practice.
He had to time me with a calendar. Running's out."

"Walking?" Philip suggested.

"Good grief, if we can't find a carriage, what's the
matter with those golf-cart things that we've been taking lately?"

"You mean the pulmonias?" His gray eyes were dancing with amusement, and Carla struggled not to succumb
to the invitation in their smoky depths.

"Whatever," she replied, pleased with herself now for
agreeing to this crazy relationship. She honestly enjoyed
this zany man.

"If you insist," Philip said blandly, and flagged down a
passing taxi when it became obvious that finding an araña
would take longer than they were willing to wait.

Back at the hotel Carla mentally chastised herself for
being so easily swayed by Philip's direct approach. She
really ought to have played harder to get.

"There's a band playing at the—"

"I love to dance," she interrupted enthusiastically. "My
feet are itching already."

Philip smoothed the hair at the side of his head. "Tell
me, why was I expecting an argument?" He was regarding her with a look of amused surprise.

"I don't know." Carla laughed gaily, happiness bubbling over.

"If you're not into sports, what kinds of things do you
like to do?" With his hand at her elbow, he escorted her
toward the lively sounds of the mariachi band.

"Play checkers," Carla responded immediately. "I've won the King County Park and Recreational checker championship three years running. It's a nice friendly game, and I've got a terrific coach I'll tell you about sometime."

Carla felt relaxed and happy as they stood in line outside the lounge. They seemed to be waiting in a lot of lines tonight, not that she minded.

Philip studied her intently; his eyes narrowed slightly as if he had trouble assimilating the fact she was nonathletic.

"No sports, you say?"

"Just checkers." Carla's gleaming eyes didn't leave his. "Knowing that I'm a champion, Philip, would you have any trouble jumping me?" She was teasing, but the responding look in Philip's eyes was serious.

"I'd consider it," he murmured, "but I think I'd probably wait until after the game."

Three

Golden moonbeams softly lighted a path along the beach. The gentle whisper of the ocean breeze was broken only by the sound of the waves crashing against the smooth white shore.

Philip slipped his arm around Carla's shoulders, and she brought her hand up so that they could lace their fingers together.

"Why didn't you tell me you could dance like that?" he murmured against her hair. "I've seen card sharks with slower moves."

Enjoying his surprise, Carla smiled softly to herself. "All I do is swing my hips a little."

"Yes, but I felt the least I could do was try to keep up with you. I'm dead."

"And I thought you police officers had to be in top physical condition." Not for a minute would she admit that she was as exhausted as Philip.

"I'm in great shape," he argued, "but three hours on the dance floor with you is above and beyond the call of duty. Next time I think I'll suggest checkers."

"You'll lose," Carla returned confidently.

"Maybe, but I have a feeling my feet won't hurt nearly as much."

Philip had been the one to suggest this stroll. But it wasn't a walk in the moonlight that interested him; Carla was convinced of that. He was seeking a few stolen kisses against the backdrop of a tropical night. And for that matter, so was she. Every time they met, Philip astonished her. One look the day on the plane and she'd instantly sized him up as dull and introspective. But he was warm, caring and witty. There wasn't any man who could make her laugh the way Philip did.

"I enjoyed myself tonight. You're a lot of fun." She felt compelled to tell him that.

"You sound surprised." Philip moved his chin so it brushed against the crown of her head. The action was strangely comforting and erotic.

"Surprised is the wrong word," she said softly, struggling to express herself. "Leery, maybe. I don't want to like you too much. That would only complicate a nice, serene relationship. We're having a good time, and I don't want to ruin it."

"In other words, you don't want to fall in love with me?"

"Exactly." Carla hated the heartless way this made her sound. Already she recognized that falling for Philip wouldn't be difficult. He was many of the things she wanted in a man. And everything she didn't.

He expelled his breath in a half-angry sigh, but it was the only indication he gave that she had displeased him.

Closing her eyes, Carla felt an unexpected rush of regret settle over her. One evening together and she was already doubting that this arrangement was going to work. Spending time with Philip might not be a good idea if they were both going to end up taking it seriously. All she wanted was a good time. And he'd claimed that was all he was looking for too. This was a holiday fling, after all, not a husband hunt.

"Don't you think you're overreacting just a little to the fact I'm a policeman?" Philip asked, his voice restrained and searching.

"Haven't we already been over this?" she answered hastily. "Besides, you have your own dating quirk. What if I'd been a flight attendant? You said yourself you prefer not to go out with them."

"But in your case I'd have made an exception."

"Why?"

"It's those lovely eyes of yours—"

"No," she interrupted brusquely, reacting with more than simple curiosity. "Why don't you like flight attendants?"

"It's a long story, and there are other things I have in mind." Clearly, he wasn't interested in relating the details of his experience, and Carla decided she wouldn't push him. When he was ready to tell her, if he ever was, she'd be pleased to listen. She found it interesting that after only a few hours' acquaintance with Philip she had released a lifetime full of bitterness about her father and his occupation. Apparently, she hadn't generated the same kind of response in him. It troubled her a little.

"You're quiet all of a sudden." His lips found her temple, and he kissed her there lightly. "What are you thinking?"

Tilting her head back, she smiled into those appealing smoky-gray eyes of his. "To be honest, I was mulling over the fact that you'll tell me about your hang-ups in time. But then it occurred to me that you might not."

"And that bothers you?" He studied her with amused patience.

"Yes and no." In a way that she didn't understand, Carla suddenly decided she didn't want to know. Obviously, Philip had loved and presumably lost, and Carla wasn't sure she wanted the particulars.

"The curious side of you is eager to hear the gory details—"

"But my sensitive side doesn't want to have you dredge up unhappy memories," she finished for him.

"It was a long time ago."

Carla slipped an arm around his waist and laid her head against his shoulder. "And best forgotten."

They continued walking along the moonlit beach in silence. Carla felt warm and comfortable having this man at her side. The realization wasn't something she wanted to explore; for now she was content.

"It's been six years since I broke up with Nicole," Philip said after a time.

Twisting in his embrace, Carla turned and pressed the tips of her fingers against his lips. "Don't," she whispered, afraid how she'd react if she saw pain in his eyes. "It isn't necessary. There isn't a reason in the world for you to tell me."

His jaw tightened, and memories played across his face. Some revealed the pleasant aspects of his relationship with Nicole, but others weren't as easily deciphered.

"I think you should know," he said, and his eyes narrowed to hard points of steel.

Carla wasn't sure which was troubling him more: the past or the sudden need to tell her about his lost love.

"Let me simplify things by saying that I loved her and asked her to marry me. But apparently she didn't care as deeply for me as I thought."

"She turned you down?" Carla murmured.

"No." His short laugh was filled with bitter sarcasm. "That's the crazy part. She accepted my ring, but she refused to move out on the guy she was living with. Naturally, neither one of us knew about the other."

Carla struggled not to laugh. "If you want my opinion, I think you made a lucky escape. This Nicole sounds a bit kinky to me."

Philip relaxed against her. His hands found the small of her back, arching her closer to him. "I don't know, there's something about me that attracts the weird ones. Just yesterday some oddball approached me in the bar with a lunatic story about me being her date for the night because I ordered a margarita."

"A real weirdo, no doubt." One brow arched mockingly.

"That's not the half of it." His head lowered with every word, so that by the time he finished, his lips hovered over hers.

"Oh?" Breathlessly, she anticipated his kiss.

"Yes." His low voice was as caressing as his look. "The thing is, I'd been watching her from the moment I walked into the lounge, trying to come up with a way of approaching her."

Before she could react to this startling bit of news, Philip brought her into his embrace. Slowly, his mouth opened over hers, taking in the softness of her trembling lips in a soul-stirring, devouring kiss. Carla stood on the tips of her toes and clung to him, devastated by the intensity of her reaction. This had happened the first time he'd kissed her. If Philip's lovemaking had been hard or urgent, maybe she could have withstood it. But he was incredibly gentle, as if she were of exquisite worth and as fragile as a rosebud, and that was irresistible.

When his tongue outlined the fullness of her mouth,

Carla's willpower melted, and she couldn't pull herself away from the fiery kiss. Desire shot through her, and when she broke away, her breathing was irregular and deep.

"I...I think we should put a limit on these kisses," she proposed shakily.

Philip didn't look any more in control of himself than she felt. His eyes were closed as he drew in a husky breath and nodded in agreement. Only a short space separated them, but he continued to hold her, his hands running the length of her bare arms.

"Let's get you back to your hotel room."

"Yes."

But they didn't move.

Unable to resist, Carla rested her head against his muscular chest, weak with the wonder of his kiss. "I don't understand." She was surprised to hear the words, not realizing she'd spoken out loud.

"What?" Philip questioned softly.

She shrugged, flustered for a moment. "You. Me. If you had come up to me yesterday and asked to buy me a drink, I probably would have refused."

He flashed a crooked grin. "I know. Why do you think I didn't?"

"Obviously, you recognized that I was about to take the initiative," she said jokingly to hide her discomfort.

Together they turned and headed back toward the hotel, taking leisurely steps. Carla's bare toes kicked up the sand.

"What would you like to do tomorrow?" she asked, not because she was especially interested in their itinerary, but because knowing she would be seeing him in the morning would surely enhance her dreams tonight.

"Shall we get together for breakfast?"

"I'd like that."

Outside her door, Philip set a time and place for them to meet in the morning, then kissed her gently and left.

Carla walked slowly inside the room and released a long, drawn-out sigh. For such a rotten beginning, the day had turned out wonderfully well.

"Is that you, Carla?" The question came from the darkened interior of the room.

"No, it's the bogeyman," Carla teased.

"I take it you met someone?" Nancy's voice was soft and curious.

"Yup."

"Tell me about your day." The moonlight silhouetted her roommate against the wall. Nancy was sitting on the side of the mattress.

"It's the guy I met yesterday." Carla couldn't disguise the wistful note in her voice.

"What happened? When I asked this morning, the looks you gave me said you didn't want to have anything to do with him."

"That was this morning."

Fluffing up her pillow, Nancy positioned it against the headboard, leaned against it and put her hands behind her head. "I'm glad things worked out."

"Me too." Carla moved into the room and began to undress.

"I can't believe how much I like Eduardo," Nancy said pensively as she stared dreamily at the ceiling. "I can't even begin to tell you what a marvelous day we had."

Carla slipped the silk nightie over her head. "The funny part was, I had no intention of seeing Philip again."

Nancy sighed unevenly and slid down so her head rested

in the thick of the pillow. "He gave me a tour of Maza-tlán that will hold memories to last a lifetime. And later tonight when he kissed me I could have cried, it was so incredibly beautiful."

"But then Philip was there, and I'd been so miserable all day, and he suggested we have dinner, and not for the life of me could I refuse."

"I've never felt this strongly about a man. And I've barely known Eduardo more than twenty-four hours."

Carla pulled back the bedcovers and paused, holding the pillow to her stomach. "I'm meeting Philip first thing in the morning."

"Eduardo says he can't believe that someone as beau-tiful as I would be interested in him. And just because he broke his leg. He keeps assuring me he really isn't a klutz. As if I'd ever think such a thing."

"I don't know if I'll be able to sleep. Every time I close my eyes I know Philip will be there. I don't know how to explain it. To look at him you'd be unimpressed. But he's the most gentle man. Tender."

"I can't sleep. Every time I try, my heart hammers and I wonder if I'm going crazy to feel like this."

The sheets felt cool against Carla's legs as she slipped between the covers and yawned. "I guess I should get some sleep. Night, Nance."

"Night," Nancy answered with a yawn of her own.

"By the way," Carla asked absently, "how'd your day go?"

"Fantastic. How about you?"

"Wonderful."

"I'm glad. Good night."

"Night."

* * *

Philip was already seated in the hotel restaurant when Carla arrived. Her gaze met his, and she smiled. She enjoyed the way he was watching her. The sleeveless pink-and-blue crinkle-cotton sundress was her favorite, and she knew she looked good. She'd spent extra time with her makeup, and one glance from him confirmed that the effort had been well spent.

"Morning." Philip stood and pulled out her chair.

"Did you sleep well?"

He leaned forward and kissed her cheek lightly. "Like a baby. How about you?"

Setting the large-brimmed straw hat on the empty seat beside her, Carla nodded. "Great."

The waiter appeared and handed them each a menu, but they didn't look at them. "What would you like to do today?"

"Explore," Carla replied immediately. "Would you mind if I dragged you to the arts and crafts center?"

Philip reached for her hand and squeezed it gently. "Not at all. And tomorrow I thought we'd take an excursion to Palmito de la Virgen."

Carla blinked. "Where?"

"An island near here. It's a bird-watcher's paradise."

The only bird Carla was interested in watching was Philip, but she didn't say as much.

"And Thursday I thought we might try our hand at deep-sea fishing."

"I'm game," she said, and giggled. "No pun intended."

"My, my, you're agreeable. Are you always like this in the mornings?"

Carla reached for the ice water, keeping her eyes lowered. "Most of the time."

"I'd like to discover that for myself."

The waiter arrived with his pen and pad, and Carla glanced up at him guiltily, realizing she hadn't even looked at the menu.

After breakfast they rode a pulmonia to the Mazatlán Arts and Crafts Center, and Philip insisted on buying her a lovely turquoise ring. Carla felt more comfortable purchasing her souvenirs from these people and not from the beach vendors. Here the price was set and there wasn't any haggling.

Tucking their purchases into a giant straw bag, Carla took off her hat and waved it in front of her face. Most of the shopping areas were air-conditioned, but once they stepped outside, the heat was stifling.

"Would you like something cool to drink?" Philip asked solicitously.

Smiling up at him, Carla placed a hand over her breast. "You, my dear man, know the path to my heart."

Unexpectedly, Philip's hand tightened on the back of her neck until his grip was almost painful. He dropped his hand and took a step forward as if he'd forgotten her completely. Surprised, but not alarmed, Carla reached for his arm. "What's wrong?"

"There's going to be a fight over there." He pointed to a group of youths who were having a heated exchange.

Although Carla couldn't understand what was being said, she assumed from the angry sound of their words that they would soon be coming to blows. Her gaze was drawn to Philip, and she was witness to an abrupt change in roles taking place within him. After all, she was a policeman's daughter. And Philip was an officer of the law. Once a cop, always a cop. He may be in Mazatlán, but he would never be entirely on vacation.

Philip's jaw hardened and his eyes narrowed with keen interest. Briefly, he turned to her. "Stay here." The words were clipped and low and filled with an authority that would brook no resistance.

Carla wanted to argue. Everything inside urged her to scream that this was none of his business. What right did he have to involve himself with those youths? Mexico had its own police force. She watched as Philip strode briskly across the street toward the angry young men. He asked them something in Spanish, and even from this distance Carla could hear the authority in his voice. She hadn't a clue of what he was saying, but it didn't matter. It was the law-enforcement officer in him speaking, anyway, and she didn't want to know.

Only one thing prompted her to stay. If the situation got ugly and Philip needed help, she could scream or do something to get him out of this mess. But he didn't need her assistance, and a few minutes later the group broke up. With an amused grin, Philip jogged across the street to her side.

"That was—"

"I don't care to know, thank you," she announced frostily. Opening her large bag, she took out the several small items he'd purchased during their morning's outing.

"What's this?" He looked stunned.

"Your things," she answered without looking up. "You couldn't do it, could you?"

"Do what?"

Apparently, he still didn't understand. "For once, just once, couldn't you have forgotten you're a cop? But no, Mr. Rescue had to speed to the scene of potential danger, defending truth and justice."

His face relaxed, and he reached for her. "Carla, couldn't you see—"

She sidestepped him easily. "You bet I saw," she shot back angrily. "You almost had me fooled, Philip Garrison. For a while there I actually believed we could have shared a wonderful vacation. But it's not going to work." Her voice was taut with irritation. With unnecessary roughness, she dumped the packages into his arms. "Not even for a few days could either of us manage to forget what you are. Goodbye, Philip." She spun and ran across the street, waving her hand, hoping to attract a pulmonia driver. At least she could be grateful that Philip didn't make an effort to follow her. But that was little comfort...very little.

A pulmonia shot past her, and Carla stamped her foot childishly. She wished she had paid closer attention to the Spanish phrase Philip called to get the driver's attention.

Already she felt the perspiration breaking out across her face as she walked along the edge of the street. The late-morning sun could be torturous. Another driver approached, and Carla stepped off the curb and shouted something in Spanish, not sure what she'd said. With her luck, she mused wryly, it was probably something to do with Cookie Monster. But whatever it was worked because the driver immediately pulled to the curb.

"Hotel El Cid," she mumbled, hot and miserable.

"*Sí, señorita,* the man already say."

Man? Tossing a look over her shoulder, Carla found Philip standing on the other side of the street, studying her. He'd gotten the driver for her. If she hadn't been so blasted uncomfortable, she'd have told him exactly what he could do with his driver. As it was, all Carla wanted to do was escape. The sooner the better.

Her room was refreshingly cool when she returned. She threw herself across the bed and stared at the ceiling.

Tears might have helped release some of her frustration, but she was too mad to cry.

After fifteen minutes, the hotel room gave her a bad case of claustrophobia. From her carryall Carla pulled the book she'd been reading on the airplane and opened the sliding glass door to the small balcony. A thorough inspection of the pool area revealed that Philip was nowhere in sight. Stuffing her book in her beach bag, Carla quickly changed into her swimsuit, slipping a cotton top over that and put on the straw hat. Not for anything was she going to allow Philip Garrison to ruin this vacation.

Carla was fortunate to find a vacant chaise longue. The pool was busy with the early-afternoon crowd. Several vacationers were in the water eating lunch at the counter that was built up against the pool's edge. Smiling briefly, Carla recalled her first glimpse of the submerged stools and wondered what this type of meal did to the theory of not swimming after eating.

Spreading out her towel, Carla raised the back of the lounger so that she could sit up comfortably and read. Her sunglasses had a tendency to slip down the bridge of her nose, and without much thought she pushed them back up. Philip's glasses did that occasionally. Angrily, she wiped his image from her mind and viciously turned the page of her suspense novel, nearly ripping it from the book.

An older man who was lying beside her stood, stretched and strolled lackadaisically toward the bar, apparently seeking something cool to drink. He was barely out of sight when a familiar voice spoke in her ear.

"Is this place taken?"

Carla's fingers gripped the page, but she didn't so much as acknowledge his presence. Without lifting her eyes from her book, she replied, "Yes, it is."

"That's fine, I'll just sit on the edge of the pool and chat," he replied casually.

Clenching her jaw so tight her teeth hurt, Carla turned a page, having no idea of what she had just read. "I'd appreciate it very much if you didn't."

Forcefully, Philip expelled his breath. "How long are you going to be unreasonable like this? All I'm asking is that you hear me out."

"How long?" Carla repeated mockingly. "You haven't got that much time. Never, as far as I'm concerned."

"Do you mean it?" The question was issued so low Carla had to strain to hear him.

Idly, she turned the next page. "Yes, I meant it," she replied.

"Okay." He took the towel, swung it around his neck and strolled away.

Carla felt a deep sense of disappointment settle over her. The least he could have done was argue with her! One would assume that after yesterday she meant more to him than that. But apparently not.

Without being obvious she glanced quickly around the pool area and discovered that Philip was nowhere in sight. Ten minutes later she did another survey. Nothing.

Tucking the book inside her beach bag, Carla settled back in her seat, joined her hands over her stomach and closed her eyes. A splash of water against her leg was more refreshing than irritating. But the cupful of water that landed on her upper thigh was a shock.

Gasping, she opened her eyes and sat up to brush the offending wetness away.

"Did I get water on you?" came the innocent question. "Please accept my apology."

"Philip Garrison, that was a rotten thing to do!" Inside she was singing. So he hadn't left.

"So was that last, untruthful remark."

"What remark?"

"That you never wanted to talk to me again." He lay down beside her on the chaise that had been previously taken by the older sunbather. "Obviously you did, or you wouldn't have made two deliberate inspections of the pool to see if I had left."

She should have realized Philip had stayed and watched her. That was a rookie's trick. And clearly Philip was a seasoned officer. Rather than argue, she lifted her glasses and turned toward him with a smug look. "I told you that place was taken," she said and repositioned herself so that the back of one hand rested against her brow. "And I don't think he'd take kindly to you lying in his place when he returns."

"Sure he would," Philip murmured confidently. "Otherwise I wasted ten very good dollars."

Struggling between outrage and delight, Carla sat up. "Do you mean to say you bribed him?" Her eyes widened as he nodded cheerfully. "What do you think you're doing, Officer Garrison? First…first you spy on me and…then… and then…" she sputtered. "You bribe the man in the chair next to me. Just how low do you plan to stoop?"

Philip yawned. "About that low."

Carla did an admirable job of swallowing her laughter.

"I suspect you aren't as annoyed as you're letting on," Philip commented.

The humor died in her eyes. "What makes you suggest that?"

"Well, you're still here, aren't you?"

Standing up, Carla pulled the thin cotton covering over her head. "Not for long," she replied, and dived into the pool.

It felt marvelous. Swimming as far and for as long as she could under the aqua-blue water helped relieve some of her pent-up frustration. Finally, she surfaced and sucked in a large breath of fresh air. In the glint of the sun, her hair was decidedly red. Carla had hoped to avoid having Philip see it wet. Like everyone else, he was sure to comment on it. Swimming at night was preferable by far.

She'd barely caught her breath when Philip surfaced beside her. Treading water at his side, she offered him a tremulous smile. "I really was angry this morning. I behaved childishly to run off like that. Thank you for seeing that I got a ride back to the hotel."

Their eyes met, and he grinned. "I know how angry you were; that's why I didn't follow you. But given time, I figured you'd forgive me." His arms found her waist and brought her close to him. Their feet kicked in unison, keeping them afloat.

"I'll forgive you on one condition," she stated firmly, and looped her arms around his neck. "You've got to promise not to do that again. Please, Philip. For me, leave your police badge in your room. We're in Mexico, and they have their own defenders of justice."

Philip went still, and she could feel him become tense. The sparkle faded from his eyes as they darkened and became more intense. "Carla, I'll do my best, but I can't change who or what I am."

Her grip around his neck relaxed, and with a sense of defeat she lowered her eyes. "But don't you see? I can't, either," she murmured miserably, and her voice fell to a whisper.

His hold tightened as he brought his body intimately close to hers in the water. "But we can try."

"What would be the use?"

"Oh, I don't know," he said softly, and brushed aside the offending strands of wet hair from her cheek. "I can think of several things." His lips replaced his fingers, and he blazed a trail of infinitely sweet kisses along her brow and eyes, working his way to her mouth.

For an instant, Carla was caught in the rapture of his touch, but an abrupt noise behind them brought her to her senses. Breaking free, she shook her head. "I…I don't know, Philip. I want to think on it."

"Okay, that sounds fair."

He didn't have to be so agreeable! At least he could have argued with her. With a little sigh, Carla turned away and said, "I think I'll go to my room and lie down for a while. The sun does me in fairly easily." She started to swim away, then rapidly changed direction and joined Philip. "I almost forgot something," she murmured as she covered his mouth with hers and kissed him thoroughly.

Obviously shaken, Philip blinked twice. "What was that for?" he asked, and cleared his throat.

"For not mentioning my frizzy hair or the color."

He cocked his head, and a puzzled frown marred his brow. "There are several other things I haven't mentioned that you may wish to thank me for."

"Later," she said with a small laugh.

"Definitely later."

Four

Amazingly, Carla did sleep most of the afternoon. She hadn't realized how exhausted she was. The sun, having taken its toll, had faded by the time she stirred. A glance at the clock told Carla that it was dinnertime. Although she hadn't made any arrangements to meet Philip, she knew he'd be looking for her.

Dressing quickly, she hunted for her sandals, crawling on the floor. Finally, she located them under the bed and was on her way into the bathroom to see what she could do with her hair when something stopped her. The faint sound of someone singing in Spanish drifted in past the balcony door that had been left ajar. Those deep male tones were unmistakable.

After eagerly parting the drapes, Carla opened the sliding glass door farther. The music and voice grew stronger, and the lovingly familiar voice sang loudly off key.

"Philip!"

Standing below, playing a guitar and singing at the top of his voice was crazy, wonderful Philip. A band of curious onlookers had gathered around him. Now, however, they focused their attention on her.

"You idiot," she cried. "What are you doing?"

"Serenading you," he shouted back, completely serious. "Do you like it?"

"I'd like it a lot better if you sang on key."

He strummed a few bars. "Can't have everything. Are you hungry?"

"Starved. I'd eat turtle tacos."

"You must be famished. Hurry down, will you? I think someone might arrest me."

Stuffing her hair under her straw hat, Carla bounded down the stairs. She paused on the bottom step, straightened her dress and took a deep breath. Then, feeling more composed, she turned the corner and found Philip relaxing on a chaise longue.

"Hi," she said, fighting the breathlessness that weakened her voice.

He rose to his feet with an ease many would envy. "I must have sounded better than I thought."

"What makes you think that?"

A grin played at the edges of his mouth as he dug inside his pocket and pulled out a handful of loose change. "People were obviously impressed. Soon after you went back inside, several started throwing coins my way."

Fighting back the bubbling laughter, Carla looped her arm around his elbow. "I hate to disappoint you, Philip, but I have the distinct feeling they were paying you *not* to sing."

The sound of his laughter tugged at her heart. "Where are we going for dinner? I wasn't teasing about being hungry."

"Anyplace you say." Tucking her hand more securely in the crook of his arm, he escorted her through the hotel to the series of stairs that led to the busy street below.

"Anyplace I say," she repeated. "My, my, you're agreeable all of a sudden."

"With a beautiful girl on my arm, and my pockets full of change, why shouldn't I be?"

She smiled, pleased by the compliment.

"Then dinner wherever the lady chooses."

"Well, I suppose I'd better choose a restaurant where I won't have to take off my hat. I didn't wash my hair after our dip in the pool this afternoon, and now it resembles Raggedy Ann's."

"Then it's perfect for what I have in mind," he said with an enigmatic toss of his head. Sandy locks of hair fell across his brow and he brushed them aside.

"Well, are you going to tell me, or do I have to guess?" she asked with a hint of impatience. She noticed that Philip had a way of arousing her curiosity, then dropping the subject. Her father did the same thing, and Carla briefly wondered if this was a common trait among policmen. They didn't want to give out too much information—keep the world guessing, seemed to be their intent. Other things about Philip reminded her of her father. He was a kind, concerned man. Like her father, he cared when the rest of the world didn't want to be bothered.

"Ever hear of La Gruta de Cerro del Creston?" Philip asked, snapping her out of her musings.

"He was some general, right?"

"Wrong," he responded with a trace of droll tolerance. "It's a cave where, it's rumored, pirates used to store their treasure. Stolen treasure, of course. It's only accessible at low tide, but I thought we might pick up a picnic lunch and eat along the beach. Later, when the tide is low, we can explore the cave."

Carla's interest was piqued. "That sounds great."

"And of course there's always the advantage of having you to myself in a deep, dark cave."

"Honestly, Garrison, cool your hormones," she joked.

One of the hot-rod golf carts Philip enjoyed so much delivered them close to the lighthouse near the heart of the city. Holding her hat, Carla climbed out from the back of the cart. Her senses were spinning, and she doubted if she'd ever get used to riding in those suicidal contraptions. The short rides weren't so bad, but anything over three miles was like a death wish.

A drop of rain hit her hand. Carla raised her eyes to examine the darkening sky and groaned inwardly. A storm would ruin everything. Besides, if Philip saw what happened to her hair in the rain, she'd never live it down. The frizzies invariably gave her a striking resemblance to the bride of Frankenstein.

"Philip?"

Preoccupied for the moment, Philip paid the driver and returned the folded money to his pocket. "Something wrong?"

"It's raining."

"I know."

Twisting the strap of her purse, she swung it over her shoulder and secured the large-brimmed straw hat by holding it down over both ears. "Maybe we should go back to the hotel."

"Why?"

She swallowed nervously. "Well, we obviously can't have a picnic in the rain, and if…my hat should come off… well, my hair—"

Suddenly, the sky opened up and the earth was bombarded with heavy sheets of rain. Giving a cry of alarm,

Carla ran for shelter. Mud splashed against the back of her legs, and immediately a chill ran up her arms.

Philip caught up with her and cupped her elbow. "Let's get out of here."

"Where?" she shouted, but he didn't answer as they raced down a side street. After two long blocks, Carla stopped counting. Placing one foot in front of the other was all that she could manage in the torrent that was beating against her.

Philip led her into a building and up two flights of stairs.

Leaning against the hallway wall, Carla gasped for breath. "Where are we?"

"My parents' condo."

Vaguely, she recalled Philip mentioning that the condo was the reason he was in Mazatlán. He'd said something about repairs, but Carla didn't care where they were as long as it was dry.

"Let's get these wet things off," Philip suggested, holding the door open for her and leading the way into the kitchen.

The condominium looked surprisingly modern, and Carla hurried inside, not wishing to leave a trail of mud across the cream-colored carpet. The washer and dryer were behind a louvered door. Philip pulled his shirt from his waist and unbuttoned it. "We'd better let these dry."

Wide-eyed, her mouth open, Carla watched him toss his drenched shirt inside. He paused and glanced expectantly at her.

"You don't honestly expect me to parade around here in my underwear, do you?"

"Well, to be honest," he said with a wry grin, "I didn't expect it, but I was hoping. Hold on and I'll get you my mom's robe."

By the time he returned, Carla had removed her sandals and found a kitchen towel to dry her feet. When she
heard Philip approach, she straightened and continued to
press her hat—still secure despite everything—down over
her ears.

"Here." He draped the cotton robe over a chair. "I'll
start a fire. Let me know when you're finished."

Shivering, Carla slipped the dress over her hips and
tossed it inside the dryer. Another towel served as a turban for her hair and hid the effects of the rain.

She tied the sash of the robe and took a deep breath.
Self-consciously, she stood just outside the living room. A
small fire was crackling in the fireplace, and Philip was
kneeling in front of it adding one stick of wood at a time.

He seemed to sense that she was watching him. "How
do you feel?" He stood and crossed the room, joining her.
Placing a hand on each shoulder, he smiled into her eyes.
"Mother's robe never looked so good."

"I feel like a drowned rat." The turban slipped over one
eye, and Carla righted it.

His hands found the side of her neck, and his touch sent
a warm sensation through her. "Believe me when I say you
don't look like one."

They continued to study each other, and Carla's heart
began to pound like a locomotive racing against time. In
some ways she and Philip were doing that. There were
only a few days left of their vacation, and then it would
be over. It had to be.

"Come in and sit down," Philip said at last, and his
thumb traced her lips in a feather-light caress. "The fire
should take the chill from your bones."

"I'm…not really cold." Not when you're touching me,
she added silently.

"Me neither."

Carla was convinced his thoughts were an echo of her own.

"Hungry?"

"Not really." Not anymore.

"Good."

Together they sat on the plush love seat that was angled to face the fireplace. Philip's arm reached for her, bringing her within the haven of his embrace.

Resting her head against the curve of his shoulder, Carla let her fingers toy with the dark hairs on his bare chest. Her body was in contact with his chest, hips and thighs, and whenever they touched, she could feel a heat building. She struggled to control her breathing so Philip wouldn't guess the effect he had on her.

"I poured these while you were changing," Philip murmured, his voice low and slightly husky. He leaned forward and reached for the two glasses of wine sitting on the polished oak coffee table.

Straightening, Carla accepted the long-stemmed crystal glass with a smile of appreciation and tasted the wine. It was an excellent sweet variety with a fragrant bouquet.

Removing the glass from her unresisting fingers, Philip set it aside. As he leaned back, his jaw brushed her chin, and his warm breath caressed her face. The contact stopped them both. He hadn't meant it to be sensual, Carla was sure of that, but her heart thumped wildly. Closing her eyes, she inhaled a quivering breath.

"Philip?" she whispered.

His mouth explored the side of her neck, sending rapturous shivers up and down her spine. "Yes?"

"Did you arrange for the rainstorm?" Carla couldn't believe how low and sultry her voice sounded.

"No, but I'm glad it happened."

Carla was, too, but she wouldn't admit it. She didn't need to.

Gently, Philip pressed her backward so that her head rested against the arm of the sofa; then his mouth claimed hers. His kiss was slow, leisurely and far more intoxicating than potent wine.

Drawing in a shaky breath, Philip diverted his attention to her neck, nuzzling the scented hollow of her throat. His hands wandered over her hips, artfully arousing her so that she shifted, seeking more. She wanted to give more of herself and take more at the same time. Her restless hands explored his back, reveling in the tightness of his corded muscles. This man was deceptively strong. Her fingers found a scar, and she longed to kiss it.

Gradually, the heat that had begun to flow through her at the tenderness of his touch spread to every part of her, leaving her feverishly warm. But when Philip's hands slid across her abdomen, she tensed slightly. He murmured her name, and his mouth lingered on her lips, moving from one side of her mouth to the other in a deep exploration that left her weak and clinging. Philip turned her so that she was sitting half-upright. As he did so, the towel that was covering her hair twisted and fell forward across her face. Gently, Philip lifted the offending material off her face, but her desperate hold on it prevented him from tossing it aside.

"Can we get rid of this thing?" he asked gently.

"No." She struggled to sit completely up. Both hands secured the terry-cloth towel.

"Your hair can't be that bad," he coaxed.

"It's worse. Turn around," she demanded as she leaned forward and rewound the turban. "I... I don't want you to see it."

Expelling his breath, Philip leaned against the back of the sofa and closed his eyes. "Would you feel better if you showered and dried those precious locks?"

She nodded eagerly.

"Come on, I'm sure Mom's got something in the bathroom that should help."

Carla followed him down a long, narrow hallway that led to a bathroom. Investigating the vanity drawers, he managed to come up with a blow-dryer and curling iron.

"I think my sister gave this to her for Christmas last year."

Carla's heart sank. "But I can't use this. The package isn't even open."

With a crooked grin, Philip tore off the cellophane. "If it bothers you, I'll tell her I used it."

Carla giggled delightedly. "I'd like to hear her answer to that."

Removing several fluffy towels from the hall closet, Philip handed them to her. "While you're making yourself beautiful I'm going to make us something to eat."

Hugging the fresh towels, Carla gave him a grateful smile. "Thank you, Philip. I honestly mean that."

He shrugged and pushed his glasses up the bridge of his nose. "Are you sure you don't need someone to wash your back?" he asked in a low, seductive voice.

"I'm sure." But the look he gave her as he turned toward the kitchen was enough to inflame her senses. Never had she felt this strongly about anyone after such a short time. Maybe that was normal. They had only a week together, and already three of those precious days had been spent. All too soon the time would come when she'd say goodbye to him at the airport. And it would be goodbye.

The water felt fantastic as it sprayed against her soft

skin. When she'd finished showering, she put the robe on and opened the bathroom door to allow the steam to escape.

"Your dress is dry if you want me to bring it to you," Philip called to her from the kitchen.

"Give me a minute," she shouted back. Carla's russet-red curls were blown dry and tamed with the curling iron in record time. Her face was void of makeup, and she knew she looked much paler than usual, but one kiss from Philip would correct that.

Tying the sash of the robe as she walked across the living-room carpet, Carla sniffed the delicate aroma drifting from the kitchen.

"Mushrooms," she announced, and picked one out of the sizzling butter with her long fingernails and popped it into her mouth.

"Canned, I'm afraid."

"No problem, I like mushrooms any way they come." She lifted out another and fed it to Philip. His shirt was dry and tucked neatly into his waistband. Her dress, she'd noticed, was hanging off a knob from the kitchen cabinet.

Peeking inside the oven, she turned around delightedly. "I don't suppose those are T-bone steaks under the grill?"

"Yup, but they'll take time. I had to get them out of the freezer." Philip set the cooking fork beside the skillet and reached for her. His hands almost spanned her waist. "But then we have lots of time."

But not nearly enough, her heart answered.

Hours later, after they'd consumed an entire bottle of wine and eaten their fill, they washed and dried the dishes. Soft music played romantically in the background.

"Philip?" Carla tilted her head as she released the plug from the sink to drain the soapy water.

He looked at her expectantly. "Hmm?"

"There's a scar on your back. I don't think I'd noticed it before. What happened?" she asked curiously.

"It's nothing." He stooped down to place the skillet in the bottom cupboard.

"It didn't feel like it. It's long and narrow, like…like…" She stopped cold. A painful sensation in the pit of her stomach viciously attacked her, and she leaned weakly against the counter. "Like a knife. You were stabbed, weren't you?"

Lifting up the frames of his glasses, Philip pinched the bridge of his nose. He muttered something she couldn't quite hear under this breath.

"You didn't want me to know. Well, I do now," she said, and gestured defiantly with her hand. "What happened? Did you decide to step in and break up a gang war all by yourself? You were willing to try your hand at that this morning." Her voice shook.

"No, it wasn't anything like that. I was—"

"I don't want to hear. Don't tell me." She searched frantically for her hat, moving quickly across one room and into the other.

"First you demand to know, then you claim you don't. I hope you realize how unreasonable you sound," he said with a low growl.

"I…don't care what I sound like." Her hat was beside her purse in the other room, and she practically raced to it. "One look at you and I should have known you were bad news. But oh, no, I had to follow this crazy scheme of Nancy's and make a complete idiot of myself. It's not going to work, Philip. Not for another day. Not for a week. Not at all. I'm going back to the hotel."

"Carla, will you listen to me?" Philip stuffed his hands

into his pants pockets, and his face hardened with a grimness she hadn't expected to see in him. "It's working, believe me, it's working."

"Maybe everything is fine for you. But I don't want to get involved. Not with you."

"You're already involved."

Defiantly, she crossed her arms in front of her. "Not anymore." Mentally and emotionally, she would have to block him out of her life before the pain became too great.

"That's twice in one day."

"Don't you see?" she cried as if shouting helped prove her point. "All right, all right, I conceded the point. I could like you very much. It probably wouldn't take very much to fall in love with you, but I just can't. Look at me, Philip." Tossing her head back, she held out her hands, palms down, for his inspection. "I'm shaking because already I care enough for you to worry about a stabbing that happened before we even met."

"Being knifed is the only thing that's ever happened to me. I was a rookie, and stupid…"

"This is supposed to reassure me?" she retorted, jamming her hat on top of her head.

He followed her to the front door and pressed a shoulder against the wood to prevent her from opening it. "Carla, for heaven's sake, will you listen to reason?"

Hands clenched at her side, she emitted a frustrated sigh. She didn't expect him to understand. "It was hopeless from the beginning."

"I'm not letting you leave until you listen to me."

Carla exhaled, her lungs aching from the effort to control her emotion. "Philip, I like you so much." Of its own volition, her hand found and explored the side of his jaw. She could feel his muscles tense as her fingertips investigated the rough feel of his day-old beard. "I won't forget you," she whispered shakily.

His hand captured hers and moved it to his mouth so that he could kiss the tender skin of her palm. As if he'd burned her, Carla jerked her fingers free.

"Come on, I'll take you back to the hotel." His quiet determination convinced her to let him escort her back. She knew him well enough to realize arguing would do little good.

Philip didn't say a word on the entire trip back. They passed a horse-drawn carriage, and Carla wanted to weep at the sight of the two young lovers who sat in the back with their arms entwined. What a perfect end to a lovely day such a ride would have been. Philip gave her a look that said he was reading her thoughts. They could have been that couple.

Bowing her head, Carla studied her clenched hands, all too aware that Philip thought she was overreacting. But she couldn't ask him to be something he wasn't, and she couldn't change, either.

His hand cupped her elbow as she climbed the short series of stairs that led to the hotel lobby. Halfway through the lobby, Carla paused and murmured, "I'll say good-bye here."

"No, you won't. I'll take you to your room."

When they reached her door, Carla's fingers nervously fumbled with the purse latch. Her hand closed around the key, and she drew in a deep, shuddering breath.

"I know you're angry," she said without looking up. Her gaze was centered on the room key. "And to be honest, I don't blame you. Thank you for today and yesterday. I'll never think of Mexico without remembering you." The brittle smile she gave him as she glanced up took more of an effort than he would ever know.

Philip's mouth drew faintly upward, and Carla guessed that he wasn't in any more of a mood to smile than she was.

Her hand twisted the doorknob.

"What? No farewell kiss? Surely, I deserve that much."

Carla meant only to brush her lips over his. Not to tease, but to disguise the very real physical attraction she felt for him. But as she raised her mouth, his hand cupped the back of her head and she was crushed in his embrace. Where Philip had always been gentle, now he was urgent, greedily devouring her with a hunger that left her so weak she clung to him. She wanted to twist away but realized that if she struggled, Philip would release her. Instead, her arms crept around his neck. Philip groaned aloud and gathered her as close as physical boundaries would allow, his arms crushing her.

A trembling weakness attacked her, and Philip altered his method of assault. He kissed her leisurely, with a thoroughness that made her ache for more. He didn't rush but seemed to savor each second, content to have her break the contact.

She did, but only when she thought her lungs would burst.

"Goodnight, Carla," he whispered against her ear, and opened the door for her.

Carla would have stumbled inside if Philip hadn't caught her. With as much dignity as possible, she broke free, entered the room unaided and closed the door without looking back.

The cool, dark interior contained no welcome. The taste

of Philip's kiss was on her mouth, and the male scent of him lingered, disturbing her further.

Pacing the floor did little to relieve the ache. Desperately, she tried watching television and was irrationally angry that every station had programs in Spanish.

After her long afternoon nap she wasn't tired. Nor was she interested in visiting the party scene that was taking place in the lounge and bars.

Her frustration mounted with every second. Standing on the balcony that overlooked the pool area, she noted again that there wasn't anyone around. A gentle breeze stirred the evening air and contained a freshness that often follows a storm. The first night she'd arrived and met Philip they had gone for a swim. And the pool had been fantastic.

Laps would help, and with the heavy tourist crowds that filled the pool during the day, it would be impossible to do them in the morning. Besides, if she tired herself out, she might be able to sleep.

Determined now, she located a fresh suit in the bottom of her carryall and hurriedly undressed. Tomorrow would be filled with avoiding Philip, but she didn't want to think about that now.

The water was refreshingly cool as she dived in and broke the surface twenty feet later. Her arms carried her to the far side, and the first lap was accomplished with a drive born of remorse. There wasn't anyone to blame for this but herself. She'd known almost from the beginning what Philip was. He hadn't tried to disguise it.

Her shoulders heaving as she struggled for breath ten

long laps later, Carla stood in the shallow end and brushed the hair from her face.

"I didn't think you'd be able to stay away," Philip said, standing beside her. "I couldn't either."

Five

Carla froze, her hands in her hair. Philip was right. When she'd come to the pool, the thought had played in the back of her mind that he would be there, too. For all her self-proclaimed righteousness, she didn't want their time together to end with an argument.

The worst part was that she'd overreacted, and like an immature child, she'd run away for the second time. It was a wonder he hadn't given up on her. "I'm sorry about tonight," she murmured in a voice that was quivery and soft. "But when I realized how you'd gotten that scar, I panicked."

Philip turned her around so that they faced each other standing waist deep in the pool's aqua-blue water. "You don't need to explain. I know."

The moon's gentle radiance revealed a thin film of moisture glistening on his torso. Carla longed to touch him. "Turn around," she requested softly, and when he did, she slid her arms around his waist, just below the water line, and pressed her cheek against the curve of his spine. Almost shyly, her fingers located the scar, and she bent down and kissed it gently. The next time, Philip might not be so fortunate; such a blade could end his life. The thought was sobering, and a chill raced up Carla's arms.

"We agreed to a week," Philip reminded her as he twisted around and looped his arms over her shoulder. "This vacation is for us. Our lives, our jobs, our friends are back in Washington state. But we're here. Nothing's going to spoil what we have for the remainder of the week." He said it with a determination she couldn't deny.

Nothing will ruin it, Carla's heart responded. Everything was already ruined, her head shouted.

They swam for an hour, making excuses to touch each other, kissing when the time seemed right. And it often seemed right.

The night had been well spent when they made arrangements to meet again in the morning. Silently, Carla climbed into the bed across from her sleeping friend. A glance at her watch told her it was after two. This time she had no trouble falling into a restful slumber.

The early-morning sounds of Nancy brushing her teeth and dressing woke Carla when the sun was barely up. Struggling to a sitting position, Carla raised her arms high above her head and yawned. "What time is it?"

"Six," Nancy whispered. "Eduardo and I are flying to Puerto Vallarta. I probably won't be back until late tonight."

Carla nodded and settled back into her bed, hugging the thick pillow.

"And before I forget, I have an invitation for you and… your friend."

"Philip," Carla supplied.

"Right." Nancy laughed lightly. "Who says my head isn't in the clouds? Anyway, you're both invited to dinner with Eduardo and me Saturday evening."

Carla's eyes remained closed, and she nuzzled the covers over her shoulder. "Sounds nice, I'll mention it to Philip." Her lashes fluttered open. "That's our last day here."

"It's really going by quickly, isn't it?" The sad note in Nancy's voice couldn't be disguised. "We've got only three more days."

"Three days," Carla repeated sleepily.

"But you have to admit, this has been our best vacation."

And our worst, Carla mused. Every year she hoped to have a holiday fling. But not next year. Her heart couldn't take this. Of course, not everyone would affect her the way Philip had, but she wasn't game to have her hopes dashed every year.

"By the way, did you hear the gossip that was going around the hotel yesterday?" Nancy didn't wait for Carla's answer. "Some crazy American was standing by the pool serenading a girl with love songs. Apparently, she's staying at the hotel."

For the third time that morning, Carla's eyes opened. A faint color began an ascent up her neck to her cheeks. "Some crazy American?"

"Right, an American. Isn't that the most incredibly romantic thing you've ever heard? Women would kill for a man like that."

"I think you're right." Carla's interest was aroused as she sat up. "Allow me to introduce you to some crazy American Saturday night."

"Philip?"

"You got it." Carla blinked twice. "And it was romantic, except that everyone at the pool was staring at us."

Nancy sighed and sat on the end of Carla's mattress. "Eduardo's romantic like that." She smoothed a wrinkle from her white cotton pants as she crossed her legs. "He says the most beautiful things to me. But half the time I don't know whether to believe him or not. The lines sound so practiced, and yet he appears sincere."

"In instances like that only time will tell," Carla said without thinking.

"But that's something we don't have. In three days I'll be flying home, and I bet I never hear from Eduardo again."

Carla searched her friend's coolly composed face, interpreting the doubts. "But I thought we were only looking for a little romance to liven up our holiday."

Nancy sighed expressively, and her eyes grew wary. "I was, but you know what? I think there's something basically wrong with me. For years now, you and I have had this dream of the perfect vacation. We've been to Southern California, Vegas, Hawaii and now Mazatlán. Every year we plan one week when we can let down our hair and have a good time." She paused, and her shoulders sagged in a gesture of defeat. "We do it so that when we get back to Seattle and our neat, orderly lives, we'll have something to get us through another year."

"But it's never worked out that way. Our vacations are as dull."

"I know," Nancy agreed morosely. "Until this year, and all of sudden I discover I'm not the type for a one-week fling. I'll never be the 'love 'em and leave 'em' type. I like Eduardo, and as far as I can tell, he likes me. But I could be one of any number of women he escorts during the course of a summer. He sees a fun-seeking American on vacation, and I doubt that he'd recognize the hardworking high school teacher that I really am." Nancy sighed and ran her fingers through her hair in frustration. "The funny part is that after all these years this was exactly what I thought

I wanted. And now that I've met Eduardo I can see how wrong I've been. When I meet a man I want a meaningful relationship that will grow. Not a one-week fling."

Carla wasn't surprised by her friend's insights. Nancy often saw things more clearly than she did, whereas she, Carla, often reacted more to her emotions. Remembering last night and the way she'd panicked at the knowledge that Philip had been stabbed produced a renewed sense of regret. With Philip her emotions had done a lot of reacting lately.

Later, when they met for an excursion to the Palmito de la Virgen, the bird-watchers' island in the bay, Carla mentioned Eduardo's invitation to dinner. Philip was agreeable, as she knew he would be.

The following morning, Philip and Carla went deep-sea fishing at the crack of dawn. Philip managed to bring in a large tuna, but all Carla caught was a bad case of seasickness.

"It wasn't the boat rocking so much," she explained later, "but the way the captain killed that poor fish, cut him up and passed him around for everyone to sample—*raw.*"

"It's a delicacy."

"Not to me."

On their last afternoon together, while Carla stood terrified on the beach, Philip went parasailing. With her eyes tightly shut, his glasses clenched in her hand, she waited until he was in the air before she chanced a look. Even then her heart hammered in her throat, and she struggled to beat down the fear that threatened to overcome her. Philip had to be crazy to allow his life to hang by a thin line. The only thing keeping him airborne was a motor boat and a cord that was attached from the boat to the parachute.

Her fear was transmitted as an irrational form of anger.

The worst part was that Carla realized she was reacting to her emotions again. She wanted Philip to behave like a normal, safe and sane male. Who would have believed that a lanky guy who wore horn-rimmed glasses defied death every day of his life?

Carla was exactly where Philip had left her when he returned. His glasses had made deep indentations in her fingers, and she didn't need to be told she was deathly pale.

Exhilarated, Philip ran to her side and took his glasses from her hand. "It was fantastic," he said, wiping the sea water from his face with a towel and placing it in her beach bag.

She gave him a poor imitation of a smile and lied. "It looked like fun."

"Then why do you resemble a Halloween ghost?"

"It frightened me," she admitted, and was grateful he didn't mention that she looked as if she were going to throw up.

"Carla, I was watching you from up there. You were more than frightened. You looked like a statue with your eyes closed and your teeth clenched, standing there frightened out of your wits."

"I thought you couldn't see without your glasses," she responded, only slightly piqued.

"My vision is affected only close up. I saw how terrified you were."

"I told you before, I'm a conservative person." She didn't enjoy being on the defensive.

"You're more conservative than a pin-striped suit," he growled. "There's nothing reckless in parasailing."

"And that's your opinion." Impatiently, she picked up her beach towel, stuffed it in her bag and turned away.

"The most daring thing you've done since we arrived

is eat chicken in chocolate sauce," Philip insisted, rushing up beside her.

If he wanted to fight, she wasn't going to back down. "What do you want from me, anyway?" she cried.

He slapped his hands against his sides. "I don't know. I guess I'd like for you to recognize that there's more to life than self-actualization through checkers."

Her hand flew to her hip, and she glared at him with a fierceness that stole her breath. "You know, I really tried to be the good sport. Everything you've wanted to do, including risking my life in that…that ocean surf." She waved her finger at the incoming tide. "Deep-sea fishing…everything. How can you say those things to me?"

"For heaven's sake, people come from all over the world to swim in this ocean. What makes it so dangerous for you?"

Several moments passed before she'd gained enough control of her voice to speak. "The very first day we arrived you warned me that the current was too strong for swimming."

"It was." He pointed to a green flag beside the lifeguard station. "The flag was red."

"Oh." Carla swallowed and forged ahead, weaving her way around the sunbathing beauties that dotted the beach. "Why didn't you explain that at the time?" she demanded.

Curious stares followed her as she ran up the concrete steps that led to the hotel's outdoor restaurant. Not waiting for Philip, she pulled out a chair and sat down, purposely placing her beach bag in the empty chair beside her.

Philip joined her, taking his short-sleeve shirt out of her bag and impatiently stuffing his arms into the sleeve.

"And I suppose you're going to make a big deal out of

the fact I didn't want to eat raw fish or dance on my hat," Carla cried, incensed. "I'll have you know—"

Before she could finish, the waiter came for their order. To prove a point, Carla defiantly asked for the hotel special, a hollowed-out coconut filled with a frothy alcoholic concoction. Philip looked at her in surprise, then ordered a cup of coffee.

"Carla," he said after the waiter had left, "what are you doing? You'll be under the table before you finish that drink. There must be sixteen ounces of booze in that coconut."

Gritting her teeth, Carla slowly shook her head. "Everything I do is wrong. There's no satisfying you, is there? If you find me so dull and boring, why have you insisted we spend this week together?"

"I don't find you dull." The paper straw he was fingering snapped in half.

"Then…then why are you so angry with me? What have I done?"

Philip ran a hand across his eyes. "Because I know what's coming. We're leaving in the morning, and when we arrive in Seattle it's goodbye, Philip. With no regrets and no looking back."

"But we agreed—"

"I know what we agreed," he growled. "But I didn't count on… Listen Carla, I didn't mean for any of this to come out this way. I think I'm falling in love with you."

Carla felt the air rush out of her. "Oh, Philip, you can't make a statement like that after only knowing me a week."

"Six days," he corrected grimly, and stared at her. His annoyance was barely in check, even now, when he'd admitted his feelings. "I'm not all that versed in love," he said stiffly. "Nicole was evidence of that. And if the truth be known, I thought for a long time afterward that there'd never be another woman I'd care about as much. But what I feel for you grows stronger every minute we're together. We have something special, Carla, and your cautious, conservative fears are going to ruin it."

Philip stopped talking when the waiter approached with their drinks. Carla stared at her drink. Normally, she didn't drink during the day, but Philip's accusations hurt. She took a tentative sip from the alcohol-filled coconut and winced. Philip was right; she was a fool to have ordered it.

"I can see what's going to happen," he continued. "And I don't like it."

Confusion raced through her. Philip was saying the very things she'd dreaded most—and most she longed to hear. "Don't you attribute this attraction to the lure of the forbidden?" She sought a sane argument. "You knew from the beginning how I feel about men in law enforcement... and maybe in the back of your mind you thought I would change."

"No," he answered starkly. "Maybe the thought flitted through my mind at one time. But I felt that chemistry between us before you ever told me about your father."

"That soon? Philip, we'd only just met."

Her answer didn't appear to please him. "Don't you think I've told myself that a thousand times?"

The silence stretched between them, tight and unbearable. Carla shifted and pushed her drink aside. Tonight was their last night, and it seemed like they were going to spend it fighting. She was more than half in love with him herself, but she couldn't let Philip know that, especially since she had no intention of continuing to see him after they returned to Washington state. What was the use? He wouldn't change, and she couldn't. There was no sense in dragging out the inevitable.

"I think I'll go up and get ready for tonight," she said, struggling to keep her voice level.

Philip didn't try to stop her as she stood, reached for her beach bag and walked away. Tears had filled her eyes by the time she reached her room. Pressing her index finger under her eye helped stop the brimming emotion. Somehow, with a smile on her face, she'd make it through tonight and tomorrow. When the time came, she'd thank Philip for a marvelous week and kiss him goodbye. And mean it.

A careful application of her cosmetics helped disguise the fact that she'd spent a good portion of the afternoon fighting back emotion. Carla thought she'd done a good job until Nancy came into the room to change, took one look at her friend and declared:

"You've been crying."

"Oh, darn!" Carla raced to the bathroom mirror. "How'd you know?"

"It was either the puffy red eyes or the extra makeup. Honestly, Carla, with a complexion like yours you can't help but tell."

"Great. Now what am I going to do?"

Nancy inspected her closet, finally deciding on a pale-blue sleeveless dress with spaghetti straps. "The same thing I'll probably end up doing. Smile and say how much you're going to miss Mexico and how this has been the best vacation of your life." She turned and laid the dress across the bed. "Now that's what you're supposed to tell everyone else. What you say to me is the truth."

"Philip claims he's falling in love with me," she declared, and sniffled loudly. Fresh tears formed, and she grabbed a tissue and forced her head back to stare at the ceiling, hoping to discourage any new tear tracks from ruining her makeup.

"And that makes you cry. I thought you really liked Philip."

"But there's something I didn't tell you. Philip's in law enforcement. He's a cop." She didn't need to say another word.

"Good grief, Carla, how do you get yourself into these things?"

"I don't know," she lamented, pressing the tissue under her eyes. "Philip was so open and honest about it when he didn't have to be, and when he suggested that we enjoy this week I couldn't turn him down. He's wonderful. Everything about him is wonderful."

"Except that he's a poiceman."

"And he's amazingly like my dad. It doesn't matter where either one of them is, the badge is always on. Even when we were shopping, Philip stopped and broke up a potential fight. Worse, Philip's been stabbed once because he was careless."

"Your dad was hurt not long ago, wasn't he?" Nancy asked from her position on the end of the bed.

"Once. He was chasing a suspect, fell and broke his arm."

Nancy nodded. "I remember because you were so furious with him."

"And with good reason. Dad's too old to be out there running after men twenty years younger than he is."

"Take my advice and don't tell him that." Nancy's comment was punctuated with a soft laugh.

Carla decided that Nancy knew her father better than most people did. "Don't worry, Mom said it for me."

An abrupt knock on the door caused them both to glance

curiously at one another. Carla's watch told her it was forty-five minutes before they were scheduled to meet the men.

Since she was ready, Carla answered the door. "Philip!" she exclaimed. How good he looked in a suit and tie! And his eyes were the deepest gray she could remember seeing. One glance at her, and their color intensified even more.

"I thought you might be ready," he said stiffly.

"Yes… I am."

"Would you have a drink with me in the lounge? Nancy and Eduardo can join us there."

He sounded as if he were preparing to read Carla her rights. "Sure," she replied, and tossed a look over her shoulder to Nancy. "We'll meet you in the lounge."

Nancy arched both brows expressively. "See you there."

Philip didn't say a word until after they'd ordered their drinks. "I owe you an apology."

Carla's smile wavered only slightly as she reached for his hand. "You can't be any sorrier than I am. I wish I could change, and if there was ever a man I'd do it for, it would be you. But you've seen how I am. I just don't want our last hours together to be spent arguing."

Philip took her hand and squeezed it tightly. "I don't either. We have tonight."

"And tomorrow," she murmured. But their flight was scheduled for the morning, and they'd be in the air a good portion of the day. Once they landed at Sea-Tac International Airport, Philip would catch a connecting flight to Spokane. They would be separated by three hundred and fifteen miles that might as well have been three thousand.

"I have something for you," he announced casually, and pulled a small wrapped package from his coat pocket.

Astonished, Carla raised questioning eyes to Philip. "We must think alike. I've got something for you, too. I'd planned on giving it to you tomorrow. I didn't want you to forget me."

"There's little chance of that," he said with a wry twist of his mouth. "Go on, open it."

Eagerly, Carla tore off the ribbon and paper and was surprised to discover it was a jewelery box. Lifting the black velvet lid, she gasped in surprised pleasure. An exquisite turquoise necklace and matching earrings lay nestled in a bed of plush velvet. The ring he'd given her earlier matched the set. "Oh, Philip, you shouldn't have." Fresh tears misted her eyes, and she bit her bottom lip in an effort to forestall their flow. "They're beautiful. I'll treasure them always."

"Would you like me to help you put it on?"

"Please." She moved to the edge of the chair, turned and scooped up her hair with her forearm. Deftly, Philip placed the turquoise necklace against the hollow of her throat and fastened it in place. Carla managed the earrings on her own.

When she'd finished, she searched through her purse for a tissue to wipe away the tears that clouded her vision. She had to be crazy to walk away from the most wonderful man in the world. Crazy and stupid.

"Here comes Nancy and Eduardo," Philip announced, and stood as the introductions were being made.

The four sat together, and Carla was surprised to discover that Eduardo wasn't anything like she recalled. Her first impression had been all wrong. The Latin good looks were in evidence, but there was a natural shyness about him, a reserve that was far more appealing than his striking good looks. When he spoke English, his Spanish inflection was barely noticeable. Carla guessed that Eduardo had traveled extensively in the United States or had lived there. But more than anything else, Carla noted the way Eduardo watched Nancy. Each time his gaze swung to her friend, the dark eyes brightened and his masculine features would soften noticeably.

Conversation between the four flowed smoothly. When it came time to leave for dinner, Eduardo told them that the hotel's most expensive restaurant had a dining area designated especially for small private parties. The room resembled an intimate dining room, and had been reserved for them. A friend of his owned the hotel, Eduardo explained, and had given his permission for them to use this room. He led the way.

"It's lovely," Carla observed at first glance, impressed with the Aztec decor.

"I chose the menu myself," Eduardo explained. "I hope you will find it to your liking."

"I'm sure we will," Carla murmured. If the meal was anything like the room, this would be a dinner she'd remember all her life.

Eduardo continued by naming the dishes that they would be sampling. Carla understood little Spanish and appreciated it when Eduardo translated for her. "The food in Mexico is a combination of indigenous Indian dishes and Spanish cuisine with some Arabic and French influences."

Carla quit counting after six courses. Replete, she settled back in her chair, her hands cupping a wineglass. "And to think none of us would be here if you two men hadn't ordered a margarita that first night." Almost instantly Carla realized that she'd said the wrong thing. Nancy's eyes widened in warning, and Carla averted her gaze to the wineglass in her hand. Apparently, Nancy hadn't explained their game to Eduardo, and Carla had just stuck her foot in her mouth.

"I'm sorry?" Eduardo questioned, and a curious frown drew his thick brows together. "I don't understand."

"It's nothing," Nancy said quickly.

"Carla said something about Philip and me ordering margaritas the day we met. I'm confused."

"Really, it's nothing," Nancy insisted, a desperate edge to her voice.

An uneasy silence filled the room. "Please explain," Eduardo said stiffly. "A man doesn't like to be the only one not in on a joke."

"It wasn't a joke." Nancy avoided meeting Eduardo's probing gaze. "It's just that Carla and I never have any luck finding decent men, and we decided... Well, you see, we were sitting in the cocktail lounge and..." She tossed Carla a frantic glare. "You explain."

Carla's eyes rounded mutinously. "Nancy—I mean... we..." Good grief, she wasn't doing any better! Silently, she implored Philip to take up the task.

To Carla's relief, Philip did exactly that, explaining at length in Spanish. Three pairs of eyes studied Eduardo, and it was easy to see that he was furious.

"And whose idea was this game?" His accent became thicker with every word.

"Mine," Nancy replied, accepting full responsibility. "But it wasn't like you think. I would never have—"

Pushing back his chair, Eduardo stood. "This has been an enjoyable time with my American friends, but I fear I have a business engagement and must cut our evening short."

Nancy stood up as well. "Eduardo, you can't leave now. We must..."

Philip leaned over to Carla.

"Let's leave these two alone to sort this out," he whispered in her ear, and they stood.

"How could I have said anything so stupid?" Carla moaned as they left the restaurant.

"You didn't know."

Philip's words did little to soothe her. "Didn't you see the look in Nancy's eyes? She'll never forgive me, and I don't blame her." Carla felt like weeping. "I've betrayed my best friend."

"Carla," Philip said, and placed an arm around her shoulder. "You can't blame yourself. Nancy should have said something to Eduardo before this."

"The bad part is that Eduardo honestly likes her, and I've ruined that." She kicked at a loose pebble. "I always did get a loose tongue when I drink too much wine."

Philip cleared his throat. "I hadn't noticed."

"And you're not helping things."

"Sorry." But his smile told her he wasn't. "You shouldn't worry. If Eduardo cares for Nancy, he'll give her the opportunity to explain."

"But I feel rotten."

"I know you do. Come on. Let's walk off some of that fantastic dinner." His arm tightened around her waist, and she propped her head against his shoulder.

The beach was possibly even more beautiful than it had been any night that week.

"Do you remember the first time we were here?" Philip asked, his voice low as he rubbed his chin along the top of her head.

Carla answered with a short shake of her head. "I remember thinking that you wanted to kiss me."

"I did."

"And at the time I was afraid you were the type of guy who would wait until the third date."

"Me?" He paused and pushed his glasses up the bridge of his nose. "And I was wondering what you'd do if I did make a pass."

A gentle breeze off the ocean carried Carla's soft laugh into the night. "No wonder you had a shocked look when we went swimming and I asked you to kiss me under water."

"I thought I'd died and gone to heaven."

The laughter faded and was replaced by a sadness born of the knowledge that within a matter of hours they would be separating. "This has been a wonderful week."

"The best."

Absently, Carla fingered the turquoise necklace. "I don't ever want this to end. This is heaven being here with you. Reality is only a few hours away."

"It doesn't have to end, you know." Philip stopped walking and turned her in his arms. His smoky-gray eyes burned into hers. "I love you, Carla."

"Philip, please," she pleaded. "Don't."

"No, I'm going to say it. Believe me, I know all the arguments. One week is all we've had, and there are a thousand questions that still need to be answered. I want to get to know you, really know you. I want to meet your family and introduce you to mine."

A bubble of pain and hysteria threatened to burst inside her. "You and my dad have a lot in common."

Philip ignored the sarcasm. "You're a beautiful, warm, intelligent woman."

"Don't forget conservative."

"And conservative," he added. "Have you ever thought how beautiful our children could be?"

"Philip, don't do this to me." She had thought about it. Blending her life with Philip's had been on her mind all afternoon. But no matter how appealing the imagery, Carla couldn't see past the police uniform and badge. "I... I think I should go back and check on Nancy. And I still have my packing to do."

Philip pinched his mouth tightly closed when he delivered her to the hotel room. "I'll see you in the morning," she promised, not meeting his gaze.

"In the morning," he repeated, but he didn't try to kiss her. Carla couldn't decide if she was grateful or not.

A muffled sound could be heard on the other side of the door. "Good night," she murmured miserably, and slipped inside her room.

Nancy was lying across the bed, her shoulders heaving as she wept. "Oh, Carla," she cried, and struggled to sit up. "Eduardo wouldn't even listen to me. He was barely polite."

Nancy and Carla looked at each other, and both burst into tears.

Six

The sun had barely crested the ocean, its golden strands etching their way across the morning beach, when Carla woke. Her roommate remained asleep as Carla slipped from the bed, quickly donning washed-out jeans and a warm sweatshirt. It wouldn't seem right to leave Mazatlán without one last walk along the water's edge.

Rushing down the concrete steps that led to the countless acres of white sand, Carla scanned the deserted area. Her spirits sank. This last stroll would have been perfect if Philip were here to share it with her.

Rolling up the jeans to her knees, she teased the oncoming tide with her bare feet. The water was warm and bubbly as it hit the shore. She vividly recalled the few times she'd swum in the surf with Philip. When the salt water had stung her eyes and momentarily blinded her, Philip had lifted her into his strong arms and carried her to shore.

With a wistful sigh, Carla strolled away from the water's edge, kicking up sand as she walked. Every memory of this vacation would be connected with Philip. She'd be a fool to think otherwise.

"Carla!"

Her heart swelled as she spun and waved her hand high above her head. Philip.

His shoulders were heaving by the time he ran the distance and joined her. "Morning." He reached for her and looked as if he meant to kiss her, then dropped his hands, apparently changing his mind.

"Morning. I was praying you'd be here."

"I thought I saw you by the pool."

The salty breeze carried her laughter. "I was there waiting for you to magically reappear."

"Poof. Here I am."

"Like magic," she whispered, and slipped her arm around his waist. They turned and continued strolling away from the hotel. The untouched morning beach meandered for miles in the distance.

"How's Nancy?"

Carla shrugged. "Asleep. But for how long, I don't know," she said as a reminder to them both that she couldn't stay long. "I guess Eduardo wouldn't let her explain that picking him up in the lounge never was a game. Not really."

"His attitude is difficult to understand, since Latin men are usually indulgent toward their women."

"Are you as indulgent toward your women?" Carla inquired with rounded, innocent eyes, determined to make this a happy conversation. She'd never be able to tell him all the things in her heart.

"I must be, or you would have shared my bed before now."

Forcing her gaze toward the sea, Carla struggled to maintain control of her poise. "You sound mighty sure of yourself, Philip Garrison," she returned. If he'd said that for shock value, he'd succeeded. The evening in his parents' condo had caught her off guard. The atmosphere had been intimate, and the wine had flown too freely.

"I don't think I'm being overconfident," Philip replied. "You wanted me as much as I did you. But whether you're willing to admit it is something else."

Carla understood what he was saying and flushed.

"What were you thinking when I called you just now?" Philip asked, breaking the uneasy silence that had settled over them. "I can't remember ever seeing you look more pensive."

"About Mexico and what a wonderful time I've had," she said, and smiled up at him. "That's mostly your doing. In my mind I'll never be able to separate the two."

"Me and Mazatlán?"

She answered with a short nod.

Her response didn't seem to please him. He glanced at his watch and applied a gentle pressure to the small of her back as he turned them around and headed for the hotel. "I'll take you back before Nancy wakes."

They didn't speak as they walked toward the El Cid. Then, Carla said somberly, "I was hoping you'd be here. My beach bag's up ahead. Your gift's inside." The hand-crafted marlin carved from rosewood had been expensive. Carla had seen Philip admire it the day they'd gone shopping at the arts and crafts center and had purchased the hand-rubbed wood sculpture for him while he had been talking to some Canadians.

Now her eyes shone with a happy-sad expression as Philip unwrapped the gift. He peeled back the paper and glanced at her wordlessly. Delight mingled with surprise as his eyes looked almost silver in the light of the morning sun.

"Thank you," he said simply.

"No," she replied, and swallowed against the hoarseness building in her throat. "Thank you. I'll never forget you, Philip, or this week we've shared. The reason for the marlin is so you won't forget me." She kissed him then, her hands sliding around his middle as her lips met his. It was meant to be a simple act of appreciation, but this kiss soon took on another, more intense significance. This was goodbye.

Philip's arms locked around her narrow waist, lifting her off her bare feet. Bittersweet memories merged with pure hunger. Mouths hardened against one another in a hungry, grinding demand. Their heads twisted slowly from side to side as the kiss continued and continued until Carla thought her lungs would burst. Incredibly, she couldn't give enough or take enough to satisfy the overwhelming passion consuming her resolve.

When they broke apart she was weak and panting. Her legs were incapable of holding her as she pressed her cheek to the hard wall of his chest and gloried in the thundering, erratic beat of his heart. Her shaking fingers toyed with the hair that curled along the back of his neck. But the comfort and security of his embrace was shattered when he spoke.

"Carla, I'm only going to ask you once. Can I see you once we're home?"

"Oh, Philip," she moaned, caught in the trap of indecision. He was forcing her to face the very question she dreaded most. Her lips felt dry, and she moistened them. She couldn't tell him "yes," although her heart was screaming for her to do exactly that. And "no" was equally intolerable. Bright tears shimmered in her eyes as she stared up at him, silently pleading with him to understand that she couldn't say what he wanted to hear.

"Listen to me, Carla," he urged gently. "What we found in Mazatlán is rare. But two people can't know if they're in love after seven short days. We both need time to discover if what we've found is real." His hand smoothed the red curls behind her ear. "What do you say? Spokane isn't that far from Seattle, and meeting would be a simple matter of a phone call."

"Oh, Philip, I'm such a coward." Her long nails made deep indentations inher palms, but she hardly noticed the pain.

"Say 'yes,'" he urged, his fingers gripping her shoulders.

Carla felt as if she were standing on the edge of the Grand Canyon looking down. She knew the pitfalls of loving Philip, and the terror of it gripped her, making speech impossible.

Trapped as she was, she couldn't agree or disagree. "I wish you wouldn't," she murmured finally.

The gray eyes she had come to adore hardened briefly before he dropped his hands to his side. "When you're through letting your fears and prejudices rule your life, let me know." Abruptly he turned, leaving her standing alone in the bright morning sunlight.

"Philip." Her feet kicked up sand as she raced after him. "We can talk more at the airport."

"No." He shook his head. "All along you've assumed I was booked on the same return flight as you. I won't be leaving for another two days."

"Oh." She was forced to continue running to keep up with his long strides. "Why didn't you say something?"

"Why? If you can't make up your mind now, flying back together shouldn't make any difference."

He stopped and caressed the underside of her face. "Goodbye, Carla." His eyes were infinitely sad, and he looked as if he wanted to say something more, but changed his mind. Without another word he turned and left.

Alone and hurting, she stood on the beach with the wind whipping at her from all directions.

"Phone. I think it's Cliff," Nancy announced on her way out of the kitchen.

Before Mexico the news would have been mildly thrilling. But Carla couldn't look at Cliff Hoffman and not be reminded of Philip. Not that the two men were anything alike. Cliff was the current heartthrob of half the medical staff at Highline Community Hospital. Carla had been flattered and excited when he'd started asking her out.

Unhooking her leg from the arm of the overstuffed chair, Carla set her book aside and moved into the kitchen, where the phone was mounted on the wall.

"Hello."

"Carla, it's Cliff."

"Hi." She hoped the enthusiasm in her voice didn't sound forced.

"How was Mexico?"

The question caught Carla off guard, and for one terrifying moment she couldn't breathe. "Fine."

"You don't sound enthusiastic. Don't tell me you got sick?"

"No… No, everything was fine." What a weak word "fine" was, Carla decided. It couldn't come close to describing the most gloriously wonderful, exciting vacation of her life. But she couldn't tell that to Cliff when she sounded on the verge of tears.

"I expected to hear from you by now. You've been back a week." She could hear an edge of disappointment in his voice, but suspected it was as phony as her enthusiasm.

From the beginning of their nonrelationship, Cliff had let it be known she had plenty of competition. Philip had once asked her if there was anyone special waiting for her in Seattle. At the time, mentioning Cliff hadn't even crossed her mind.

"It's been hectic around here...unpacking and all." No excuse could have sounded more lame.

"I was thinking we should get together soon." Cliff left the invitation open-ended.

If he expected her to jump at the opportunity to spend time in his company, he was going to be disappointed. "Sure," she agreed without much enthusiasm.

"This weekend?"

Why not? she mused dejectedly. She wouldn't be doing anything by moping around the apartment, which was exactly what she and Nancy had been doing since their return. "That sounds good."

"Let's take in a movie Saturday night, then."

"Fine." There was that word again.

Five minutes later, Carla returned to the living room and her book.

"These arrived while you were on the phone." A huge bouquet of three dozen red roses captured her attention. Philip. Her heart soared. That crazy, wonderful man was wooing her with expensive flowers. It was exactly like him. She'd phone him and chastise him for being so extravagant, and then she'd tell him how miserable the last week had been without him.

Nancy sniffled and wiped the tears from her cheeks. "Eduardo sent them."

"Eduardo?"

"He sent the flowers in hopes that I'll forgive him for his behavior our last night in Mazatlán."

Carla felt like crying, too, but not for the same reasons as her roommate. "I'm really happy for you." At least one of them would be lifted from the doldrums.

"You might still hear from Philip."

"Sure," Carla said with an indifferent shrug. If anyone did anything to improve the situation between her and Philip, it would have to be she. And she couldn't, not when seeing him again would make it all the more difficult. As it was, he dominated her thoughts.

Fifteen minutes later the phone rang again. Carla's immediate reaction was to jump up and answer it, but Nancy was sitting closer to the apartment telephone and for Carla to rush to it would be a dead give away. Although Carla pretended she was reading, her ears were finely tuned to the telephone conversation. When Nancy gave a small, happy cry, Carla's interest piqued. Eduardo, it had to be, especially since Nancy was exclaiming how much she loved the roses. She told him how sorry she was about the mix-up and how everything had changed since Mexico.

When her friend started whispering into the receiver, Carla decided it was time to make her exit. "I think I'll go visit Gramps," she said, reaching for her bulky knit sweater and her purse.

Nancy smiled in appreciation and gave a friendly wave as Carla walked toward the door.

The sky was overcast, and Carla swung a sweater over her shoulder as she walked out the front door. Summer didn't usually arrive in the Pacific Northwest until late July.

"See you later," Nancy called with a happy lilt of her voice.

Carla's Grandpa Benoit was her mother's father. He lived in a retirement center in south Seattle not far from

Carla's apartment. Whereas Carla had always felt distant from her mother, she shared a special closeness with Gramps. Grandpa Benoit loved cards and games of any kind. From the time Carla could count, he had taught her cribbage, checkers and chess. The three essential C's, Gramps called them. It was because of Gramps that Carla had won the checkers championship through the King County Parks Department.

Pulling into the parking lot, Carla sat in her car for several minutes. If she showed up again today, Gramps's questions would only become more probing. From the day she'd returned to Seattle he'd guessed something had happened in Mexico. At first he hadn't pried; his questions had been general, as if her answers didn't much concern him. But Carla knew her grandfather too well to be tricked by that. Yesterday, when she'd stopped by on her way to work, they'd played a quick game of checkers, and Carla had lost on a stupid error.

"I guess that young man from Mexico must still be on your mind?" His eyes hadn't lifted from the playing board.

"What young man?"

"The one you haven't mentioned."

Carla ignored the comment. "Are you going to allow me a rematch or not?"

"Not." Still he didn't lift his gaze to hers. "Don't see much use in playing when your mind isn't on the game."

Carla bristled. She'd lost plenty of games to Gramps over the years, andit was unfair of him to comment on this one.

"Seems you should have lots of things you'd rather be doing than playing checkers with an old man anyways."

"Gramps!" Carla was shocked that he'd say something

like that. "I love spending time with you. By now, I'd think you'd know that."

His veined hands lifted the round pieces one by one and replaced them in the tattered box. "Just seems to me a woman your age should be more interested in young men than her old Gramps."

Carla started picking up the red pieces. "His name's Philip. Does that satisfy you?"

The blue brightened on his ageless face. "He must be a special young man for you to miss him like this."

"He is special," Carla agreed.

Gramps hadn't asked anything more, and Carla hadn't voluntarily supplied additional information. But if she were to show up again today, Gramps wouldn't let her off as lightly.

Backing out of the parking space, Carla drove to a local Hallmark shop and spent an hour reading through cards. She selected two, more for the need to justify spending that much time in the store than from a desire for the cards.

That evening, as a gentle drizzle fell outside, Carla sat at the kitchen table and wrote to Philip. The letter seemed far more personal than an email. It was probably the most difficult of her life. Bunched-up sheets littered the table-top. After two hours, she read her efforts with the nagging feeling that she'd said too much—and not nearly enough.

Dear Philip,
You told me to let you know when I was ready to let go of the fears that rule my life. I don't know that I'm entirely prepared to face you in full police uniform, but I know that I can't continue the way I have these last two weeks. Nothing's the same anymore, Philip. I lost a game of checkers yesterday, and Gramps said

I shouldn't play if my mind isn't on the game. The only thing on my mind is you. The moon has your image marked on its face. The wind whispers your name. I can't look at the ocean without remembering our walks along the beach.

I'm not any less of a coward than I was in Mazatlán. But I don't know what to do anymore.

I used to be happy in Seattle. Now I'm miserable. Even checkers doesn't help.

Once a long time ago I read that the longest journey begins with a single step. I'm making that first attempt. Be patient with me.
Carla

The letter went out in the next morning's mail. Since she didn't have Philip's address, Carla sent it to him in care of the Spokane Police Department. His return letter arrived four torturous days later.

Dear Carla,
My first reaction was to pick up the phone and call, but if I said everything that was going through my mind, I'd drive you straight to Alaska and I'm afraid you'd never stop running.

My partner must have thought I was crazy when the watch commander handed me your letter. I've read it through a thousand times and have been walking on air ever since. Do you mean it? I never dreamed I could take the place of checkers.

Carla, I don't know what's been going through that beautiful head of yours, but with every minute that passes I'm all the more convinced that I'm in love with you. I didn't want to blurt it out like this in a letter, but I'll go crazy if I hold it inside any longer. Get used to hearing it, love, because it feels too right to finally be able to say it.

You asked me to be patient. How can I be anything else when that first step you're taking is on the road that's leading you back to me?

Hurry and write. Your last letter is curling at the edges from so much handling.

I love you.

Philip

P.S. I can tell I'm going to like your grandfather.

If Philip claimed to have read her letter a thousand times, then Carla must have doubled his record. Her response, a twelve-page epic, went out in the next day's mail.

Monday evening the phone rang. Nancy called Carla from the kitchen. "It's for you. Cliff, I think."

Carla was tempted to have her roommate tell him she wasn't home. Their date Saturday night had been a miserable failure. The movie had been a disappointment, and their conversation afterward had been awkward. But the problem wasn't Cliff, and Carla knew as much. Nothing was wrong with Cliff that substituting Philip wouldn't cure.

"Hello."

"Who the hell is Cliff?"

"Philip," Carla cried, and the swell of emotion filled her breast. "Is it really you? Oh, Philip, I've missed you so much." Holding the phone to her shoulder with her ear, she pressed her fingertips over her eyes. "Good grief, I think I'm going to cry."

"Who's Cliff?" he repeated.

"Trust me no one important." How could he even think anyone meant half as much to her as he did? "We went out last Saturday night, and I think he was thoroughly pleased to be done with me. I'm rotten company at the moment." Her laugh was shaky. "It seems my thoughts are preoccupied of late."

"Mine, too. Jeff's ready to ask for a new partner. I haven't been worth much since I got back."

Carla stiffened, and her hand tightened over the receiver. If Philip was being careless, he could be stabbed again. Or worse.

"What's wrong? You've gone quiet all of a sudden."

"Oh, Philip, please be careful. If anything happened to you because you were thinking about me, I'd never forgive myself."

"Carla, I can take care of myself." The tone of his voice told her he was on the defensive.

Carla paused, remembering that he'd already been stabbed once. "I... I just don't want anything to happen to you."

"That makes two of us."

"I'm so glad you called," she said, and leaned against the countertop, suddenly needing its support. "I've never felt like this. Half the time I feel like I'm living my life by rote. Every day I rush home and pray there'll be something in the mail from you."

"I do, too," he admitted, his voice low and husky. "Listen, Carla, I've got two days off next Thursday and Friday. I'd like to come over."

"Philip, I'm scheduled in surgery both days."

"Can you get off?"

Carla lifted the hair from her forehead and closed her eyes in frustration. "I doubt it. This is vacation time and we're shorthanded as it is." Their mutual disappointment was clearly evident. "Don't be upset," Carla pleaded softly.

"If it was up to me, I'd have you here in a minute. What about the weekends? Unless I'm on call I'll be free."

"But I won't."

"Right." She sucked in an unsteady breath. For a moment she'd forgotten that he didn't work regular hours. His life had to be arranged around his job. Even love came in a poor second to his responsibility to the force.

The awkward stillness fell between them a second time.

"Now you're upset?"

"No." The denial came automatically. "I understand a lot better than you realize. I can remember how rare it was to have Dad home on a weekend. Nothing has changed to make it any easier for you."

"You're wrong." Philip's voice dropped to a husky timbre. "Everything's changed. My life is involved with this incredible person who fills every waking thought and haunts my sleep."

"Oh, Philip."

"The worst part is that I get discouraged. You asked me to be patient and I promised I would be. I guess I'm looking for you to make leaps and bounds and not small steps."

Her throat tightened and she struggled not to give into tears. "I'm trying. Really trying."

For a long moment he didn't speak, but when he did, his voice was ragged. "Please, Carla, don't cry."

"I'm not," she lied, sniffling. "I wish I could be the kind of woman you want…"

"Carla—"

"Maybe it would be better if you quit wasting your time on me and found someone who can adjust to your lifestyle." Her voice shook. "Someone who doesn't know the score… Someone who doesn't understand what being part of the police force really means. Believe me, ignorance is bliss."

"Maybe I should," Philip said sharply. "There's not much to be said about a woman who prefers to live with her head buried in the sand."

Carla placed her hands over her eyes. All this time they'd been fooling themselves to think that either of them could change.

"I think you're right," she whispered in voice that was pitifully weak. "Goodbye, Philip."

He started to say something, but Carla didn't wait to listen. Very gently, very slowly, she replaced the receiver. She expected a flood of tears, but there were none—only a dry, aching pain that didn't ease. In some ways Carla doubted that it ever would.

Ten minutes later the phone rang again. Carla didn't answer it, knowing it was Philip. The phone was silent for the remainder of the evening.

Carla found two messages on the kitchen counter when she returned home from work the following afternoon. PHILIP PHONED. CLIFF DID, TOO.

Carla returned Cliff's call. They made arrangements to go to dinner Thursday night. Carla wasn't particularly interested in continuing her non-relationship with Cliff. But not for the world would she let someone—anyone—accuse her of burying her head in the sand. That comment still hurt. Most girls should consider themselves lucky to be going out with Cliff. Obviously, there was something about him she was missing. Thursday she'd make a determined effort to find out what it was.

Two days later a letter arrived from Philip, and Carla silently cursed herself for the way her heart leapt. She managed to make it all the way into the apartment, hang up her sweater and pour a cup of coffee before she ripped open the envelope.

Dearest Carla,
I promised myself I wouldn't rush you, and then I do exactly that. Can you find it in your heart to forgive me? At least give me the chance to make it up to you. Be patient with me, too, my love.
Philip

Carla read the letter twenty times nonstop. Never had any two people been more mismatched. Never had any two people been more wrong for each other. But right or wrong, Carla couldn't ignore the fact that she'd never felt this strongly about a man. If this was what it meant to love, she hadn't realized what a painful emotion it could be.

Dear Officer Garrison,
It's been brought to my attention that two people who obviously care deeply for one another are making themselves miserable. One has a tendency to expect overnight changes, and the other's got sand in her eyes from all those years of protecting her head. I'm writing to seek your advice on what can be done.
Carla
P.S. I'll be more patient with you if you're still willing to stick it out with me. P.P.S. I've got a date with Cliff Thursday night, but I promise not to go out with him again. Maybe I should cancel it.

Two days later Carla got a phone call from Western Union.

"Telegram from Mr. Philip Garrison for Miss Carla Walker."

She had never received a telegram before, and her heart

leapt to her throat as she searched frantically for a pencil. "This is Carla. Will I need a piece of paper?"

"I don't think so. There are only two words: 'Break date.'"

Seven

Early Thursday evening Carla rushed home from the hospital. "Did Philip call yet?" she asked breathlessly as she scurried inside the apartment.

Nancy looked up from her magazine, happiness lighting up her face. "Philip didn't, but Eduardo did. He's in Colorado on a business trip and wanted me to hop in the car and join him."

"You're joking?"

"No," she countered, "I'm totally serious. Obviously, he had no idea how far Seattle is from Denver. We did have a nice talk though."

From the look on her roommate's face, Carla could see that the conversation with Eduardo had been satisfying. Fleetingly, she wondered where the relationship would go from here. It was obvious the two were strongly attracted to each other. For Eduardo to have swallowed his pride and contacted Nancy, revealed how much he did care.

"So Philip hasn't phoned?" Disappointment settled over Carla. Everything was going so well with Nancy that she couldn't help feeling a small twinge of envy.

"Not yet. But it's a little early, don't you think?"

Carla had already kicked off her shoes and was unbuttoning the front of her uniform. "It's not nearly early enough. I guess I can wait a few more minutes." In some ways, she'd been waiting a lifetime for Philip.

"What makes you so sure he's going to phone?" Nancy asked, following her down the hallway to the large bedroom they shared.

Carla laughed as she pulled the uniform over her head. "Easy. He'll want to know if I broke the date or not."

"And did you?"

"Of course. I'm not all that interested in Cliff anyway."

Nancy released a sigh of relief. "I'm glad to hear that."

"Why?" Carla turned to her roommate as she slid pale blue cotton pants over her slender hips.

"Because he asked me out."

Carla was shocked. "Cliff did? Are you going?"

Nancy's eyes were evasive. "You don't mind, do you?"

Carla couldn't have been more shocked if Nancy suddenly had announced that she'd decided to date a monkey. Her roommate had practically jumped for joy because Eduardo had phoned her, yet she was going out with Cliff. It didn't make sense.

"I don't mind in the least. But…but why would you want to? I thought you'd really fallen hard for Eduardo."

"I have," Nancy admitted freely, "maybe too hard. I want to know if what I feel is real or something I've blown out of proportion. We were only together for six days. And although I've been miserable without him ever since, I need to test my feelings. Eduardo's culture is different from ours, he thinks and reacts to things completely opposite of the way I do sometimes and that frightens me."

Nancy revealing she was frightened about anything was a shock. Of the two roommates, Nancy was by far the more stout-hearted. But she was the type who would be very sure before committing herself to Eduardo and once she did, it would be forever.

"But why date Cliff?" Carla wondered aloud.

"To be honest," she said a little shyly, lowering her eyes, "I've always been attracted to him, but you were seeing him and I'd never have gone out with him while you were."

"You like Cliff?"

Nancy nodded, indicating that she did. "But if it troubles you, I'll cancel the date."

"Don't," Carla said without the least hesitation. "As far as I'm concerned, Cliff is all yours."

The doorbell chimed and Nancy glanced at the front door. "That must be Cliff now. You're sure you don't mind?"

"Of course not. Enjoy yourselves, I'll talk to you later."

Too excited to bother eating dinner, Carla brought in a chair and placed it beside the phone. As an afterthought, she added a pencil, some paper and a tissue box in case she ended up crying again. Satisfied, she moved into the living room to watch the evening newscast.

When the phone rang, she was caught off guard and glanced at her wristwatch before leaping off the sofa.

"Hello," she answered in a low, seductive voice that was sure to send Philip's heartbeat racing.

There was a lengthy pause on the other end of the line. "Carla?"

"Mom." Embarrassed, Carla stiffened and rolled her eyes toward the kitchen ceiling. "Hi... I was expecting someone else."

"Obviously. Is it someone I know?"

"No, his name's Philip Garrison. I met him in Mazatlán." She briefly related the story. "I thought he might be phoning tonight." Take the hint, Mom, and make this short, Carla pleaded silently.

"You and...Philip must have hit it off for you to be answering the phone like a seductress."

"I like him very much," was all Carla would admit.

"Since you're so keen on this young man, when do your father and I get to meet him?"

Clenching a fist at her side, Carla struggled to hold on to her temper. She resented her mother for asking these questions, and she wanted to get off the phone in case Philip was trying to get through to her. "I don't know. Philip lives in Spokane."

"Spokane," her mother mused aloud. "Your father and I knew some people named Garrison. Delightful folks—"

"Mom," Carla interrupted, "would you mind if we talked later? I really do need to get off the phone."

"No, that'll be fine. I just wanted to know if you could come to dinner tomorrow night."

"Sure." At this point she would have agreed to anything. "What time?"

"Seven."

"I'll be there. Talk to you later."

"Goodbye, dear. And Carla, it might help if you're a little more subtle with...what's his name again?"

"Philip."

"Right. I'll see you tomorrow. And, Carla, do try to be demure."

"Yes, Mother, I'll try."

After hanging up, Carla took several calming breaths. She had never gotten on well with her mother. Over the years, Rachel Walker had admirably portrayed the role of a docile wife, but Carla had always thought of her as weak willed: there were too many times when she'd witnessed the anger and hurt in her mother's expressive eyes. She had wanted to shout at both her parents. Her father should have known what his career was doing to the rest of the family. Her mother should have had the courage to speak up. Carla had tried at sixteen and had been silenced immediately, so she'd moved away from home as soon as possible, eager to leave a situation that made her more miserable every year. And now…here she was following in her mother's footsteps. A knot tightened in the pit of her stomach. Dear heavens, what was she getting herself into with loving Philip? Again and again she'd tried to tell herself that what they shared was different—that she and Philip were different from her parents. But their chances of avoiding the same problems her parents had dealt with were slim—likely nonexistent. With stiffening resolve, Carla vowed she would never live the type of life her mother had all these years. If that meant giving up Philip, then she'd do it. There wasn't a choice.

The phone rang again a half hour later. Carla stared at it as if it were a mad dog, her eyes wide with fear. Chills ran up and down her spine. This was Philip phoning—the call she'd anticipated all day.

Trembling, she picked up her purse and walked out the door. A movie alone was preferable to listening to the phone ring every half hour. If she let Philip assume that she had gone out with Cliff, then maybe, just maybe, he'd give up on her and they could put an end to this misery. Her instincts had guided her well in the past. Now, more than at any other time in her life, she had to listen to her intuition—for both their sakes. Philip deserved a woman who would love him for his dedication to law and order and his commitment to protect and serve. He needed a wife who would learn the hazards of his profession a little at a time. Carla knew too much already.

Nancy wasn't back when Carla returned to the dark, lonely apartment. And within five minutes the phone rang. She ignored it. Coward, she taunted silently as she moved into the bedroom. But if she was behaving like a weakling, it shouldn't be this difficult. It wasn't right that it hurt this much.

Nancy was still asleep when Carla dressed for work the following morning. She penned her roommate a note and left it propped against the sugar bowl on the kitchen table: *If Philip contacts you, please don't tell him I didn't go out with Cliff last night. I'll explain later. Also, don't bother with dinner. I'm going to my parents'. Am interested in hearing how things went with Cliff. Talk to you tonight.*

Carla's first surgery was an emergency appendectomy, a teenage boy who was lucky to be alive. Carla had witnessed only a handful of deaths in the last couple of years. She didn't know how the rest of the staff dealt emotionally with the loss of a patient, but each one had affected her greatly.

When she had finished assisting with the appendectomy, she found a message waiting for her. She waited to read it until she was sitting down, savoring a cup of coffee in the cafeteria. Call Nancy, it read. A glance at the wall clock confirmed that there wouldn't be enough time to call until after lunch. When she phoned at one-thirty, however, there wasn't any answer, so Carla assumed it couldn't have been that urgent. She'd wait to talk to Nancy at home.

Three hours later Carla headed for the hospital parking lot, rubbing the ache in the small of her back to help relieve some of the tension accumulated from a long day on her feet. Dinner with her parents would only add to that tension. And eventually she would have to talk to Philip—he'd demand as much. But she didn't want to think about that now. Not when her back hurt and her head throbbed and she was facing an uncomfortable dinner with her parents.

Carla was soaking in a tub full of scented water when Nancy knocked on the bathroom door. "Carla."

"Hmm," she answered, savoring the luxurious feel of the warm, soothing water.

"I think you should get over to your grandfather's as soon as possible."

Carla sat up, sloshing water over the edge of the bathtub. "Why? What happened?"

"I can't explain now, I'll be leaving any minute. Cliff's on his way. He's taking me to the Seattle Center for the China Exhibit."

"Is anything wrong with Gramps?" Carla called out frantically. Already standing, she reaching for a thick towel to dry herself.

"No, nothing like that. It's a surprise."

"What about you and Cliff? Things must be working out if you're seeing him again." Carla could feel Nancy's hesitation on the other side of the bathroom door.

"They're working out, but not as I'd expected. I'm giving it a second chance to see if it's any better the second time."

"Oh?" Carla hoped that Nancy wasn't going to make her ask that she explain that.

"Cliff's all right, I guess."

Behind the closed door, Carla smiled smugly. That was how she felt about Cliff. He was fine, but he wasn't Philip, and now apparently he wasn't Eduardo either.

"Does Eduardo know? I mean did you tell him you were seeing another man?" Carla hated to think what would happen if he discovered Nancy was dating Cliff. Eduardo's male pride was bound to cause him to overreact.

"I... I told him yesterday."

"And?"

"Oh, he understands. In fact, he encouraged me to see Cliff again. I told him he should do the same thing and you know what he said? He said he didn't need to see another woman to know how he feels about me. He mentioned something about me flying to Mexico City to meet his family, but I didn't let him know one way or the other." As if regretting she'd revealed that much, Nancy added hastily, "Listen, Carla, I promise that you'll like your surprise. I'd hurry if I were you."

The doorbell sounded and was followed by a clicking sound that told Carla she wouldn't get any more information from her friend. A surprise! Presumably, this was why Nancy had contacted her at the hospital.

Dressing casually in cotton pants and an antique white blouse with an eyelet collar, Carla hardly bothered with her hair. A quick application of lip gloss and a dab of perfume and she was out the door.

Her heart was hammering by the time she arrived at the retirement center. Her shoes made clicking sounds as she hurried inside, pushing open the double glass doors with both hands. She took the elevator to Gramps's room on the third floor, thinking it would be faster than running up the stairs.

Gramps's door was closed. Carla knocked loudly twice and let herself inside. "Gramps, Nancy..." The words died on her lips as her startled eyes clashed with Philip's. He was sitting opposite her grandfather, playing a game of checkers.

"Philip." She stood there, stunned. "What are you doing here?"

Gramps came to his feet, using his cane to help him stand. "Nancy brought your young man over to meet me."

"I asked her to," Philip added. "Your grandfather was someone I didn't want to miss meeting."

"Mighty fine young man you've got yourself," said Gramps, his blue eyes sparkling with approval.

"He could be saying that because he beat me in checkers," Philip explained, grinning.

Gramps's weathered face tightened to conceal a smile. "Leave an old man to his peace. Knowing my daughter, she'll have your hide if either of you is late for dinner."

"Dinner," Carla repeated with a panicked look.

"Yes, your mother was kind enough to include me in the invitation."

"My mother."

"Something's wrong with my hearing aid," Gramps complained, tapping lightly against his ear. "I'm hearing an echo."

Philip chuckled and cupped Carla's elbow. "Nice meeting you, Gramps," he said as he led the way out the door and into the hallway.

"Philip Garrison, what are you doing here?" Carla demanded. Her hands rested defiantly on her hips.Oh my, he looked good. His sandy-colored hair was combed to the side, and a thick lock fell carelessly across his wide brow. His appealing gray eyes were dark and intense as they met hers. To Carla he had never looked more compelling. Staying out of his arms was growing more difficult every minute.

"Are you trying to drive me crazy? Because you're

doing a mighty fine job of it. Why wouldn't you answer the phone?"

"I…couldn't." She wouldn't lie outright, but she had no compunction about letting him believe she'd been out with Cliff.

"And while we're at it, you can explain this." He took Carla's note to Nancy from his pocket. "'Don't tell Philip I didn't go out with Cliff,'" he read with a sharp edge in his voice. "It seems to me we've got some explaining to do."

"Y-yes…yes, I guess I do."

"Then let's go back to your place. At least there we can have some privacy." He flashed a look down the wide corridor.

They rode back to the apartment in silence.

"How'd you get here?" Carla asked shakily as she pulled into her assigned parking space.

"I flew in at noon. Nancy picked me up at the airport."

"When are you going back?"

His gaze cut into hers, and one thick brow arched arrogantly. "Can't wait to be rid of me, is that it?"

"No…yes… I don't know." She replied, her voice trembling.

Her hands were unsteady as she unlocked the apartment and stepped inside. Philip had come all this way because she hadn't had the courage to talk to him last night. She'd been foolish to believe he wouldn't find out why. "Would you like a cup of coffee?" she asked, hanging her purse over the inside doorknob of the coat closet.

Gently, Philip settled a hand on each shoulder and turned her around so that he could study her. Carla's gaze fell to the floor.

"Carla, my love." Philip's voice was low, sensuously seductive. "You know what I want."

She did know. And she wanted it, too. "Oh, Philip," she groaned, and slipped her arms over his shoulders, linking her fingers behind his neck. "It's so good to see you."

His mouth claimed hers in a series of long, intoxicating kisses that left her weak and trembling. Philip was becoming a narcotic she had to have; his touch was addictive.

His hands roamed over her back, pulling her soft form against his muscular frame. A warmth spread through her limbs, and she turned her head when his lips explored the smooth curve of her shoulder and the hollow of her throat.

Taking a deep breath to keep the room from spinning, Carla pushed against his chest, leaving only a narrow space between them.

"How can you refuse to speak to me, deceive me by letting me think you'd gone out with this other guy, and then kiss me like that?" Philip asked in a voice husky with emotion.

Melting against him, she explored his earlobe with her tongue as her fingertips caressed his clenched jaw. "I think I'm going crazy," she murmured at last. "I want you so much my heart's ready to pound right out of me."

"Then why?" he groaned against her ear. "Why are you running from me so hard I can barely keep up with you?"

"I'm so scared." Her low voice wavered. "I don't want to be like my mother."

"What's that got to do with anything?" He continued to nibble the side of her neck, making it impossible for her to think clearly.

"Everything," she cried desperately. "I'm not the right person for you."

"But I won't want anyone else."

"Philip, be reasonable."

"You're in my arms. I can't think straight." He bit gently

at the edge of her lips. "Carla, I'm going crazy without you. I want you to marry me. I want to share my life with you, because heaven knows I can't take much more of this."

Carla's eyes shot open. "How can you talk about marriage?" she asked, struggling to break free of his hold.

"It's the normal process when two people feel as strongly about one another as we do."

"But I don't want to love you," she cried. "When my husband leaves for work in the morning I don't want to worry about him risking his life on the streets of the city."

"Carla—"

"And when he comes home at night I don't want him to drag his job with him. I want a husband, not a hero—"

His mouth intercepted her words, muffling them until she surrendered to his kisses, arousing her until she clung to him, seeking a deeper fulfillment. "Kissing me won't settle a thing," she murmured, breaking free with her last reserves of strength.

"I know, but it keeps you from arguing."

"When you're holding me like this," she admitted shyly, "there's not much fight in me."

"Good. All I need to do for the next seventy years is keep you at my side. Agree, and I'll whisk you to a preacher so fast it'll make your head spin."

"You're incorrigible."

"I'm in love." His hands were linked at the small of her back and slipped over her buttocks, arching her backside, lifting her up to meet his descending mouth. The kiss was shattering.

"Can we talk now?" Every minute in his arms made it more difficult to think clearly.

"Okay, explain what happened yesterday," he said as

they sat in the living room. "Why wouldn't you talk to me last night?"

"I already told you why," she said, and exhaled slowly. "I don't want to be like my mother."

"Carla." Philip captured both her hands in his and kissed her knuckles. "That doesn't make any sense. You're who you are, and I'm me. Together we'll never be like anyone else."

Carla bowed her head, and her lashes fluttered until they closed completely. "Mom and I are a lot alike. You'll understand that when you meet her later. But she's weak and afraid and never says what she's really thinking. And Philip, I'm trying so hard to be different."

"That still doesn't explain why you wouldn't talk to me."

Carla swallowed uncomfortably. "Mom called just before you did, and everything she said reminded me how unhappy she's been all these years."

"Ah," Philip said, and nodded thoughtfully. "And the note to Nancy?"

"I… I was thinking that if you assumed I was still dating Cliff, you'd give up on me."

He tucked his index finger under her chin and lifted her eyes to his. "I think there's something you'd better understand. I'm not giving up on you. Never. I love you, Carla."

"But loving someone doesn't make everything right," she argued. "We're different in so many ways."

"I don't see it like that. We complement each other. And although it seems like I'm the one who's asking you to make all the changes, I'm not. When we're married I promise that you and our family will be my first priority. Nothing will ever mean more to me than you."

"Oh, Philip." She felt herself weakening. "But it's more than that."

"I know, love." Slowly, deliberately, his eyes never leaving hers, he pulled her toward him. His mouth sought her lips, exploring their softness as if he would never get enough of the feel of her.

"Philip," she groaned, her voice ragged. "We have to leave now for my mother's."

"Your mother's," he repeated as if he needed something to bring him back from the brink.

"You'll be meeting my dad," she said softly, teasing his neck and ear with small, biting kisses.

"Mom and Dad, I'd like to introduce Philip Garrison." Carla stood just inside her parents' living room. "Philip, my mom and dad, Joe and Rachel Walker."

Joe stepped forward and shook Philip's hand. "Nice to meet you, Philip."

Carla felt the faint stirrings of pride. Her father, although graying, was in top physical condition. Over the years he hadn't lost the lean, military look of his younger days. Intuitively, Carla knew that in twenty years Philip wouldn't, either.

"It's a pleasure to have you join us," Rachel added warmly. "Carla said you live in Spokane."

"Yes, I flew in this afternoon."

The four of them sat in the large living room, and Philip immediately took Carla's hand in his. The action didn't go unnoticed by either of her parents. Rachel's blue eyes sought Carla's, and she gave her daughter a small wink, indicating that she approved of this young man. Maybe Carla should have been pleased, but she wasn't. Having her family like Philip would only complicate her feelings.

"And when will you be leaving?"

Carla was as interested in his answer as her parents.

"Tonight; I'd like to stay longer, but I'm on duty tomorrow morning."

"Carla said that you two met in Mazatlán."

"Yes, the first day she arrived." Philip looked at Carla, and his dark eyes flickered with barely concealed amusement.

Her eyes widened, silently warning him not to mention *how* they'd met. Then flustered, she cleared her throat and said, "Philip helped me out with my Spanish."

"You speak Spanish?" Joe asked, but his narrowed gaze studied Carla. Her father was too observant not to recognize that there was a lot going unsaid about her meeting with Philip. Fortunately, he decided not to pursue the subject.

Rachel glanced at her gold wristwatch. "Excuse me a minute."

"Can I help, Mom?" Carla asked, and uncrossed her long legs.

"No, everything's ready, I just want to check the corn. Your father's barbecuing chicken tonight."

"You're in for a treat," Carla told Philip proudly. "I've been telling Dad for years that when he retires he should open a restaurant. He makes a barbecue sauce that's out of this world."

"It's an old family recipe that's been handed down for generations."

"He got it out of a Betty Crocker cookbook," Carla whispered, grinning. Then before her father could open his mouth, she stood. "I'll see what I can do to give Mom a hand." Although her mother had refused her offer, there was undoubtedly something she could do to help.

Rachel was taking a large bowl of potato salad from the refrigerator when Carla came through the swinging kitchen doors. "I like your young man," she announced without preamble.

Carla couldn't hold her mother's gaze. She should have been surprised; Rachel had disapproved of most of the men Carla dated. Her excuses were usually lame ones— this boy was careless, another boy was lazy. By the time Carla moved out, she had stopped introducing her dates to her parents. Somehow, though, she'd known her mother would approve of Philip.

"He's clean-cut, polite and he has a nice smile."

Carla bit into a sweet pickle from the relish tray. "And his eyes are the most incredible gray. Did you notice that?" Naturally, they wouldn't discuss any of the important aspects of her relationship with Philip.

"You two make a nice couple."

"Thank you," Carla answered with a hint of impatience. She opened the silverware drawer and counted out forks and spoons. "I'll set the table."

Philip was holding a beer, watching her father baste the chicken with a thick coating of pungent sauce, when Carla joined them on the sunny patio. He slipped an arm over her shoulder. His thumb made lazy, sensuous forays at the base of her neck.

Annoyed, she shrugged her shoulder and Philip dropped his hand to her waist. She didn't want him to make this kind of blanket statement to her family about their relationship. *He* was serious about her, but she had yet to deal with her feelings about him. When she stepped free of his hold, Philip firmly but gently cupped her shoulder.

"Philip," she groaned in an irritated whisper. "Please don't."

His eyes sparkled as he leaned toward her. "I told your father outright that I'm going to marry you."

"You didn't!" she cried in angry frustration.

Joe turned aside from the barbecue. "Hand me a spoon, would you, Carla?" he requested, and his gaze followed her as she moved to the picnic table and brought back a spoon. "Problems, Princess?"

"No." She shook her head, the red curls bouncing with the action. "I'm just sorry that Philip made it look like we're more serious than we are."

"He was rather forthright in his feelings."

Carla swallowed. "I know."

"But aren't you sure?"

"I won't marry a cop." Years of self-discipline masked any physical reaction from her father.

"I can't say I blame you for that," he said after a long moment. Some of the brightness faded from his eyes as he concentrated on his task.

"I love you, Dad, you know that. But I won't live the life Mom has."

With practiced skill he turned the chicken over with a pair of tongs. "She's never complained."

"Oh, Dad," Carla said with a rush of inner sadness. She respected and admired her father and had never thought of him as oblivious of the stress his career had placed on their family. "Are you really so blind?"

His mouth tightened, and the look he gave her was piercing. "I said she's never complained. It takes a special kind of woman to love a man like me."

Carla lifted her gaze to Philip, who was examining the meticulously kept flower beds, and her father's words echoed in her mind. Carla didn't know if she could ever be that special kind of woman.

Rachel appeared at the sliding glass door. "Carla, would you help me carry out the salads?"

"Sure, Mom." Carla followed her mother into the kitchen.

Rachel stuck a serving spoon in the potato salad, handed it to Carla and turned away. "Philip mentioned that he had to be back tomorrow because he's on duty. You did say he was a doctor, didn't you?" Her voice was unnaturally high, and her hands were busily working around the sink.

"No, Mom." She'd wondered how long it would take for her mother to pick up on that. "Philip's a police officer."

A glass fell against the aluminum sink and shattered into little pieces. Rachel ignored it as she turned, her face suddenly waxen. "Oh, Carla, no."

Eight

"**Y**our flight will be boarding in a minute." Carla stood stiffly in the area outside of airport security. The lump in her throat was making it hard for her to talk. The crazy part was that she didn't want Philip to leave and at the same time she couldn't bear to have him stay.

The meal with her parents had been an ordeal. As she had suspected, Philip and her father had gotten on like soul mates. They were alike in more ways than Carla had first suspected. Their personalities, ideas and thoughts meshed as if they were father and son.

Rachel had remained subdued during most of the meal. Later, when Carla had helped clear the picnic table and load the dishwasher, a strained tension had existed between them. Her mother had asked a few polite questions about Philip, which Carla had answered in the same cordial tone.

"I don't think it would be a good idea for you to become too serious with this young man," Rachel said as they were finishing. Her casual attitude didn't fool Carla.

Fleetingly, Carla wondered what reason her mother would give. Philip wasn't the careless type, and even the most casual observer could see he wasn't lazy. She was bound to say everything but what was really on her mind.

"Why not?" Carla implored. "I thought you said you liked him."

"I do," Rachel replied quickly in a defensive tone. "But he's too much like your father, and I'll love that man to my death." The poignant softness of Rachel's voice cracked the thin wall that stood between mother and daughter.

"And you," Rachel continued with a wry grin, "are too much like me: vulnerable, sensitive, tender-hearted. Our emotions run high, and when we love, we love with a fervor. Philip could hurt you, Princess."

Her mother so rarely called her by that affectionate term that Carla lifted her head in surprise.

"There are plenty of men in this world who will make life a thousand times easier for you than someone involved in law enforcement."

"But you married Dad," Carla argued, studying her mother intently. This was as close as they had ever come to an open conversation.

"Your father joined the force after we were married."

"I... I didn't know that."

"Something else you may not know is that Joe and I separated for a time before you were born."

Shocked, Carla's mouth dropped open. "You and Dad?"

Rachel busily wiped off the kitchen counter, then rinsed out the rag under the running faucet. "There are certain qualities a policeman's wife should have. I... I've never been the right woman—" She stopped in midsentence as Philip and Joe sauntered into the kitchen.

Mother and daughter had been unable to finish the conversation, but Carla had felt a closeness with her mother she had never experienced. She realized now that they had always been too much alike to appreciate each other.

"Carla?"

Philip's voice brought her back to the present, and to the reality of his leaving.

"You're looking thoughtful." His fingers caressed the gentle slope of her neck, trailing down her shoulder. "I expect a kiss goodbye, one that will hold me until I see you again."

A smile briefly touched Carla's eyes. "I don't think that kind of kissing is allowed in public places."

"I don't care." His voice was low and husky as he ran his hands up and down the length of her silken arms. "Seeing each other again has only made things worse, hasn't it?"

"No," she denied instantly. "I think it's been good for us both."

"Good and bad," he growled, and the frustration and longing in his eyes deepened. "Good, because holding you lessens the ache I feel when we're apart." His hands gripped the back of her collar, bringing her closer into his embrace. "And bad, because I don't know how much longer it'll be before I hold you again."

Their gazes met and held, and Carla felt as if she were suffocating. His eyes, steel-gray and narrowed, slowed the torment within him, and Carla realized hers were filled with doubt. Her lips started quivering, and she pressed them tightly together.

Philip's hands tightened on Carla's blouse, and he dipped his head forward so that their foreheads touched. "I hate this."

Her arms slid around his waist, and she pressed her face to his shirt. "I do, too." Her voice was scratchy and unnaturally high as she swallowed hard, determined to be strong. "You should go," she said, and gave him a brave smile.

"Not until the last minute. Not until I have to." His voice wasn't any more controlled than her own. "Carla"—he breathed in deeply—"I want to do everything right for you. You need me to be patient and wait; then I'll do that."

"Oh... Ph... Philip. How can you love me? I'm so wrong for you."

"No one has ever been more right," he insisted, his words muffled against her hair. "I love you, and someday we'll have beautiful redheaded children."

"With warm gray eyes."

"Tall," he added.

"Naturally," she said, and offered him a shaky smile.

"Does this mean that you've reconsidered and will marry me? Because let me warn you: if it does, I'll make the arrangements tomorrow."

She couldn't answer him. Something deep and dark in her soul wouldn't allow her to speak. Instead she blinked her eyes in an effort to hold back the emotion that threatened to overtake her.

Disappointment, regret, pain and several other emotions Carla couldn't name played across Philip's face.

"Soon?" he asked in a whisper.

Carla forced a smile. "Maybe."

"That's good enough for now. Just make it soon, my love. Make it very soon."

Philip waited until the very last minute before going through security. Carla waited and once he was through, he tossed an impatient glare over his shoulder and disappeared down the corridor, rushing to make his flight. His kiss had been short, but ardent. As she watched him go, Carla pressed four fingers to her lips and closed her eyes.

She didn't leave the terminal until the plane was out of sight and her tears had dried. Her spirits were at an all-time low as she headed to the airport parking lot, fighting back questions that tormented her from all sides.

Philip's letter arrived in Saturday's mail.

My dearest love,

It's been only a few hours since I left you in Seattle. I couldn't sleep, and it's too late to phone. As I flew back tonight I couldn't drop the picture of you from my mind. This week is hectic, but I'll phone you Tuesday night. I'm involved with three other friends from the force in a canoe race—don't laugh. Ever hear of the Great Soap Lake Canoe Race? Well, yours truly is captain of the motley crew. We're planning to arrive in Soap Lake Friday afternoon. The race begins early Saturday morning. The others have their own cheering squads. I have only you. Tell me you'll come. I want to introduce you to my friends and their wives. And for all the trouble I've been giving Jeff Griffin, my partner, since Mexico, he claims he has a right to meet you. Let me warn you now that you shouldn't believe everything he says. Jeff likes to tease, and believe me he's had a lot to kid me about the last few weeks. I want you to talk to Jeff's wife when you come. Sylvia is pregnant with their first child. I know you'll like her. Please tell me you'll be there.

This is torment, Carla. I can feel your kiss on my lips, and the scent of your perfume lingers, so all that I need to do is close my eyes and imagine you're with me. And, my love, don't ever doubt I want you with me. I'm praying that this feeling can hold me until Friday.

I love you.

Philip

Carla read his letter again and again, savoring each word, each line. Several times she ran her index finger back and forth over his declaration of love. Philip sounded so sure of things. Sure that they were right for each other. Sure that she could put her insecurities behind her. Sure that she would eventually marry him.

And Carla felt none of it. Every day the list of pros and cons grew longer. Philip, like her father, was an idealist. Carla wasn't convinced that being in love made everything a rose garden.

As for his invitation to have her come and root for him in the canoe race, Carla was sure that the real reason was so she could meet his friends. And she didn't need to be told that policemen usually socialized with other policemen. Her parents had few friends outside the force; the same undoubtedly held true for Philip. Friday was only a few days away and finding someone willing to trade work days would be difficult with half the staff scheduled for vacation time. It was a convenient excuse until she made up her mind what to do.

"Have you decided what you're going to tell him?" Nancy asked Tuesday evening as she carted her luggage into the living room. After her last date with Cliff, Nancy had returned convinced she knew what she was feeling for Eduardo. When he'd pressed the invitation for her to meet his family she hadn't hesitated.

"No," Carla answered dismally. "I'm afraid that I'll be

dragged into his life little by little until we're married and I don't even know what happened."

"I think Philip's counting on that."

"I know." Carla nibbled on her bottom lip. Philip would be phoning later, and she still didn't know what she was going to tell him. If she told him outright that she wouldn't come, he'd accuse her of burying her head in the sand again. And he'd be right. But if she did agree, Carla realized that things would never be quite the same again. He had come to Seattle and invaded her world. He'd played checkers with Gramps and had dinner with her parents. She didn't feel safe anymore. Inch by inch he was entwining their lives until it would be impossible for her to escape.

A happy, excited Nancy had left for Mexico by the time Philip phoned. Carla stared at the phone for five long rings before she had the courage to answer.

"Hello." As hard as she tried, she couldn't disguise her unhappiness.

"Carla, what's wrong?" She wanted to cry at the gentle concern that coated his voice. "You aren't coming," he said before she could answer.

"I… I don't know. Friday's a busy day at the hospital, and finding a replacement—"

"You don't want to come," he interrupted impatiently.

"It's not that." Carla leaned her hip against the counter and closed her eyes in defeat. "It's too soon for this sort of thing. I don't think I'm ready."

"For a canoe race!" Carla could feel his anger reverberate through her cell.

"You said you'd give me time and then you immediately start pushing at me. You're not playing fair, Philip

Garrison. Don't force me into something I'm not ready to deal with yet."

"You mean to say you can't handle a social outing with my friends?"

"I don't know," she cried.

An unnatural, tension-filled silence followed. Carla struggled for some assurance to give him and found none. Maybe Philip was seeking the same. A full minute passed and neither spoke, yet neither was willing to break off the connection.

Carla heard Philip take a deep breath. "All right, I won't push you. I said I'd be patient. When you decide if you're going to come, phone me." From the tone of his voice, she knew that he was hurt and discouraged. "I'll be out most of the week—practicing with the rest of the team." Apparently, he wanted her to realize why he wouldn't be available. "If you can't reach me, I'll be waiting at the B and B Root Beer stand in Soap Lake from seven to nine Friday night. It's on the main road going through town. You can't miss it. If you don't come, I'll understand."

"I'll call you before then." The lump in her throat made her voice sound tight.

"I'd appreciate that."

Again there was silence, and again it was obvious neither of them wished to end the conversation.

"I...I have some good news about Nancy," Carla said at last. "She's flying to Mexico City to meet Eduardo's family. From the way things have been progressing I wouldn't be surprised if Nancy returned wearing an engagement ring."

"You could be too." Philip told her in a tight voice and Carla regretted having said anything. It'd been a mistake to bring up the subject of Nancy and Eduardo in the light of their own circumstances.

"I know."

"But you're not ready? Right?"

"Right," Carla returned miserably.

The strained silence returned until Philip finally spoke, his voice devoid of anger. "Eduardo's a good man."

So are you, Carla mentally added.

"So you think Nancy may marry Eduardo."

"It wouldn't surprise me," Carla said, forcing an air of cheerfulness into her voice. "Nancy's a lucky girl." The second the words were out, Carla desperately wanted to take them back. "Philip," she said contritely, and swallowed. "I didn't mean that the way it sounded."

"The problem is, I believe it's exactly what you mean. I'm not a good-looking, Latin American who's going to impress your friends." His words were as cold as a blast of wind from the Arctic.

"Philip, you're everything I want in a man except..."

"Except... I've heard it all before. Goodbye, Carla, if I see you Friday, that's fine. If not, that's fine too."

The phone clicked in her ear and droned for several moments. The entire conversation had gone poorly. She'd hoped to at least start off in a lighter mood, and then explain her hesitancy about meeting him for the weekend. But she'd only succeeded in angering Philip. And he'd been furious. She knew him well enough to realize this type of cold wrath was rare. Most things rolled off him like rain water on a well-waxed car. Only the important matters in his life could provoke this kind of deep anger. And Carla was important.

She still hadn't decided what to do by the time she joined her grandfather after work on Thursday for their regular game of checkers. Carla hoped he wouldn't try to influence her to go. She'd taken Gramps out to dinner Sunday afternoon, and he had done little else but talk about what a nice young man Philip was. By the end of the day, Carla had never been more pleased to take him back to the retirement home. She prayed today wouldn't be a repeat of last Sunday.

"Afternoon, Gramps," she greeted him as she stepped into his small apartment.

Gramps had already set up the board and was sitting in his comfortable chair waiting for her. "The more I think about that young man of yours, the more I like him."

"Philip's not my young man," she corrected more tersely than she had intended. Carla had suspected this would happen when Philip met her family. Gramps and her dad had joined forces with Philip—it was unfair!

"'The lady doth protest too much'—Shakespeare."

Carla laughed, her first real laugh in two days. She and Gramps played this game of quotes occasionally. "'To be is to do'—Socrates," she tossed back lightly as she pulled out the rocking chair opposite him and sat down.

Gramps's eyes brightened and he stroked his chin, deep in contemplation. "'To do is to be'—Sartre." He nodded curtly to Carla, and the set of his mouth said he doubted that she could match him.

"'Do be do be do'—Sinatra," she said, and giggled. For the first time in recent memory she'd outwitted her grandfather. Soon Gramps's deep chuckles joined her own, and his face shone with pride. "I'm going to miss you, girl."

"Miss me?" She opened the game of checkers by making the first move.

"When you and Philip marry you'll be moving to Spokane to live with him."

Miffed, Carla pressed her lips tightly together and re-moved her hand from the faded board. "Did he tell you that?"

"Nope." Gramps made his return move.

With her fingers laced together in her lap, Carla paused and looked up from the checkers. "Then what makes you think I'm going to marry him?"

"You'd be a fool not to. The boy clearly loves you, and even more obvious is the way you feel about him."

Carla returned her gaze to the checker pieces, but her mind wasn't on the game. "He's a cop, Gramps."

"So? Seems to me your daddy's been a fine officer of the law for twenty-odd years."

"And Mom's been miserable every minute of those twenty-odd years."

"Your mother's a worrier. It's in her blood," Gramps countered sharply. "She'd have fretted about your dad if he was the local dogcatcher."

"But I'm afraid of being like Mom," Carla declared vehemently. "I can't see myself pacing the floors alone at night when Philip's called on a case, or when he isn't and just goes away for a while to settle things in his head. Don't you have any idea of how much time Mom spends alone? She's by herself when she needs Dad. But he's out there"—she pointed to the world outside the apartment window—"making the city a better place to live and for-getting about his own wife and family." Her voice was high and faltering as she spewed out her doubts in one giant breath. "Gramps, I'm afraid. I'm afraid of loving the wrong man." Her fists were tightly clenched, and her nails cut painfully into her skin.

"And you think Philip is the wrong man?"

"I don't know anymore, Gramps. I'm so confused."

His gnarled hand reached across the card table and patted her arm. "And so in love."

Talking out her fears with Gramps had a releasing effect on her, Carla realized as she walked around the lonely apartment hours later. Only a few days ago Philip had been sitting on that couch, holding her as if he'd choose death rather than let her go.

Her gaze was drawn to her cell. She'd promised to call him by now and let him know if she was coming. Her heartbeat accelerated at the thought of hearing his voice. With trembling resolve, she reached for her phone, and waited for the electronic bleeps to connect their lines.

Philip answered on the first ring with a disgruntled "Yes?"

"Do you always answer your phone like you want to bite off someone's head?" Just hearing his voice, unwelcome and surly as it was, had her heart pounding erratically.

A long pause followed. "Carla?"

"The one and only," she answered. Her voice throbbed with happiness. She'd pictured him lying back in an easy chair and relaxing. Now she envisioned him sitting up abruptly and rolling to his feet in disbelief. The imagery produced a deep smile of satisfaction.

"You called!" This time there was no disguising his incredulity.

"I said I would," she murmured softly.

"You've decided about the canoe race?"

"Yes."

"And?"

"First, I need to know if you're wearing your glasses."

"Good grief, Carla, what's that got to do with anything?"

"Do you have your glasses on or don't you?" she demanded arrogantly.

"Why?"

Carla was learning that he could be just as stubborn as she. "Because what I'm about to say may steam them up, so I suggest you remove them."

Washington was known as the Evergreen State, but there was little evidence of any green in the eastern portion of the state—and none at all in the sagebrush, desert-like area in which Carla was traveling. Divided by the Cascade mountain range, Washington had a wet side and a dry side. In Seattle, summers and winters were less extreme—for example, although it was already mid-July, there had been only a handful of days above eighty-five degrees.

Carla shifted in the driver's seat of her compact car, hoping to find a more comfortable position. She'd been on the road for almost four hours and was miserably hot. Her bare thighs stuck to the seat of her car, and rivulets of perspiration trickled down the small valley between her breasts. Even Mazatlán hadn't seemed as hot.

Exiting off the interstate freeway at the town of George, Carla gassed up her car at Martha's Inn and paused to read over the map a second time. Within an hour or so she would be meeting Philip. They'd been apart only six days, yet it felt more like six years. Carla didn't know how she was going to endure any long separations.

As he'd said he would, Philip was sitting at a picnic table in front of the B and B Drive-In. Carla savored the sight of him and did a quick self-inspection in her rearview mirror. Instantly, she was sorry she hadn't stopped at a service station outside of town to freshen her makeup.

As she pulled into the drive-in's parking lot, she noticed that Philip had spotted her and was heading for her car. Carla's throat was dry, and she couldn't think of a thing to say.

"Hi." Philip opened the driver's side and gave her his hand, his face searching hers all the while as if he couldn't quite believe she wasn't an apparition. The hand gripping hers tightened. "How was your trip?"

"Uneventful" was all Carla could manage.

Lightly, Philip brought her into his arms and brushed her cheek with his lips. Their eyes met as they parted, and still he didn't smile. "You really came," he said hoarsely.

She answered with a short nod. Philip had known without her fully explaining what her coming meant. The doubts, her determination to fight this relationship, were slowly dissolving. And coming here to meet his friends was a major step on her part.

"Jeff and Sylvia will be by in a few minutes." He led her to a picnic table. "Sit down and I'll get you something cool to drink."

"I can use that." Now that she was outside the car, the heat was even more sweltering.

Philip returned with two cold mugs of root beer. He set them on the table and sat opposite her. "I can't believe this. My heart's beating so fast I feel like an adolescent out on his first date."

"I feel the same way." She lowered her gaze to the root beer. Her fingers curled around the mug handle, and she took her first long drink. "I noticed in your note you said that you wanted me to talk to Sylvia."

Philip's hand reached for hers. "I think you two will have a lot in common."

"Does she feel the same way about Jeff's job as I do?" Carla asked tentatively.

"No." His voice was gently gruff. "But you're about the same age."

"Didn't you say she was pregnant with their first child?"

"Very." He said it with an odd little smile. "You'll be beautiful pregnant."

Carla could feel herself blushing. "Honestly, Philip," she murmured, her eyes looking troubled. "I wish you wouldn't say things like that."

"Why not? Last night after we finished talking I was so happy that I lay in bed thinking I could run ten miles and not even feel it. But I didn't run. Instead I lay there and closed my eyes, picturing what our lives would be like five years from now."

"And?" She was angry with herself for going along with this fantasy, but she couldn't help herself.

"You were in the kitchen cooking dinner when I walked in the back door. A little redheaded boy was playing at your feet, banging pots and pans with a wooden spoon. When you turned to me, I saw that you were pregnant. I swear, Carla, you were so beautiful I went weak. My heart stopped beating and my knees felt like putty. I don't think anything's ever affected me like that. I've never made any pretense about wanting you, and I'm not going to start now."

Carla busied herself by running her finger along the rim of her mug, and when she lifted her gaze, their eyes met. "That's beautiful," she said, and was shocked at how low her voice was. The closeness she felt with him at that moment was beyond anything she had ever known. But she wished he wouldn't say such things to her. It only made her more miserable.

Silence fell between them, but Philip seemed content to watch her. Her hands trembled as she lifted the mug for another long drink. "Philip," she moaned, finding his continued scrutiny uncomfortable, "please stop looking at me like that. You're embarrassing me."

Immediately, he dropped his gaze. "I didn't mean to. It seems I do everything wrong where you're concerned. I thought I'd play it cool today when you arrived. And the minute I saw you every nonchalant greeting I'd practiced died on my lips."

"Mine too," she confessed shakily.

"I'm still having trouble believing that you came."

"We both need to thank Gramps for that."

"I think we should name our first son after him."

Carla shook her head. "He'd never forgive us for naming a boy Otis."

"All right, we'll name him after your dad."

"He'd like that." Good heavens, the sun must have some effect on her mind. Here they were discussing the names of their children, and Carla wasn't even convinced she should marry Philip!

"Jeff and Sylvia are here," he announced, and his expression became sober. Carla turned and noticed a sky-blue, half-ton pickup kick up gravel as it pulled into the parking lot.

A lanky fellow with a thick patch of dark hair jumped down from the driver's seat and hurried around to help his obviously pregnant wife.

Sylvia, a petite blonde with warm blue eyes, pressed a hand to the small of her back as she ambled toward them. Carla guessed that Jeff's wife must be seven or eight months pregnant.

"Hi, you must be Carla." Jeff held out his hand, not waiting for an introduction.

"Hi. You must be Jeff."

Sylvia offered her a gracious smile. "I'm glad you could make it."

"The whole team's ecstatic she could make it. Philip hasn't been worth a damn since he got back from Mexico. I certainly hope you're going to put this poor guy out of his misery and marry him."

Carla's startled eyes clashed with Philip's. This was exactly what she'd feared would happen. She didn't want to have to answer these kinds of questions. They were bad enough coming from Philip and Gramps.

"I... I'm not sure what I'm going to do," she answered stiffly, her eyes challenging Philip.

Nine

The warm sun had disappeared beyond the horizon, and the sun-baked land cheerfully welcomed the cool breath of evening. The flickering flames of a campfire licked at the remaining pieces of dry wood.

Sylvia and Carla were the last to remain by the dying fire. The other women were busy tucking their little ones into bed, and the sound of their whispers and hushed giggles filled the still evening air. Carla and Sylvia glanced at each other and grinned. Next year Sylvia would be joining the other young mothers. And next year Carla… She closed her eyes and shook her head. She didn't know what she'd be doing.

Jeff, Philip and the rest of the ten-man relay team were meeting to plan their strategy for the coming race. An air of excitement drifted through the campgrounds. The Great Soap Lake Canoe Race had dominated the conversation all afternoon. This was the first year the Spokane Police Department was competing, and their cheering squad held high expectations. For the last couple of years, the eighteen-and-a-half-mile course had been won by a two-man marathon team in the amazing time of two hours and thirty minutes. Philip's teammates seemed to think that ten men in top physical condition could easily outmaneuver two. The most incredible fact, Carla thought, was that every team that had ever entered this outrageous competition had finished. "Carla?" Sylvia's voice broke into her reverie, and she looked up.

"Hmm?"

"Jeff didn't mean to put you on the spot this afternoon— about marrying Philip, I mean," Sylvia said shyly. "It's just that we all like him so much."

"I…like Philip, too." The toe of Carla's sandal traced lazy patterns in the dirt. "In fact, I love him."

"You didn't need to tell me that. It's obvious."

A sad smile played at the edges of Carla's mouth. She liked Sylvia. She'd discovered that she liked all of Philip's friends. They had welcomed her without hesitation and accepted her as a part of their group, going out of their way to include her in the conversation and activities. One of Philip's friends had worked in Seattle for a short time and remembered Carla's father. Perhaps that was the reason she was accepted so quickly, but Carla didn't like to think so.

"The natural thing to do when two people love one another is to get married," Sylvia suggested softly.

"Not always," Carla answered with an emotional tremor in her voice. "Oftentimes there are…extenuating circumstances. My father's a policeman."

"I heard." Sylvia slipped her arms into the sleeves of the thin sweater draped over her shoulders and leaned back against the folding chair. "I can understand your hesitancy. Being a policeman isn't the kind of work I would have chosen for Jeff. There are too many worries, too many potential dangers that affect both our lives. But Jeff's career is an important part of who he is. It was a package deal, and

I've had to learn to accept it. Each police wife must come to grips with it sooner or later."

"Philip's got to be the most patient man in the world to put up with me."

"He loves you." Sylvia smiled. "I remember the first week after Philip returned from Mexico. Jeff complained every night." She paused and laughed softly. "A lovesick Philip took us all by surprise. We just didn't expect him to be so human. He's been as solid as a rock, and we were shocked to discover he's as vulnerable as the rest of us."

"He was in love with a flight attendant a few years back. Did you ever meet Nicole?"

"No." Sylvia shook her head slowly. "That was before I married Jeff. But I can remember him mentioning how hard Philip took it when they split up. I think Jeff's worried the same thing is going to happen again."

Rather than offer reassurances she didn't have, Carla said, "Philip's like that. Everything is done full measure."

"Everything," Sylvia agreed.

"Nicole was a fool to let him go." Carla paused and sucked in her breath, realizing what she'd just said. She'd be a fool to allow her fears and inhibitions to ruin her life. Yet something within her, some unresolved part of herself, couldn't accept what Philip was. The other wives had come to terms, appreciating their men for what they were. Carla hadn't honored Philip's commitment to his career, just as her mother had never been able to fully respect her father's dedication to his. The thought was so profound that it caused Carla to straighten. Maybe for the first time in her life she needed to talk with her mother.

"Would you like some help out of that chair, Mommy?" Jeff asked as he stepped behind his wife and lovingly rested his hand on her shoulder.

"Next time, I'm going to let him be the one to get pregnant," Sylvia teased, and extended her hand, accepting her husband's offer of assistance.

With their arms wrapped around each other, Jeff and Sylvia headed toward their tent.

"Night, Carla," Sylvia called back with a yawn. "I'll see you in the morning."

"Night."

"Are you tired?" Philip asked as he took the chair Sylvia had vacated.

"Not yet." Not when she could spend a few minutes alone with Philip. Not when they could sit undisturbed in the quiet of the night and talk. There were so many things she wanted to tell him. But in the peaceful solitude by the campfire, none of them seemed important.

"It's a beautiful night," he murmured as he leaned back and stared up at the sky. "In fact, tonight reminds me of Mexico and this incredibly lovely woman I once held in my arms."

"If I close my eyes, I can almost hear the surf against the shore," Carla responded, joining his game. "And if I try, really try, I can picture this incredibly wonderful man I met in Mexico sitting across from me."

Philip's chuckle was deep and warm. "How hard do you need to try?"

"It's not so difficult, really."

"I should hope not." Philip smiled and moved his chair so that they were sitting side by side. When he sat back down and reached for her hand, Carla glanced at him. His strong face was profiled in the moonlight, his look deep and thoughtful.

"Have you got your strategy all worked out, oh master of the canoe race?" she asked lightly. His pensive look troubled her. She didn't want anything to ruin these few minutes alone together; this wasn't the time to discuss her doubts or find the answers to nagging questions.

"Pretty much." He grimaced and quickly disguised a look of pain.

"Philip, what's wrong?" Her voice was unnaturally high with concern. "You're not feeling well, are you?" Immediately, she knelt at his side and touched his brow, which was cool and revealed no sign of a fever.

"It's nothing." He tried to dispel her worry with a wide grin. "Nerves, I think. I'm always this way before a race."

Returning to her chair, Carla nodded. "I had the lead in a play when I was in the eighth grade, and I was deathly sick before the first performance. I know what you mean."

"Have you and Sylvia decided where you're going to position yourselves to cheer us on?"

Apparently, Philip didn't want to talk about his nerves; this Carla understood and could sympathize. "At the finish line. Sylvia isn't in any condition to go running from lake to lake with the rest of the team. So we've decided to plant ourselves there and wait for our dedicated heroes to bring in the trophy."

"You may have a long wait," Philip said wryly and grimaced again.

Carla decided not to comment this time, but she was concerned. "Five lakes, Philip. Are you guys honestly going to canoe across five lakes?"

"We're going to paddle like crazy across each one, then lift the boat over our heads and run like madmen to the checkpoint. From there the next two-man team will take the canoe and the whole process will start again."

"Which lakes?" Carla had heard them mentioned only fleetingly.

"Park, Blue, Alkaline, Lenore and Soap."

"I think you're all a little nuts."

"We must be," Philip agreed soberly. "But to be honest, I'd swim, hike, canoe and run a lot farther than a few miles for an excuse to have you with me." He raised her fingers to his lips and kissed the back of her hand.

He studied her in the moonlight, and, feeling wretched, Carla lowered her eyes. "I don't know how you can love me," she murmured.

"Patience has its own rewards."

"I do love you." But a declaration of love, she knew, was only a small part of what he wanted from her.

"I know." He stood and offered her his arm. "I think we should both turn in. Tomorrow's going to be a full day." His voice was bland, almost impersonal, but his tone was at odds with the look in his eyes. Carla would have sworn he was hiding something from her and it was a whole lot more than nerves.

Philip's kiss outside her tent was brief, as if he were more preoccupied with the race than he was with having her near. It could be nerves, but they'd only seen each other twice since Mexico and she'd thought he'd do a whole lot more than peck her cheek when it came time to say good-night. A hand on her hip, Carla tipped her head to one side and flashed him a confused glance as he turned toward the tent he was sharing with another officer. Carla didn't know what was troubling Philip, but she'd bet hard cash it had nothing to do with her or the race. But whatever it was, he wasn't going to tell her. That hurt; it seemed to prove that Philip didn't feel he could discuss his problems with her. He wanted her to share his life, but there was a part of himself he would always hold back. The same way her father had from her mother.

* * *

Carla hadn't known there were this many people in all Eastern Washington. The start of the race was jam-packed with participants, friends, casual observers and cheering fans. Some of the contestants wore identifying uniforms that would distinguish themselves as being looney enough to participate in such a laughable race.

Everyone had been laughing and joking before the race, but when the gun went off, the competition began in earnest; each team was determined to win.

Jumping up and down with the others and clapping as hard as she could, Carla was caught up in the swirl of craziness that seemed to have engulfed the entire city of Soap Lake.

Three hours later, when Philip and Jeff crossed the finish line, placing a respectable fifth, Carla and Sylvia had cheered and laughed themselves weak.

Dramatically throwing themselves down on the grass, both men lay staring at the cloudless blue sky, panting.

Jeff spoke first. "Next year," he managed breathlessly, "we'll go after the trophy."

Sitting around the picnic table at the campgrounds later that afternoon, Philip positioned himself by Carla's side and casually draped his arm over her shoulder. "Do you think we should compete again next year?"

Carla lowered her hot dog to the plate. "It'd be a shame not to. You were only twenty minutes off the best time, and with a little practice you're bound to improve. Don't you agree?"

"On one condition. That you promise to be on my cheering squad again next year." His eyes searched hers, seeming to need reassurance.

Confidently, Carla placed her hand on his. "You got it."

The sun beamed off the gold band of her watch, and Carla noticed the time and groaned.

"What's the matter?"

"I've got to leave."

"Now?"

Sadly, she shook her head. "Soon. In order to have Friday afternoon free, I traded days with another girl who's on call tomorrow."

"Which means?" His eyes narrowed.

"Which means I have to be back tonight by midnight in case there's an emergency."

Standing, Philip tossed his paper plate in the garbage can. Carla dumped the remainder of her lunch away and followed Philip to a large oak tree, where he stood, staring at the ground.

"It was hardly worth your while to make the trip. I'm surprised you came."

"I'm glad I did. I enjoyed meeting your friends, especially Sylvia and Jeff."

He pursed his lips, and Carla studied him suspiciously. He looked as if he wanted to argue and she couldn't understand why. Planting herself in front of him, her legs braced slightly apart, she stared at him until he met her gaze. "It's not going to work, you know."

He frowned. "What's not going to work?"

"Starting an argument. I refuse to react to your anger. I wish I could stay. If it was up to me, I would. But circumstances being what they are, I've got to leave this afternoon." She paused and drew a long breath. "Now. Will you walk me to the tent and spend the next few minutes saying goodbye to me properly, or are you going to stand here and pout?"

Philip bristled. "I never pout."

"Good." She smiled and reached for his hand. "Then let's escape for a few minutes of privacy before someone comes looking for us."

The sun was setting, whisking back the splashes of warm, golden rays, by the time Carla pulled into her apartment parking space. After emerging from the car, she stretched, raising her arms high above her head and yawning. The trip back had been leisurely and had taken the better part of four hours. Philip had promised to connect as soon as he was back in Spokane. That brooding, troubled look had returned when he'd kissed her goodbye. Carla didn't know what was bothering him, but she guessed that it had nothing to do with her. Already he was acting like her father, afraid to tell her something he knew could upset her. If she was going to consider being his wife, she didn't want him treading lightly around information she had a right to know. She'd ask him about it Monday night.

Sunday afternoon, while on call at the hospital, Carla drove to her parents' house.

"Hi, Mom," she said as she let herself in the front door. Rachel Walker was sitting on the worn sofa, knitting a sweater.

"Who's this one for?" Carla asked as she sat across from her mother, admiring the collage of colored yarn. Rachel was constantly doing something—idle hands led to boredom, she had always said. She was a perfectionist housekeeper, and now that Carla and her brother had left home, she busied herself with craft projects.

"Julianne," her mother replied without a pause between stitches, her fingers moving with a skill that was amazing. "She'll need a warm sweater this fall for first grade. She's six now, you know."

"Yes." Both her nieces had always been special to Carla, and she'd missed them terribly since her brother and his wife had moved to Oregon.

"Where's Dad?"

Briefly, a hurt look rushed across her mother's face. "He's playing on the men's softball team again this year." The Seattle Police Department had several teams, and Carla's father loved to participate, but her mother had never gone to watch him play, preferring to stay at home. What Joe did outside the house was his business, because it involved the police force—and Rachel had never had anything to do with the force.

"Actually, I'm glad Dad isn't here, because I'd like to talk to you alone."

"To me?" Momentarily, Rachel glanced up from her handiwork.

"I'm in love with Philip Garrison," Carla announced, and closed her eyes, preparing for the backlash that was sure to follow.

"I think I already knew that," her mother replied calmly. "In fact, your father and I were just talking about the two of you."

"And?"

"We agreed that you and Philip will do fine. What I said to you the other night isn't altogether valid. We are alike, Carla, in many ways, but in others we're completely different."

Carla marveled at the way her mother could talk so frankly with her and at the same time keep perfect pace with her knitting.

"Joe pointed out that your personality is stronger than I've given you credit for. You're not afraid to say what you feel or to speak out against injustice. Your work at the hospital proves that..." Rachel paused and after taking a shuddering breath, she bit her bottom lip.

Carla moved out of the chair and kneeled at her mother's side. Rachel tossed her yarn aside and leaned forward to hug her daughter as she hadn't since Carla was a child. "I would have chosen another man for you, Princess. But I can't hold against Philip the very things that make me love your father. Be happy, baby. Be happy."

"I love you, Mom," Carla murmured. She'd never thought she'd feel this close to her mother. Philip had done that for her. He had given her the parent she had never thought she'd understand—the closeness every daughter yearns to share with her mother.

Carla laughed and said, "It's not every day your only daughter decides to get married. Could we do something together? Just you and me."

Leaning back in the cushioned sofa, Rachel reached for a tissue and blew her nose. "What do you want to do?"

"Can we go to Dad's softball game?"

For a second Rachel looked stunned. But gradually a smile formed at the edges of her mouth. "I've been waiting twenty years for an excuse to do just that."

Monday afternoon, on her way home from the hospital, Carla stopped off to visit Gramps, but she stayed just long enough for a single game of checkers and to tell him she'd made a decision about Philip.

"So you've come to your senses and decided you're going to marry him?"

"If he'll have me."

"No worry there," Gramps said with a chuckle. "The problem, as I see it, is if you're ready to be the right person for a man like Philip."

Carla didn't hesitate. "I know I am. Philip is a policeman, and I should know what that means. After all, I've been a policeman's daughter all my life."

His eyes beamed with pride as he slowly shook his head. "I see you've come to terms with that. Now I pray that you'll be as good a wife as your mother has been all these years."

"I hope I can, too," Carla added soberly.

The phone rang just as she she let herself into the apartment. Carla dumped her purse on the kitchen table and grabbed her cell.

"Hello."

"Carla. Thank heaven I caught you. Where have you been? This is Jeff, Philip's partner."

Carla felt the blood rush from her face. Jeff would be phoning her only if something had happened to Philip. Her knees went weak, and she leaned heavily against the counter. "We aren't allowed to keep our phones with us while on duty. What is it?"

"Apparently, you didn't check your messages either. Philip's in the hospital. I think you should get here as soon as possible. I checked with Alaska Airlines, and there's a flight leaving Seattle in two hours. If you can be on it, I'll pick you up in the patrol car and take you directly to him."

Ten

"What happened?" Somehow Carla managed to get the words past the bubble of hysteria that threatened to overtake her.

"We were on patrol and… It was my fault, I should have known what was happening. With all the medical training I've had, I can't believe I didn't know what was going on. But I got him to the hospital in record time. Listen, Carla, I can't explain everything now. Just get here. Philip asked for you when he came out of surgery. I want to tell him that you're coming."

"Yes…of course, I'm on my way now. And Jeff." Her hand tightened around her phone. "Thanks for letting me know."

Unable to move, Carla felt an almost tangible fear move through her body. Her senses reeled with it. Her mouth was dry, her hands were clammy, her knees felt weak. Even the rhythmic beating of her heart slowed. It seemed unfair that once she had reconciled herself to who and what Philip was, her newfound confidence should be severely tested this way. With a resolve born of love, Carla had thought she could face anything. Now she realized how wrong she was. She would never come to terms with losing Philip.

By rote, she reached for her phone and contacted her parents. "Mom," she cried, not waiting for a greeting, "Philip's been shot." Carla heard her mother's soft gasp and fought her own rising panic. "He's just out of surgery and I'm flying to be with him. Call the hospital and explain that I won't be in. And let Gramps know."

"When's your flight."

Carla ran her hands through her hair. "In two hours... There's a flight on Alaska but I...I..."

"You pack," her mother said, taking over. "I'll call the airport for you. Your father will be there in ten minutes to drive you. Don't worry, Princess, Philip will be fine." Her mother hadn't any more information than Carla, but the gentle reassurance gave her the courage to think clearly.

Yanking clothes off the hanger, Carla stuffed them in an overnight case. After adding her toothbrush, curling iron and a comb, she slammed the lid closed. She'd be fine if only she could stop shaking. Pausing, she forced herself to take several deep, calming breaths. The shock of Jeff's call prevented tears, but she knew those would come later.

The doorbell rang, and Carla rushed across the living room to open the door.

"You ready?" Her father looked as pale as she did, Carla realized, but she knew he was far too disciplined to display his emotion openly.

She gave an abrupt nod, and he took the small suitcase out of her hand and cupped her elbow as they hurried down the flight of stairs to the apartment parking lot. During the ten-minute drive to Sea-Tac International Airport, Carla could feel her father's concerned scrutiny.

"Are you going to be all right, Princess? Do you want your mother with you?"

"No, I'm fine," she said, and with a sad smile amended, "I think I'm fine. If anything happens to Philip, I don't know that I'll ever get over it."

"Cross that bridge when you come to it," he advised. "And phone as soon as you know his condition."

"I will," she promised.

Jeff was nervously pacing the tiled airport floor when Carla spotted him just minutes after stepping off the plane. Without hesitation she ran to him and gripped his forearm. "How's Philip?" Her eyes pleaded with him to tell her everything was fine.

"There weren't any complications. But apparently I misunderstood him. He said he *didn't* want you to know."

"Didn't want me to know?" she echoed incredulously. If that bullet didn't kill him, she would. Philip was lying on a hospital bed wanting to protect her from the unpleasant aspects of his occupation. It infuriated her, and at the same time she felt an overpowering surge of love.

"Just before I left, the doctors told me it would be several hours before he wakes."

Carla weighed Jeff's words carefully. "Take me to the hospital. I want to be there when he wakes."

A smile cracked the tight line of Jeff's mouth. "As the lady requests. Tell him the decision was yours and I'm not responsible."

"I'll tell him," she said and winked.

"Great." He looked at his watch. "I'm afraid I can't take you to the hospital personally; I'm still on duty. But another friend of ours will get you there safely. If you like, I can take your things and drop them off at Philip's condo."

"Yes...that'll be fine."

Jeff introduced Bill Bower, a ruddy-faced officer Carla didn't recognize from the previous weekend. Bill nodded politely, and after saying goodbye to Jeff, the two of them headed for Bill's car.

"Can you tell me what happened?" she asked Bill when they were on the freeway. During the flight she had prepared herself to hear the details of what exactly had gone wrong. In some ways Carla realized that she didn't want to know. It wasn't important as long as Philip was alive and well. There would be time for explanations later when Philip could make them himself. But knowing that he would make light of the incident, she'd hoped to get a fuller version of the story on the way to the hospital.

"I wasn't there," Bill stared matter-of-factly, "so I don't know how it happened. But apparently Philip was in tremendous pain, and Jeff may have saved his life by getting him to the hospital as quickly as he did."

Carla paled at the thought of Philip in agony. He'd be the type to suffer nobly. Her lips felt dry, and she moistened them.

The stoic-faced offer must have caught her involuntary action. "I wouldn't worry. Philip's healthy and strong. But he's bound to be in a foul mood, so don't pay any mind to what he says."

"No, I won't," she replied with a brave smile.

The hospital smelled fainty of antiseptic. Carla was admitted into Philip's room without question, which surprised her. Seeing him lying against the white sheets, tubes coming out of his arms, nearly undid her. She sank gratefully into the chair beside his bed.

"The doctor will be in later, if you have any questions," the efficient nurse explained.

"I'll be leaving now," added Bill. "If you need anything, don't hesitate to call. Jeff will be back later tonight."

"Thanks, Bill."

"All the thanks I want is an invitation to the wedding."

"It's yours." She tried to smile, but the effort was painful.

Still wrapped in the warm comfort of sleep, Philip did little more than roll his head from one side to the other during the next two hours. Content just to be close to him, Carla did little more than hold his fingers in hers and press her cheek to the back of his hand.

"Carla?"

Forcing herself to smile, Carla raised her head and met Philip's gaze.

"Is it really you, or is this some befuddling dream?"

"If I kiss you, you'll know for sure." Gently, she moved to the head of his bed and leaned forward to press her lips to his. Philip's hand found her hair, and he wove his fingers through its rusty curls.

"Oh, Philip, are you going to be all right?" she moaned, burying her face in the side of his neck.

"Stay a while longer, and I'll prove it," he whispered against her temple.

He lifted his gaze to hers, and the intense look in those steel-gray eyes caught her breath. A muscle worked in his lean jaw as his gaze roamed possessively over her face. "I didn't want Jeff to contact you."

"I know, but I'm here now and nothing's going to make me leave." Her hand clasped his as she took the seat beside the bed.

"What did Jeff say when he phoned? He has a high sense of theatrics, you realize."

"You warned me about that once before. He said that you'd just come out of surgery and had asked for me."

"What I asked was that he not contact you. I didn't want you worrying."

"Philip Garrison, if you think you can keep something like getting shot from me"—she tried to disguise the hurt in her voice—"you've got a second think coming, because I can assure you, wild canoe racers wouldn't keep me away from you at a time like this."

"Shot?" His breath quickened as he raised his head slightly to study her. "Jeff told you I was shot? I'll kill him."

"Well, good heavens, something like a gunshot wound is a little difficult to keep from me. Just how were you planning to tell me about it? 'Carla, darling'" she mimicked in a deep rumbling voice, "'I guess I should explain that I got scratched while on duty today. I'll be in the hospital a week or so, but it's nothing to worry about'"

"Carla…" His voice was a husky growl. "If I told you I'd been shot, paranoia would overtake you so quickly that I'd never catch you, you'd be running so fast."

"It's a high opinion you've got of me, isn't it?" she asked in a shaky voice. "You're missing the point. I did learn what happened, and I'm here, because it's exactly where I want to be."

"Only because Jeff made it sound as if I were on my deathbed."

"He said you asked for me—that's all."

"And I hadn't."

Sitting became intolerable, and she stood, pacing the floor with her arms gently wrapped around her to ward off the chill in his voice.

"As it is, you've wasted a trip. There won't be any

deathbed scene. I was never in any danger from a gun-shot wound. I had my appendix out."

Carla pivoted sharply and her mouth dropped open. "Your appendix out?"

"If you need proof, lift the sheet and see for yourself."

She ignored the heavy sarcasm lacing his voice. "Then why did Jeff—" What kind of fool game was Philip's friend playing anyway? Did he feel he needed to fabricate stories to convince her to come?

"That's exactly what I intend to find out."

Silence hovered over them like a heavy thundercloud.

"I don't mean to be rude, but I'm not exactly in the mood for company, Carla."

She'd thought he'd been shot and all the while it was his appendix. To her humiliation, she sniffled and her soft breath became a hiccuping sob. Frantically, she searched for her purse, needing to get out of the room before she humiliated herself further.

"Carla. Don't go," he groaned in frustration. "I didn't mean that. I'm sorry."

"That's all right," she mumbled shakily, wiping the tears from her pale cheeks. A kaleidoscope of emotions whirled through her—shock, relief, hurt, anger, joy. "I understand."

"This is exactly what I didn't want. If it had been up to me, you wouldn't even have known I was in the hospital. I don't want you worrying about me."

"You didn't even want me to know you were in the hospital?" Carla closed her eyes. She didn't want to think about the life they'd have if Philip insisted on shielding her from anything unpleasant. She wondered how he'd feel if the tables were turned. By heaven she was going to get Jeff for this. She'd arrived expecting something far worse and he'd let her believe it!

"I may be out of line here, but didn't you ask me to marry you not long ago?" she reminded him.

Philip looked at her blankly. "What's that got to do with anything?"

"Doesn't a wife or a fiancée or even the woman in your life have a right to know certain things?"

His hand covered his weary eyes. "Do you mind very much if we discuss this at another time? Go back to Seattle, Carla. I'll call you when I'm in a better frame of mine and we can discuss it then."

Placing four fingers at her temple, she executed a crisp military salute. "Aye aye, Comandant."

Carla couldn't tell whether the sound Philip made was a chuckle or a snort, and she didn't stay long enough in his room to find out.

Luckily, Jeff was due to arrive at the hospital within a half hour. Her anger mounted by the time Philip's partner arrived. The minute he appeared she stood, prepared for battle.

"That was a rotten trick you pulled," she declared with clenched teeth.

"Trick?" Jeff looked stunned. "I didn't pull any trick."

"You told me Philip had been shot."

Jeff looked all the more taken aback. "I didn't."

"You implied as much," she returned, barely managing to keep her voice even.

"How could you have thought he'd been shot? Especially since he was feeling so crummy during the canoe race. Saturday night someone suggested it could be his appendix and..." Jeff swallowed, looking chagrined. "That's right, you left early. Phil was feeling even crummier later and I think we all should have known what was wrong. Listen,

I apologize, I thought you knew. You must have been frantic. I wouldn't have frightened you had—"

"It's all right," Carla accepted his apology with a wry grin. Obviously, she had read more into his comments than he had intended. The misunderstanding hadn't been intentional.

"I'd better explain to Philip," Jeff said with a thoughtful look. "He's probably mad as hops."

"It's best to let the beast rest for now. If you want you can explain later."

One glance at Carla was apparently enough to convince him that Carla knew what she was talking about. The ride through Spokane seemed to take forever and when Jeff stopped at a traffic light, Carla couldn't hold back a giggle.

"What's so funny?" Jeff glanced at her curiously.

"I don't know…just my thoughts, I guess. I assumed that someone as wonderful as Philip would be a good patient. I thought he'd be the type of man to suffer silently…and he's terrible. Just terrible."

"Give him a day or two," Jeff advised good-humoredly. "He'll come around."

Philip's condominium was located in the heart of the city near the Spokane River. "Here are the keys to his car," Jeff said, handing them to her after unlocking the front door. They stood just inside the entryway. "Bill dropped it off on his way home tonight. Listen…" Jeff paused and ran his hand along the side of his short-cropped hair. "Sylvia called and said she was feeling strange. I don't know what that means, but I think I should head home. I have this irrational fear that the baby is going to come into this world without me coaching, and I'd hate to think that all those classes would go to waste. Call if you need anything, all right?"

"Sure. Go on, and give Sylvia my best."

"I will. Thanks."

Jeff was out the door, and Carla turned to interrupt Philip's orderly life even more by invading his home. Maybe he was right; maybe she should take her things and head back to Seattle. No, she wouldn't do that. Things between them had to be settled now.

The first thing that caught Carla's attention was the hand-carved marlin that she'd given Philip. He'd set it on the fireplace mantel. A photo of them together in Mexico sat on his dresser. Carla was smiling into the camera as the wind whipped up her soft russet curls. Philip's head was turned and his eyes were on her. There was so much love in his expression that Carla breathed a soft sigh as she examined the framed photo.

Her letters to him were stacked on the kitchen table. Each one had been read so many times that the edges had begun to curl. Carla took one look and recognized again that there wasn't any man on earth who would love her as much as Philip. And more important, there would never be anyone she could love as much.

After a reassuring phone call to her parents, she took a long shower and slept fitfully.

She waited until noon the next day before venturing outside the condominium. Driving Philip's car to the hospital proved to be eventful. Twice she got lost, but with the friendly help of a local service-station attendant, she finally located the hospital.

A nurse on Philip's floor gave her a suspicious look as she walked down the wide corridor carrying a guitar.

One loud knock against his door was all the warning she gave.

"Carla."

She suspected it was relief she heard in his voice, but she didn't pause to question him. Instead she pulled out the chair beside his bed, sat at an angle on the cushion and strummed one discordant chord. With that she proceeded to serenade him in the only song she knew in Spanish.

He started to laugh but quickly grimaced and tried to contain his amusement. "Why are you singing to me the A, B, C's?"

"It's the only Spanish song I know all the way through. However, if you'd like to hear parts of 'Mary Had a Little Lamb,' I'll be happy to comply."

Extending a hand to her, he shook his head. "The only thing I want is you."

"That's a different tune than you were singing yesterday."

"Yesterday I was an unreasonable boor." He pulled her closer to his side. "I'm glad you're here. Today I promise to be a much better patient."

"Once we're married I suspect I'll have ways of helping you out of those irrational moods."

The room went quiet as Philip's eyes sought hers. "Once we're married."

"You did ask me, and you better not have changed your mind, because I've already given my two-week notice at the hospital."

"Carla." His gray eyes reflected an intensity she had rarely witnessed. "Do you mean it?"

"I've never been more serious in my life. But I won't have you holding out on me. If I'm going to be your wife, I expect you to trust me enough not to try to shield me from whatever comes our way. I'm stronger than I look, Philip Garrison."

"Far stronger," he agreed as his hand slipped around her waist. "You've already convinced me of that. I love you, Carla Walker—soon to be Carla Garrison."

Tenderness surged through her as she slipped her arms over his shoulders. "But not near soon enough," she said with a sigh of longing as her mouth eagerly sought his.

* * * * *

YESTERDAY ONCE MORE

One

Julie Houser pushed the elevator button and stepped back to wait. An older woman whose office was on the same floor joined her and they exchanged smiles.

Absently, Julie glanced at her watch; she'd have plenty of time to finish unpacking tonight. Not wanting to prepare a meal, she considered picking up something from the local deli.

The elevator doors swooshed open, and the two women entered, then moved to the back, anticipating the five-thirty rush. By the time the car arrived at the ground floor it would be filled to capacity.

The next floor down it stopped, and three men boarded. Julie was concentrating on the lighted numbers above the door when the elevator came to a halt again. Another man got in and Julie squeezed herself into the far corner to make room.

The strap of her purse slid off her shoulder and as she eased it back up she felt someone's eyes on her. Accustomed to the appreciative gaze of men, Julie ignored the look and the man. The close scrutiny continued and she could practically feel his stare. Abruptly, Julie turned her head, wondering who he was.

But when she finally saw her admirer, she nearly choked. She felt chilled and on fire at the same moment. Her heart hammered wildly, and her hand tightened around the purse strap as if that would hold her upright.

"Daniel." The name fell from her lips as her eyes met those of the man standing closest to her. His dark eyes narrowed and an impassive expression masked his strikingly handsome face.

Unable to bear his gaze any longer, Julie glanced away.

The elevator stopped and everyone filed out until she stood there alone, her breath coming in uneven gasps. So soon? She'd only been back in Wichita for six days. Never had she dreamed she'd see Daniel so quickly. And in her own building. Was his office here? *Oh, please,* she begged, *not yet. I'm not ready.*

"You coming or going?" An irritated voice from the foyer broke into her thoughts and Julie moved out of the elevator on unsteady legs.

Her heels clicked noisily as she hurried across the marble floor and outside. The downtown sidewalks were filled with people rushing and Julie made her way through the crowds, uncertain where she'd parked her car that morning. Pausing at a red light, she realized she was walking in the wrong direction and turned around. Ten minutes later she'd found her car. Her hand trembled uncontrollably as she opened the door.

She felt as if she'd been running a marathon as she slipped into the driver's seat and pressed her forehead against the steering wheel. Nothing could have prepared her for this meeting. Three years had passed since she'd last seen Daniel. Years of change. She'd only been twenty-one when she'd fled in panic. He had cause to be bitter and she was sorry for what she'd done. The regret she felt at hurting the man she loved was almost more than she could bear.

And she had loved Daniel. The evening he'd placed the diamond engagement ring on her finger had been the happiest of her life.

Julie's thoughts drifted back to that night as she started her car and headed toward her apartment. Daniel had taken her to an elegant French restaurant. The lights were dim, and flickering candlelight sent shadows dancing over the white linen tablecloth. Julie tried not to reveal how ill-at-ease she was in such a fancy place. She'd been so worried that she'd pick up the wrong fork, or worse, dump her soup in her lap. She was so much in love with Daniel and desperately wanted to please him. Julie let herself remember...

"Happy?" he asked.

She glanced over the top of the gold-tasseled menu and nodded shyly. Everything on the menu was in French with an English translation below. Even with that she didn't recognize half of what was offered. "What would you suggest?"

Daniel set his menu aside, his expression preoccupied. Julie noticed that from the moment he'd picked her up that evening he'd been unnaturally quiet. Nerves tightened her stomach.

"Daniel, is something the matter?" she ventured.

He stared at her blankly.

"I'm not wearing the right kind of dress, am I?" She'd changed clothes three times before he'd arrived, parading each outfit in front of her mother until Margaret Houser had demanded that Julie stop being so particular. Any one of the outfits was perfectly fine.

"You're beautiful," Daniel whispered and the look in his eyes confirmed the softly murmured words.

Julie lowered her gaze. Her hand smoothed an imaginary crease from her crisp skirt. "I wanted everything to be perfect tonight."

"Why?"

Julie answered him with a delicate shrug of one shoulder. She wanted everything to be perfect for Daniel all the time. "You've been very quiet," she said. "Have I done something to upset you?"

He chuckled, shaking his head. "Oh, my adorable Julie, is it any wonder I love you?" His hand reached for hers. "I've been trying to find a way to ask you a question."

"But, Daniel, all you need to do is ask."

He sighed expressively. "It's not that simple."

Julie couldn't imagine what was troubling him. Daniel was always so thoughtful; he did everything possible to make her comfortable. When they met his friends, he kept her beside him because he knew how reserved she was. A thousand times over the past six months, he'd been so loving and caring that it hadn't taken Julie long to lose her heart to him. Slowly, he'd brought her into his world. He often took her to the Country Club and had taught her how to play golf and tennis. Gradually, his friends had become hers until, reticent though she was, Julie had flowered under his love.

But she knew that a blossom had its season and would soon wilt and droop. Maybe Daniel was trying to think of a way to let her down gently. Maybe he was tired of her. Maybe he didn't want to see her again. Panic filled her and she clutched the linen napkin in her lap, praying that she wouldn't make a fool of herself and burst into tears when he told her.

"I've been accepted into the law practice of McFife, Lawson and Garrison."

Julie jerked her head up. "That's wonderful news! Congratulations."

He smiled. "It's only a junior partnership."

"That's the firm you were hoping you'd get into."

"Yes, it is, for more reasons than you know."

Now she understood why he'd chosen such an expensive restaurant. "We're here to celebrate, then."

"Not quite yet." He leaned forward and clasped her hand in both of his. "These last few months have been the happiest of my life."

"Mine, too," she whispered.

"I know you're only twenty-one and I should probably wait a couple of years." He paused. "Julie…"

Her heart was pounding so loudly she was afraid he could hear it. Her eyes met his. "Yes, Daniel?"

"What I'm trying to say is… I love you, Julie. I've never kept that a secret. Now that I've been accepted by a good law firm and can offer you a future—will you marry me?"

Julie closed her eyes, savoring the warmth of his words.

"For heaven's sake," Daniel said. "Say something."

Julie bit her bottom lip, convinced she'd start to cry if she tried to speak.

"Julie," he pleaded.

She nodded wildly.

"Does that mean yes?"

Her voice trembled. "Yes, Daniel, yes! I love you so much. Nothing would make me happier than to spend the rest of my life with you."

The look in Daniel's eyes was enough to melt her bones. "I didn't think anything this delicate could be so heavy," he said, pulling a jeweler's box from his jacket pocket. He lifted the lid, revealing a diamond so large, Julie gasped.

Tears blurred her gaze. "Oh, Daniel."

"Do you like it? The jeweler said we can exchange it if you'd prefer something different."

"It's the most beautiful ring I've ever seen."

"Here." He took her hand again and slipped the diamond onto her finger...

Julie fought to suppress the memory of that night. She pulled into the apartment parking lot and turned off the engine. Her fingers toyed with the gold chain that hung around her neck, seeking the diamond ring she'd kept there these past three years. She'd continue to wear it this way until it was back on her finger where it belonged. But after seeing Daniel today, Julie realized how difficult that would be. Daniel wouldn't forgive her easily.

Determined, she climbed out of her car and walked to her uninspired furnished apartment.

The bright, sunny place she'd left in California had been shared with good friends, people who cared about her.

The most difficult decision she'd ever made was to flee Wichita three years ago. The second hardest was to come back. But she had no choice. She loved Daniel, and if at all possible, she needed to set things right with him.

Julie hung her coat in the closet. She entered the living room to find several stacks of boxes, but felt too exhausted to unpack.

Until today, everything had happened exactly as she'd hoped. Her job had been lined up before the move, and she'd managed to locate an apartment with no lease that was within her budget, and in a relatively good area. The transition had been smooth. But running into Daniel after only six days was something she hadn't counted on. She sat on the couch and rested her head against the back cushion for a few minutes.

Julie moved onto the floor, then crawled along the carpet until she got to the box containing their engagement portrait. She stared at the two smiling faces. They'd been so much in love. As tears filled her eyes, the happy faces swam in and out of her vision.

She traced her fingers across the image of Daniel's face and recalled their encounter that afternoon. His carefree smile had disappeared. The years had added a harshness to him, an arrogant aloofness. Even his sandy-colored hair was no longer casual but styled.

Julie's finger idly moved over the lean, proud jaw, pausing at the tiny cleft in his chin. She smiled sadly as she recalled how she'd loved to kiss him there. To tease him with her lips. And he'd been so wonderful, so understanding of her need to take things slow. Julie wondered if he regretted that now. There'd been many opportunities to consummate their love, but Daniel had always been the one to put a stop to it. She'd respected and loved him for that. He'd refused the ring when she'd tried to return it, which was how she'd come to wear it around her neck, keeping it close to her heart, no matter how many miles stood between them. Or how much pain.

Early the next morning Julie arrived at work intent on checking the list of occupants in her office complex. The Inland Empire Building housed fifteen floors of offices. As she studied the directory in the foyer, the listing for Daniel Van Deen, Attorney, seemed to leap off the board. Only one floor separated her from Daniel. For five of the six days she'd been in Wichita, they'd been this close without even knowing it.

A shiver ran down her spine and she slowly turned to see Daniel approaching the elevator, a newspaper wedged under his arm. He pushed the button and the wide doors opened. He stepped inside and turned around, his eyes locking with hers from across the foyer.

She watched as frustration swept over his features. His dark eyes narrowed as he stared back at her—and then the elevator doors glided shut.

Julie released a deep breath. Daniel hadn't forgiven her. The seething look he'd just sent her confirmed that.

Her legs felt unsteady as she took the next elevator up to the office of Cheney Trust and Mortgage Company. Grateful that she was the first one in that morning, she sat at her desk, trying to calm her nerves. Her hand trembled as she opened the bottom drawer of her desk and set her purse inside.

Sherry Adams, Julie's pretty blonde coworker, strolled in about fifteen minutes late. Their employer, Jack Barrett, had arrived before Sherry and had pointedly frowned at the empty desk, silently noting her absence. Julie had only been working at the office a few days and she didn't know Sherry well, but she could see that, despite her faults, the young divorcee was a valuable asset to the company.

"Morning," Julie said. "You seem to be in a good mood."

"I am." Sherry gave a brilliant imitation of a fashion model, her skirt flaring as she whirled around.

"I take it you want me to guess?" Julie asked.

Sherry shrugged playfully. "Not really. I just thought you'd be interested to know that I was asked out by the most eligible man in town."

"Congratulations."

"Thank you." Sherry smiled. "Actually, this is the culmination of five weeks of plotting and fine-tuning my womanly charms. I must admit, this guy's been one tough fish to catch."

"Well, double congratulations then," Julie said with a laugh.

Sherry sat and rolled her chair over to Julie's desk. "I don't suppose…you-know-who…is in yet?" Sherry inclined her head toward the closed door of Jack Barrett's office.

"'Fraid so," Julie said. "About fifteen minutes ago."

"Did he say anything about me being late?" Sherry asked, not looking the least bit concerned.

"Not to me he didn't."

"One of these days, old Barrett's going to fire me—and with good reason."

"I doubt that," Julie assured her. "Now tell me about your hot date."

"It's with Danny Van Deen."

Julie bit back a gasp and lowered her gaze, hoping to hide her surprise.

"He's a lawyer in the building," Sherry continued. "I've had my eye on him for a while. He's only taken a nibble so far, but it won't be long before I reel him in."

Julie forced her voice to maintain the same level of cheerfulness. "Good luck."

"Of course, I can't let him know how interested I am. That would be the kiss of death with a guy like Danny. But keeping my cool shouldn't be too difficult. By the time we're standing at the altar, he'll think it was his idea."

"I thought you didn't believe in wedded bliss anymore."

"Sure I do. It just didn't work out with Andy. I feel bad about that, but we fell out of love with each other. Not much either of us could do about it, really."

"And…this Van Deen…has he ever been married?"

"Nope. I can't understand it. He's perfect husband material—handsome, intelligent and sensitive under that cool exterior of his. He dates often enough, but nothing ever comes of it. Until now." She laughed softly. "I'll have him at the altar before he knows what hit him."

"Good luck," Julie murmured.

"I'm going to need all the luck I can get," Sherry added, straightening her desk. "Are you taking the first lunch today?"

"If you'd like," Julie replied absently as she flipped through the pages of a report on her desk.

"Would you mind cutting it short so I can get out of here by twelve-thirty? I'll make it up to you later, I promise." Sherry's brilliant blue eyes held a pleading look. "There's a dress I saw this morning and I want to try it on. That's actually the reason I was late. Wait until Danny Van Deen sees me in that."

"Sure," Julie agreed. "I can be back early."

The remainder of the morning was quiet. The two women took turns answering the phone. Because she wasn't fully accustomed to the office, Julie relied on Sherry for help, which she willingly supplied. Sherry was a generous person, who seemed to harbor no ill against anyone. That was what made her divorce so hard to understand. Julie couldn't imagine a woman like Sherry giving up on something as important as a marriage.

Shortly after noon, Sherry reminded Julie of their agreement. Julie removed her purse from the desk drawer and stood, ready to leave for her lunch break when Jack Barrett strolled out of his office.

"Are you going for lunch?" the balding man asked.

"Yes," Julie replied. "Would you like me to get you something?"

"Not today, thanks." He handed her a large manila envelope. "But would you mind dropping this off at Daniel Van Deen's office?"

Two

Panic filled Julie's eyes as she cast a pleading glance at Sherry.

"Go on. You might catch a glimpse of him and then you'll know what I mean!" Sherry seemed oblivious to the real reason behind Julie's reluctance.

Jack Barrett looked suspiciously from one to the other. "Is there a problem?"

"No problem," Sherry said.

Julie nodded her agreement, hoping to bow gracefully out of the situation.

"His office is one floor down. Number 919, I think." Sherry wrinkled her nose. "His name should be on the door."

Julie managed a smile and walked out of the office. By the time she reached Daniel's floor, the envelope felt as if it weighed fifty pounds.

Her hand was clammy as she turned the knob and entered the office.

A round-faced secretary glanced up and smiled. "Can I help you?"

The first thing Julie noticed was the woman's ring. She

was married. But why should it matter that Daniel's secretary was married?

"I...have a package," she stammered. "For Mr. Van Deen. From Jack Barrett."

"Agnes, did you find—" Abruptly, Daniel had appeared, his words cut short as he caught sight of Julie. For a moment there was a hard look in his eyes, but then they softened and an expression Julie couldn't define came over his features.

"Mr. Barrett's sent the papers you asked about this morning," Agnes said, and although Julie heard her speak, it somehow felt as if she and Daniel were alone in the room.

"You did ask about the Macmillan papers?" The woman's words sounded distant.

"Yes," said Daniel, his words breaking the spell as he continued to stare at Julie.

The secretary took the envelope from Julie's limp hand, her sharp gaze shifting from one to the other. "Was that all?"

Julie snapped to attention. "Pardon?"

"Was there something else?"

"No," she mumbled. "Thank you."

A puzzled look appeared on the woman's face. "Thank you for dropping this off."

Julie smiled and turned, walking out of the office with her head held high.

The rest of the day passed in a blur and by the time she got home that night, Julie felt physically and mentally drained.

As she entered her apartment, Julie discovered her new phone had been installed. She decided to call her mother.

"Hi, Mom," she said, trying to sound cheerful.

"Julie. How are you?" Her mother sounded concerned.

Margaret Houser lived in San Diego, where she'd moved when she was widowed. With Julie's older brother, Joe, in Montana, none of her family lived in Wichita anymore.

"Fine, Mom. Everything's fine."

"I'm so glad you called. I've been worried. Have you looked up any of your old high school friends?"

"Not yet," said Julie, though truthfully, she doubted she would. The only real friends she'd had in Wichita had gone elsewhere. "Mom." She took in a deep breath. "I've seen Daniel."

The concern in her mother's voice returned. "How is he?"

"We…we haven't talked. But I can tell he's changed. I feel like I hardly know him. He never understood why I left. He's not likely to understand why I came back."

"Don't be so sure, sweetheart." Her mother's voice was reassuring. "He's been hurt, and it makes sense that he's changed over the years."

"Mom, I don't think he'll talk to me."

"I've never known you to be a defeatist," her mother said in a supportive tone. "But I do worry about Daniel's mother. Be careful if you have to deal with her."

"I will." Julie's fingers flipped through the white pages of the telephone directory. Clara Van Deen's number was unlisted, but Daniel's was there. As her mother continued, Julie ran her finger back and forth over his name. The movement had a strange, calming effect on her, as if she were reaching out to him.

"Did you hear me, Julie?"

The question pulled Julie back into the conversation. "I'll be careful around Mrs. Van Deen, I promise."

"That woman can be completely unreasonable," her

mother went on. "Don't forget, I was the one who had to deal with her after you left."

"I know and I'm sorry about that."

"I still think you did the right thing, honey."

Even after three years, Julie wasn't certain. She'd been so naive. There'd been many times she should have objected more strongly, should have forced a stop to the outrageous wedding plans. But like Daniel, she'd been overwhelmed by his mother's dominant personality. Even when Julie had tried to tell Mrs. Van Deen how she felt, her wishes were quickly pushed aside.

"Julie, are you still there?" her mother asked.

"Yes, I'm here. Sorry, Mom, it's been a long day. I'll talk to you next week."

"I'll be thinking about you."

"Thanks, Mom." Her mother's support had gotten her through some difficult times in the past and she was grateful to have it now.

Julie replaced the receiver, then slumped forward on the couch, burying her face in her hands. A tightness was building in her throat. It felt as though no time had passed. Her anxiety was as keen now as it had been three years ago.

Julie had been aware right from the start that Daniel's mother wanted her son to marry a more socially prominent girl. To her credit, Clara Van Deen had accepted Julie as Daniel's choice, but then she immediately set to work making Julie into something she'd never be. First came the makeover. Julie's hair was cut and styled to meet Clara's standards. Clara then purchased an entire wardrobe of what she claimed were outfits better suited for her new role as Daniel's wife.

Julie had found herself swallowing her pride a hundred

times over. She tried to do exactly as Mrs. Van Deen asked. She wanted to make Daniel proud. He was climbing the corporate ladder and Julie didn't want to do anything that might jeopardize his success.

The out-of-control wedding plans were what had finally caused Julie to run. All she'd wanted was a simple ceremony with only their immediate families, but before she knew it, Daniel's mother had issued invitations to four hundred supposedly close and intimate friends she couldn't possibly insult by not including.

"But, Daniel," Julie had protested, "I don't know any of these people."

"Don't worry about it," Daniel had said, kissing the tip of her nose. He'd never fully understood the depth of her anxiety. "They'll love you as much as I do."

Daniel had negated any further protests with a kiss that left Julie unable to argue.

As the date drew closer, Julie's marriage to Daniel became the talk of the town, making Julie herself the reluctant focus of many a social gathering.

After each event, Mrs. Van Deen would run through a list of things that Julie had done wrong. No matter how hard Julie tried, there was always something worth criticizing.

"I can't take it anymore," Julie cried to her mother one night.

"You need to speak up," her mother advised. "Tell her how you feel."

"Don't you think I've tried?" Julie hid her face in her hands. "This isn't a wedding anymore, it's a Hollywood production."

Every day the pressure mounted. The wedding plans grew until what had started out as a simple ceremony was now a monster that threatened to devour Julie whole. Everything was beyond her control—the caterers, musicians, flower girl, bridesmaids and dresses. Even their honeymoon had been arranged by Mrs. Van Deen.

"Daniel, please listen to me," Julie had begged a week before the wedding. "I don't want any of this."

"Honey, I know you're nervous," he'd said soothingly. "But it's only one day and then we can go ahead with the rest of our lives."

But Julie had doubted they could. Every incident with his mother just reinforced her belief that the wedding was only the beginning. Eventually, Mrs. Van Deen would take over every aspect of their marriage, and when Daniel's mother made a large down payment on a house for them, Julie's suspicions were confirmed.

"It's her wedding gift to us," Daniel had explained. But the house was just a short distance from his mother's and the writing on the freshly painted walls was clear. His mother had insisted on helping Julie decorate. Such important details couldn't be left in the hands of an immature twenty-one-year-old, she'd implied.

"Doesn't it bother you that she's taken over our lives?" Julie had asked plaintively.

She could see that Daniel did care, but would do nothing.

"For the first time since Dad died, my mother has a purpose. Can't you see how much happier she is now?"

But Julie couldn't see anything other than a growing case of claustrophobia.

That night she couldn't sleep, and by the time the sun rose the next morning, Julie had packed her bags.

"You can't do this," her mother protested when she realized her daughter's plans.

"I've got to," Julie said, her eyes red from crying. "I wouldn't be marrying Daniel. I'd be marrying his mother."

"But the wedding's in five days!"

"There isn't going to be a wedding," Julie said adamantly. "What should have been a simple and beautiful ceremony has turned into a three-ring circus and I won't be part of it."

"But Julie—"

"I know what you're going to say," she interrupted. "But this isn't just pre-wedding jitters. Daniel and I are never alone anymore. His mother's taken over every aspect of our relationship."

"Talk to him, sweetheart. Explain how you feel," Margaret advised. "At least do that much. This is a serious step you're considering."

Julie took her mother's advice and went to Daniel's office. They met as he was on his way out the door.

"Julie." He seemed surprised to see her.

"I need to talk to you," said Julie, her hands tightly clenched.

Daniel glanced at his watch. "Can it wait? I'm short on time."

She shook her head forcefully. "No. It can't wait."

Daniel seemed to notice her agitated manner. He pressed a hand to the small of her back and led her into his office. "Honey, I know things have been hectic lately, but it's bound to improve once we're married. We'll have lots of time together then, I promise."

"That's just it, Daniel," Julie said. "We aren't going to be married."

Daniel inhaled sharply. "What do you mean? What's this all about?"

With a trembling finger, she removed the diamond ring and held it out to him. "I can't marry you, Daniel."

"Julie!" He was completely stunned. "Put that ring back where it belongs!"

"I can't."

He slumped onto the arm of his office chair. "I don't understand."

"I didn't expect you would." Julie bowed her head. "Do you remember last week when I suggested we drive across the border and elope? You laughed." Her voice wavered. "But I was serious, Daniel. Dead serious."

"My mother would never forgive us if we did something like that."

Julie sighed. "That's the problem, Daniel. You wouldn't dream of crossing your mother, but you don't seem to care what all of this is doing to me."

"My mother loves you."

"She loves the woman she's created. Haven't you noticed? Look at me, Daniel. Am I the same woman you proposed to three months ago?"

Daniel averted his eyes. "I don't know what you're talking about."

"Look at me," she repeated. "My hair is different, my nails are manicured, and my...my clothes..." Tears welled up in her eyes as her voice broke. "Do you realize she expects me to call her every morning to ask what I should wear? I haven't worn a pair of jeans in weeks," she exclaimed. "I'm slowly being molded into what she thinks your ideal woman should be. I can't take it anymore."

Daniel stood, threading his fingers through his hair. "Why didn't you refuse?"

"Don't you think I've tried? No one listens to me—not

even you, Daniel. What I think or feel doesn't seem to matter anymore. I'm…not sure how I feel about you anymore."

"Is that so?" he demanded.

"It is," Julie said defensively. "I want out. Here." Again, she tried to return the ring.

Daniel stared at her for a long moment before dropping his gaze to the diamond in her hand. He turned and stalked to the window on the far side of the room, his back to her. "Keep it."

"But, Daniel," she began. "I'm—"

"I said keep it," he broke in. He turned to face her, his mouth a rigid line. His dark eyes were clouded with hurt and pain. "Now get out of my life and stay out."

Tears ran down her face as she drove straight to her mother's. The clothes, the wedding dress—she left everything Mrs. Van Deen had purchased strewn across her bed. Julie then loaded her suitcases into the back of her car and drove to her aunt's in California.

That had been three years ago and every night since she'd wondered if she'd done the right thing. She straightened on the sofa. The guilt had been weighing on her, but her love for Daniel had never died. She'd hurt him and his mother. Right or wrong, there were better ways to handle the situation.

Now, she'd come back to ask for Daniel's and Mrs. Van Deen's forgiveness.

Three

The next morning, Julie waited in the Inland Empire foyer for Daniel to enter the building. She needed to talk to him. She'd dreamed of it for months, praying that a heartfelt apology would wipe out the pain she'd caused him. Then—and only then—could they start to rebuild their relationship.

She spotted him the moment he pushed past the double glass doors.

Julie watched him approach the elevator. Without a sound, she moved closer so that when the doors opened, she could enter behind him.

Frustration knotted her stomach as two other people boarded the elevator.

If Daniel was aware of her, he didn't let on. But Julie had never been more aware of anyone or anything in her life. She felt his presence beside her. The years had been good to him. He'd been boyishly attractive three years ago; even though he'd lost the relaxed, carefree quality he'd had then, he was still devastatingly handsome. No wonder Sherry had set her sights on him.

A long moment passed and Julie yearned to reach out

and touch him, anything to force him to acknowledge that she was there. He couldn't ignore her forever. Sooner or later, they'd have to talk.

He stared straight ahead as the creases around his mouth hardened. Julie's stomach tightened. She couldn't take her eyes off him. His features were so achingly familiar, but on closer inspection, the changes in his appearance were even more prominent. Streaks of gray mingled with the sandy-colored hair at the side of his head and Julie had to restrain herself from brushing her hand across his temple. She leaned against the back wall for support.

The two strangers exited on the fifth floor, leaving Julie alone with Daniel. This was exactly what she'd hoped for, and yet her tongue was suddenly uncooperative. There was so much she wanted to say, and she'd practiced exactly how to begin so many times. But now that the opportunity was there, she found herself incapable of uttering a single word.

"Hello, Daniel," she managed after an awkward silence. The air between them felt charged, adding to Julie's discomfort.

Daniel ignored her, staring straight ahead.

"We need to talk," she continued, her voice barely above a whisper.

Silence.

"Daniel, please."

The thin line of his lips tightened as he directed his attention away from her.

She laid her hand gently on his forearm and sighed. The hopelessness of the situation overwhelmed her. The man who stood beside her became a watery blur as tears filled her eyes. Julie dropped her hand. The elevator stopped and she watched him leave.

Julie was grateful to be the first one in the office again.

She collapsed into her chair, fighting off waves of nausea. Pain pounded at her temples. It was too soon. She'd been expecting too much. Daniel needed more time; she had to be patient. When he was ready, she'd be waiting.

Sherry strolled into the office five minutes early, a wide grin on her face. "Morning," she said.

Julie pretended to be absorbed in reading a paper on her desk.

"Aren't you going to ask how my hot date went?"

Julie didn't want to hear it, but knew she should play along. "Sure." She swallowed hard and banished the mental image of Daniel holding Sherry in his arms.

"Awful," Sherry admitted with a wry grin. "Talk about disappointing! I could've had two heads for all the attention he paid to me and my new dress."

"Maybe he was worried about a case or something." Julie couldn't repress her delight. If Sherry became involved with Daniel, things would become unpleasant.

"Or something is right," Sherry shot back.

"If last night was such a disaster, how come you're so cheerful this morning?"

"Because Danny apologized and asked me out again this weekend," Sherry said. "And when he takes a woman out, he spares no expense. We went to the best restaurant in town—what a waste. Danny barely touched his dinner."

Danny! Julie shuddered at the casual use of his name. Daniel used to hate it. No one called him Danny.

Julie smiled stiffly. "I hope everything works out better next time."

"It will," Sherry said confidently. "Next time, he won't be able to take his eyes off me." She laughed lightly. "I won't let him." She smiled and hung her jacket in the closet.

"Are you doing anything special this weekend?" Sherry asked a while later.

"Painting my living room," Julia said. Such distractions were vital at the moment. Anything to keep her mind from the thought of Sherry and Daniel falling in love. Throughout the morning, Julie debated whether or not she should say something to Sherry. But what? She had no claim to Daniel now.

When Julie woke on Saturday morning, the sun was shining. It was far too beautiful a day to spend indoors. She recalled how Daniel's mother loved to garden; Clara Van Deen grew the most gorgeous irises.

When Julie climbed into her car, her destination had been the paint store, but as she drove, she found herself on the street that led to Clara's house instead.

She pulled to a stop across from the lovely two-story home with the meticulously landscaped front yard. A fancy sports car was parked in the driveway. Julie doubted that Mrs. Van Deen would ever drive something like that.

The long circular driveway was bordered on both sides by flowering red azaleas. Julie stared at the house for a long time, undecided about whether or not she should approach Daniel's mother, having had no luck with Daniel himself. She wondered what had become of Clara Van Deen, realizing that she could be a greater challenge than her son.

No. Julie shook her head. Now wasn't the time. Not when she was dressed in jeans and a sweatshirt. She'd need to look and feel her best when she faced Mrs. Van Deen. Her desire to get the confrontation over with as quickly as possible would benefit neither of them. Before she could change her mind, she pulled away from the curb and headed toward the closest shopping center.

The paint she chose for the living room was an antique white that would brighten the place up. Her spirits lifted as she returned to the apartment. She was actually looking forward to a quiet afternoon painting.

She unhooked the drapes and carefully laid them across the back of the sofa. As she began to spread out newspapers, a knock at the door caught her off guard. She rushed to answer, stumbling over the ottoman on her way.

Stooping to rub her injured shin, she opened the door.

Daniel stood there, and he did not look amused.

"Leave my mother alone," he said.

Julie stared back at him, completely speechless.

"Did you hear what I said?" he demanded, his expression cold.

She nodded.

"I saw you parked in front of her house this morning. Stay away from her, Julie. I'm warning you."

Julie jutted her chin out defiantly. "The time will come when I'll have to talk to her." She retreated into the living room.

Daniel entered and followed, closing the door behind him. "Not if I can help it."

Julie turned to face him. "You can't."

"Don't bet on it," he snarled.

"Daniel, I've come a thousand miles to talk to you and your mother."

"Then you wasted your time because neither of us cares to see you."

Julie met his gaze. "I didn't come back to hurt either of you. I've come to make amends."

"Amends?" He threw the word back at her as he paced

the carpet, his hands buried deep in his pockets. "Do you really think you could ever undo the humiliation I suffered when you walked out?"

"I'm sure I can't, but I'd like to try. I was young and stupid. Don't you understand? A thousand times I've regretted what I did—"

"Regretted," he repeated sarcastically. "I used to dream you'd say that to me. Now that you have, it means nothing. Nothing," he muttered. "I look at you and I don't feel a thing. You came back to apologize? Fine. You've made your peace. But don't go to my mother, bringing up the past. She has no desire to see you. Whatever you and I shared is over and done with."

Julie closed her eyes, warding off the sting in his voice. She wouldn't be so easily swayed from her goal. "You don't mean that," she whispered.

"I've blocked you from my mind," he continued. "But unfortunately, my mother has never been the same. I can't forgive you for what you've done to her."

"But that's the reason I've come back," Julie said, trying to stay calm although her stomach churned uncomfortably. "I want to make it up to you both. Can't you see how sorry I am? I never stopped thinking about you. Not for a day. Not for a minute. You've haunted me all this time."

"Do you expect me to pat you on the head and tell you everything's just fine? That we can pick up where we left off?" His eyes narrowed. "It's not that easy."

Julie struggled to keep her composure. "You've changed so much." She raised her hand to his mouth, her touch light against his lips. Daniel abruptly jerked his head away and took a step back.

"I don't want to hurt you or your mother," she said again.

"Then leave before you do."

"I can't. This is too important to me. I've got to make things right."

"You'll never be able to do that. Sometimes it's best for the past to remain buried."

"Believe me, I've tried to put this behind me. I can't."

Daniel looked exhausted. "Leave, Julie. You'll only make everything worse."

"I won't go," she insisted. "Not until I've talked to your mother. Not until I pay her back every penny."

"Why now?" He sank onto the sofa and leaned forward until his elbows rested on his knees.

"You're not the only one who's changed, Daniel. I'm not a naive twenty-one-year-old anymore. I'm an adult willing to admit I made a terrible mistake. I was wrong to have run away instead of confronting the problems we faced. I regret what I did, but more than that, I've realized there isn't anyone I could ever feel as strongly about as you. Whenever another man held me, I found myself wishing he was you. It's you I came back for, Daniel."

He stared at her disbelievingly. "You mean to tell me what? That your conscience hasn't quit bothering you?"

"Yes, but it's so much more than that. I want to make everything up to you."

"Well, that's fine and dandy, Julie. You've come here, we've talked and now you can go. I absolve you of everything. Just stay out of my life—understand?"

Pain flashed across his face, and for a fleeting moment, Julie saw a glimmer of the old Daniel. Something was troubling him, something deep beneath the surface.

"Daniel." She moved to sit beside him, wishing she could comfort the man she loved. She weighed her words carefully. "Something's wrong. Won't you tell me what it is?"

He looked right through her and Julie knew his thoughts were elsewhere.

He stood, impatiently shaking off his mood. "Leave my mother alone," he said again. "Do you understand?"

"I'm so sorry." Julie hung her head in defeat. Everything she'd tried to explain had meant nothing.

As he started to go, she stood and faced him. "I promise not to do anything to hurt her. Will you trust me?"

"I shouldn't." A nerve moved in his jaw and again Julie was aware of some internal struggle. Without another word, he walked out of the apartment.

Julie remained exactly where he'd left her, numb and completely unaware of how much time passed. Finally forcing herself into action, she finished covering the floor with newspapers and opened the first gallon of paint.

She worked until well past midnight. By the time she finished, the room was barely recognizable. The sense of accomplishment helped lift her spirits.

Her hand skimmed the ring dangling from her neck. Her body ached as she cleaned the paintbrushes under the kitchen faucet, but her mind raced.

Maybe Daniel was right. Maybe contacting Clara Van Deen would do more harm than good.

Later that night, as she lay in bed, staring at the darkened ceiling, Julie couldn't let the thought go. She'd come this far. The clock dial illuminated the time—2:00 a.m. Although she was exhausted, she hadn't been able to sleep. Julie pounded her pillow and rolled over to face the wall.

Write to her.

The idea suddenly flashed through her mind. She threw back the covers and sat up, eager to search for a pen and pad.

Sitting on the bed, Julie drafted the letter:

Dear Mrs. Van Deen:
I know this letter will come as a shock to you. My
hope is that you're willing to hear what I have to say.

   I wonder if you've ever done anything in your
life that you've regretted. Something that's haunted
you over the years. Something you'd give anything
to do over again. I have. For three years I've carried
the guilt of what I did to you and Daniel. I know
there's nothing I can say that would ever undo the
embarrassment or hurt I caused, but I do beg your
forgiveness, and ask that you allow me to make this
up to you in some way. I'd do anything for that opportunity.

   You'll find my address above, along with my
phone number. Please contact me if you're willing
to talk.

Julie read the letter again the following morning and
typed it into her computer, printed it and mailed it off. The
next move would be Mrs. Van Deen's.

A week passed before Julie received a response, but
she saw Daniel almost every day in between. Not once
did he speak to her, but his eyes held an unspoken warning that made Julie wonder if his mother had told him
about the letter.

The scented envelope addressed in delicate handwrit-
ing caught her attention the minute she picked up her mail
on Saturday afternoon. Julie's heart soared.

She'd hardly got inside her apartment before she ripped
open the envelope. Her fingers shook as she removed the
single sheet of stationery.

It read simply: *Saturday at four.*

"That's today," Julie said aloud. Frantically, she glanced at the kitchen clock. It was just after one—only three hours to prepare. Surely, Mrs. Van Deen had done that deliberately, hoping to catch her off guard. But she'd be disappointed. Julie was ready. She knew what she had to say and she was eager to finally say it.

After carefully surveying her wardrobe, Julie decided on a simple blue business suit. It was the same one she'd worn to her job interview with Mr. Barrett six weeks earlier. She wanted to show Mrs. Van Deen that she wasn't an awkward young girl anymore.

At precisely four o'clock, Julie pulled into the curved driveway. Mrs. Batten, the elderly cook who'd been with the family for years, answered the door. She didn't appear to recognize Julie.

"Yes?" The woman's tone wasn't particularly civil.

"Good afternoon. I'm here to see Mrs. Van Deen."

Mrs. Batten hesitated.

"We have an appointment today at four," Julie added.

Again the woman paused, but then stepped aside, allowing Julie to enter the foyer.

The interior of the house was exactly as she remembered it. The same mahogany table and vase sat beside the carpeted stairway that led to the second floor. To her left was the salon, as Mrs. Van Deen called it; at one time Julie had regarded it as a torture chamber. To her right was the massive dining room.

"This way," Mrs. Batten instructed, her voice only slightly less frosty.

Like an errant student being led to the principal's office, Julie followed two steps behind the elderly woman.

She was escorted through the house to the back garden Mrs. Van Deen prized so highly.

"You may wait here." Mrs. Batten pointed to a pair of cast-iron chairs separated by a small table.

Julie did as she was told.

"Would you like something to drink while you wait?" the woman asked, refusing to look at Julie.

"No. Thank you," she mumbled, clasping her hands in her lap.

Fifteen minutes passed and still Julie waited. Daniel's mother was doing this deliberately. Testing her. But Julie was determined to sit there until midnight if necessary.

She tensed at the sound of footsteps behind her.

"Hello, Julie." The words were said in a low and trembling voice.

Julie stood and turned to see Daniel's mother—frail and obviously weak. She leaned heavily on a cane, her back hunched, and yet she was elegant as ever. Her hair was completely white now and she was thin, far thinner than Julie remembered.

"Sit down." Mrs. Van Deen motioned with her hand and Julie perched on the hard metal chair, grateful for its support.

Daniel's mother took the seat beside her, both hands resting on her wooden cane. "To say I was surprised to receive your letter would be an understatement."

Julie's grip on her purse tightened. "I'd imagine so."

"Does Daniel know you're back?"

Julie nodded. "We work in the same building."

Mrs. Van Deen didn't comment, but smiled weakly.

The changes Julie had noticed in Daniel were nothing compared to those she saw in his mother.

"You have a Wichita address?"

"Yes." Julie's voice quavered slightly. "I moved back here."

"Why?"

"Because—" Julie swallowed "—because I hope to make amends and I didn't think I could do that if I flew in for a weekend."

Mrs. Van Deen smiled knowingly. "That was wise, dear."

"I came because I deeply regret my actions—"

"Do you still love my son?"

Julie focused on her hands, which were tightly coiled around the small leather purse. The question was one she'd avoided since her return, afraid of the answer. "Yes," she admitted. "Yes, I do, but I..."

"But you hate me?"

"Oh, no." Julie met her gaze. "The only person I've hated over the years was myself."

The old woman's smile was thin. "There comes a time in a woman's life when she can look at things more clearly. In my life, it comes as I face death. As you've probably guessed, I'm not well."

Julie's vision blurred with sudden tears. She hadn't expected Daniel's mother to be so kind or understanding.

"There's no need to cry. I've lived a full life, but my heart is weak and I can't do much of anything these days. Ill health gives one an opportunity to gain perspective."

"Then you forgive me?" Julie whispered, her voice close to cracking.

The frail hand tightened around the cane. "No."

Julie closed her eyes. An apology would have been too easy; she should have realized that. Daniel's mother would want so much more. "What can I do?" Julie asked softly.

"I want you to forgive me." Mrs. Van Deen's voice was

gentle. She reached across the space that separated them and patted Julie's hand. "I was the reason you did what you did. I've buried that guilt deep in my heart. I behaved like an interfering old woman."

Julie noticed several tears sliding down Mrs. Van Deen's weathered cheek, and knew that her own face was wet, too.

"We've both been fools," Julie said.

"But there's no fool like an old one." Mrs. Van Deen wiped her tears with the back of her hand. She looked pale and tired, but her eyes held an unmistakable radiance.

As if on cue, Mrs. Batten carried in a silver tray with a coffeepot and two china cups. Mrs. Van Deen waited until the woman left before asking Julie to do the honors.

Julie poured the coffee with a smile, stirring sugar into Mrs. Van Deen's before presenting it to her.

Mrs. Van Deen nodded approvingly. "Very good."

Julie laughed, perhaps her first real laugh in three years. "I had a marvelous teacher." She sat back and crossed her legs, her own cup and saucer in one hand.

"Tell me what you've done with yourself all this time." Mrs. Van Deen looked genuinely interested.

"I went to school in California for a while and lived with my aunt. My mother joined me later on and I got a job as a bank teller before working my way into the loan department. From there, I got a job in a trust company. Nothing too exciting."

"What about men?"

The abrupt question flustered Julie. "I...dated some."

"Anyone serious?"

Julie shook her head. "No one—did Daniel find any-one...serious?"

The former radiance dimmed. "He never tells me."

"He's changed."

"Yes, he has," his mother admitted. "And not for the better, I fear. He's an intense young man. Some days he reminds me of..." She paused.

"Mrs. Van Deen, are you okay?"

"I'm fine, Julie. You sound like Daniel. He's always worried about me. And please, I'd prefer it if you called me Clara."

Even when she was engaged to Daniel, Julie had never been granted the privilege of using Mrs. Van Deen's first name. Permission to do so now confirmed their new understanding.

"All right then. Clara." The name felt awkward on Julie's tongue.

"I do have regrets." The older woman looked as if she were someplace far away. "I would so have liked to hold a grandchild."

Julie took a sip of her coffee, hoping the warm liquid would ease the tightness in her throat.

"I know what it's cost you to come here," Mrs. Van Deen continued. "You have far more character than I gave you credit—" The woman paused to take several deep, labored breaths. "I'm sorry, Julie, but I'm suddenly not feeling very well." Mrs. Van Deen raised her hand to cover her heart.

A wave of panic swept through Julie. Daniel's mother wasn't just weak, she was on the verge of collapse. "I'm calling for help," Julie said.

She retrieved her cell phone from her purse and dialed 911, trying to remain calm as she relayed the address to the operator.

After being told that an ambulance was on its way, Julie struggled to recall the lessons she'd taken in CPR.

She moved to kneel next to Daniel's mother, taking one weathered hand in hers.

"Don't worry, child," Clara assured her. Her voice was weak.

Julie began loosening the older woman's clothes, words of reassurance tumbling from her lips. Clara was slowly losing consciousness. How soon would help arrive? Julie eased her onto the ground. Sirens could be heard in the distance and Julie breathed a little easier.

The ambulance pulled up and Julie stumbled aside as two men approached and set to work on the now-unconscious woman. They lifted her onto a stretcher, then transported her to the waiting vehicle.

Julie's heart pounded wildly as she followed close behind. Mrs. Batten joined her on the front lawn and the pair watched as the EMTs loaded Daniel's mother into the ambulance.

"What happened?" Mrs. Batten asked. Her face was pale.

"We were just talking," Julie explained. "And then she suddenly had trouble breathing. She just…collapsed."

Mrs. Batten raised her hand to her chest in silent prayer.

"I'm going to the hospital," Julie said. She knew she'd go crazy waiting around here.

The hospital was a whirlwind of activity when she got there. She almost collided with Daniel as she hurried down the wide corridor. He stopped and glared at her accusingly, as though he blamed her for his mother's poor health. He entered the waiting room, leaving Julie alone in the hall.

Daniel didn't want her there, but she couldn't leave without knowing how Clara was.

The hospital's chapel offered her the solitude she sought. She sat in the back pew and covered her face with her hands. An eternity seemed to pass before she felt strong enough to stand.

Daniel was pacing the small waiting area when she returned. He swiveled to face her as she walked into the room.

"Don't ask me to leave," she said.

He ran his fingers through his already rumpled hair. "The EMT told me you're the one who called in time to save her life."

Julie didn't answer. Her arms cradled her stomach as she paced alongside him. They didn't speak. They didn't touch. But Julie couldn't remember a closer communication with anyone. It was as if they were emotionally connected, offering each other hope.

The universe seemed to come to a stop as soon as the doctor stepped into the room. "She's resting comfortably," he announced.

"Thank God," Daniel said. He released a shuddering breath.

"Your mother's a stubborn woman. She insists on seeing both of you. But, please, take only a minute. Is that clear?"

Julie glanced at Daniel. "You go."

"She asked for both," the doctor repeated. "She was very specific about that."

Clara Van Deen looked as pale as the sheets she was lying against when Julie and Daniel entered her room in the intensive care unit.

She opened her eyes and attempted to smile when she saw them. "My dears," she said, "I'm so sorry to cause you all this trouble."

"Don't worry about that," Daniel whispered. "You need to rest."

"Not yet," she murmured. "Julie, you said you'd do anything to gain my forgiveness?"

"Yes," Julie said, her voice hardly sounding like her own.

"And Daniel, will you do one last thing for me?"

"Anything. You know that."

Clara Van Deen's tired eyes closed and opened again as if she was on the brink of slipping away. "I would like the two of you to marry—for my sake."

Four

Julie woke in the gray light of early morning. She hadn't slept well and imagined Daniel hadn't either. They'd hardly spoken as they left the hospital; they'd scarcely even looked at each other. The tight clenching of Daniel's jaw said plenty about his feelings on the matter of any marriage between them.

When she'd arrived home Julie changed into something comfortable and made herself a cup of strong coffee. She sat in the living room, bracing her feet against the coffee table as she slouched on the sofa. Daniel's mother was so different from what Julie had been expecting. She'd been so sure that Clara would lash out at her, but instead she'd discovered a sick, gentle woman who suffered many regrets. Julie longed to ease Clara's mind, knowing that as she lay weak in a hospital bed, facing death, she needed the assurance that her son would be happy.

But, Julie also knew that she and Daniel could never grant her request, not when Daniel resented Julie so much.

Later that evening, as she lay awake in bed, a calm came over her. She loved Daniel, had never stopped—and, if possible, found she loved him even more now. Every time she looked at him, she felt it. As she closed her eyes, Julie reminded herself of the reasons she'd returned to Wichita.

When she got to the hospital the next morning, the parking lot was full. Although she hadn't reached a decision, Julie felt a sense of peace. She'd talk to Daniel—really talk—and together they'd decide what to do.

A faint antiseptic odor greeted her as she pushed through the glass doors that led to the hospital foyer.

Daniel was in the waiting area outside the intensive care unit. He glanced up as Julie approached, his eyes heavy from lack of sleep.

"Good morning," she said. "How's Clara?"

"My mother," he returned stiffly, "is resting comfortably."

Julie took the seat across from him. "Can we talk?" Sitting on the edge of the cushion, she leaned toward him, clasping her hands together.

Daniel shrugged.

"Did you sleep at all?" she asked.

A quick shake of his head confirmed her suspicions. "I couldn't. What about you?"

"Some." She noticed that Daniel wouldn't look at her, not directly. Even when she'd entered the room his gaze had met hers only briefly before shifting to something behind her.

"The doctor's with her now," he said.

"Daniel." Julie found it difficult to speak. "What are we going to do?"

His laughter was mirthless, chilling. "What do you mean, *do?* My mother didn't know what she was saying. They gave her so many drugs yesterday she wasn't thinking straight. Today she won't remember a word."

Julie didn't believe that any more than she thought Daniel did, but if he wished to avoid the issue there was little she could say.

They sat in silence, his eyes still refusing to meet hers, which allowed Julie the opportunity to study him. The lines on his face were more pronounced now, deeply etched with his concern. His brow was furrowed. Julie knew that Clara was all the family he had.

The coffee machine across the hall caught her attention and Julie walked over to it, retrieving enough change from her purse for two cups. She added sugar to each and cream to Daniel's. He glanced up briefly as he accepted the paper cup. He looked surprised that she remembered how he liked his coffee.

They both set their cups aside and stood when the doctor came into the room.

"How is she?" Daniel asked.

"She's very weak, but better than we'd expected. The fact that she survived the night is nothing short of a miracle." The doctor paused to study them both. "Your mother seems to be a fighter. And since she's come this far, the chances of her making a complete recovery are good."

Julie felt as though a weight had been lifted from her shoulders.

"She's resting now, and both of you should do the same."

Daniel nodded. "I didn't want to leave until I was sure she'd be all right."

The doctor shook his head. "I don't know what you talked about last night, but it's certainly made a world of difference in her attitude. She's been improving ever since."

Julie's eyes met Daniel's. All the color had drained from his face.

"Go home and get some rest. There's nothing you can do here. I'll call you the minute there's any change."

"Thank you, Doctor," Daniel said.

They remained standing even after the doctor left. Daniel closed his eyes and released a long sigh.

"Can I give you a lift?" Julie asked quietly. Daniel didn't look as if he was in any condition to drive.

He shook his head. "No."

"You'll call me if you hear anything?"

Daniel nodded that he would.

"Everything's going to work out for the best," Julie whispered. She turned and walked away, ready to head home to her apartment.

Julie didn't mean to fall asleep, but after calling her mother to tell her about Clara Van Deen's attack, she decided to stretch out on the sofa and rest her eyes for a few minutes. The next thing she knew, someone was knocking on the door.

Julie glanced at her wristwatch and was shocked to see that it was after two.

"Just a minute," she called and hurriedly slid her feet back into her shoes as she ran her fingers through her tangled hair. "Who is it?" she asked before releasing the lock.

"It's Daniel."

Julie immediately threw open the door. "Is she all right? I mean, she's not worse, is she?"

"No, she's doing remarkably well."

"Thank God," Julie whispered as she stepped aside to let Daniel in.

"Did I wake you?" he asked.

With a wry smile, Julie nodded. "It's a good thing you did or I wouldn't be able to sleep tonight."

"They let me see her for a few minutes," Daniel said. He stood uneasily in the center of the living room.

"And?"

"And—" he paused and ran a hand through his hair "—she asked when we were planning to have the wedding."

Julie sat down on the sofa. "I was afraid of that."

Daniel remained standing. "Apparently, she's been talking to the nurses about us. The head nurse told me she firmly believes that the fact you and I are going to be married was what kept my mother alive last night."

"And," Julie finished for him, "you're afraid that telling her otherwise could kill her."

Daniel moved to the far side of the room and spoke with his back to Julie. "I talked to the doctor again. He explained that if my mother can grow strong enough in the next few months, there's a possibility that heart surgery could correct her condition."

"That's wonderful news!"

He turned to her with a hard look in his eyes. "Yes, in some ways it's given me reason to hope. But in others…" He shook his head and let the rest of his words fade away. "Why did you come back, Julie? Why couldn't you have left well enough alone?"

"I already explained," she answered. "I want—no," she amended, "I need your forgiveness."

"My forgiveness," he repeated and lifted his head so she could read the conflict in his eyes. "I wish to God I'd never seen you again."

The pain of his words slammed into her and she struggled to remain composed. "But I am here and I won't leave until I've accomplished what I came to do."

He muttered a curse under his breath. "I don't know

what to do. I can't see us getting married. Not with the way I feel about you now."

"No," she agreed. "I can't see adding that complication to our relationship."

"We don't have a relationship," he reminded her. Then he left the apartment, slamming the door behind him.

On her way home from work on Monday, Julie dropped by the hospital with a flower arrangement. Mrs. Van Deen remained in intensive care. Julie doubted she'd be able to see her, but when she reached the nurses' station, she was informed that special permission had been granted for her to visit. The same five-minute limitation applied.

Clara Van Deen opened her eyes and gave Julie a feeble smile as she entered the room.

"I'm so pleased you came," Clara whispered, reaching out to squeeze Julie's hand.

"I can only stay a few minutes," Julie told her in a soft voice.

"I know."

"How are you feeling?"

"Much better now that I know Daniel will be happy."

A strangling sensation gripped Julie's throat. She couldn't think of any way to tell Clara that she and Daniel weren't going to be married.

"It was all my fault," Clara said. "With you and Daniel married, I can undo some of the harm I did."

"But…" Julie groaned inwardly. "Marriage isn't something to rush into. I'm still very much in love with Daniel, but he's been badly hurt and needs time to forget the past."

Clara closed her eyes. "Daniel loves you. He always

has. His pride's been hurt, but he'll come around. I know he will."

So much for that argument, Julie mused, recalling her conversation with him the day before.

"Trust me, Julie," Clara said, opening her eyes once more. "The reason he's hurting so much is because he loves you."

The nurse came into the room. "I'm sorry, but I'm going to have to ask you to leave now."

Julie leaned down and gently kissed Clara on the cheek. "You rest now. I'll stop in tomorrow afternoon."

"Tell Daniel you love him," she whispered, her voice barely audible. "He needs to know that."

Julie didn't answer one way or the other. How could she admit that to a man who fought her every chance he got? Julie couldn't set herself up for that kind of pain.

Daniel was in the waiting room when she entered. He stood and looked at her expectantly.

"She seems much better today," Julie said.

He nodded. "Can we go someplace to talk?" he asked.

The hospital cafeteria was almost empty, with only a few people sitting at tables near the window.

"Go ahead and sit. I'll bring us something. Iced tea?" he suggested, arching a questioning brow.

The day had been warm for early spring and Julie smiled her thanks.

He carried the two glasses on an orange tray, setting them down before taking a seat himself.

"I talked to Dr. Givens," he said, staring into his tea.

Julie's hand curled around the icy glass, the cold seeping up her arm.

"He seems to feel that if we...if I...were to disappoint

my mother over this marriage it could be detrimental to her recovery."

The cool sensation stopped at Julie's heart. "Does this mean you want to go ahead with the wedding?" she asked softly.

"No." He sighed. "A marriage between us would never work. Any possibility of finding happiness together ended when you left. But my mother's health—"

"Daniel," she said, her voice gaining strength, "I know you may find this hard to believe, but I never stopped loving you."

His gaze hardened. "If you'd loved me, you'd never have walked out. I don't think you know what it is to love, Julie."

Her mouth trembled with the effort to restrain an angry retort. She'd done what Daniel's mother suggested; she'd humbled herself. Daniel had to know how difficult it was for her to say those words and yet he threw her declaration of love back in her face. "If you honestly believe that, there's no point in having this discussion." She stood and hurried from the room. Tears blurred her vision as she made her way to the parking lot.

Before she could reach her vehicle, a hand gripped her upper arm, spinning her around.

"Running away again?" he said coldly. "Not this time. I need you to marry me, Julie. As soon as I can make the arrangements."

"I'd have to be crazy to marry a man like you!"

"Do you want to carry the guilt of my mother's death on your shoulders? If you leave now, that's what'll happen. It'll kill her. Are you ready to face that, Julie? Or don't you care?"

Julie pulled herself free of his grip. "Daniel," she said, "marriage is sacred."

"Not always," he insisted. "This'll be one of convenience."

"Will it stay that way?" Her questioning eyes sought his.

"Yes." His gaze was steady. "I couldn't touch you."

Biting her inner cheek, Julie refused to reveal the hurt he'd inflicted. It shouldn't matter. Considering how he felt, Julie didn't want Daniel to make love to her. "And after your mother…" She couldn't bring herself to mention the possibility of Clara Van Deen's death.

"You'll be free to go—no strings attached. An annulment should be fairly simple."

"I don't know." Julie smoothed a hand across her forehead. "I need time to think."

"No," Daniel shot back. "I need to know now. "

What choice did she have? Slowly, deliberately, Julie nodded. "All right, Daniel, I'll marry you. But only for your mother's sake."

His lip curled sardonically. "Do you think I'd marry you otherwise?"

"No, I don't suppose you would." Unfastening the chain from around her neck, Julie handed him her original engagement ring.

"You kept it?" Shock rang through his voice.

Julie stared into his dark eyes. "I couldn't bear to part with it. I wore it all these years. Close to my heart. That must tell you something."

He laughed shortly. "It must have given you a sense of triumph to have kept that all this time. To be honest, I'm surprised there's only one. In three years I would have expected you to add at least that many more."

"No," Julie answered, lowering her gaze, "there was never anyone but you."

"You don't honestly expect me to believe that, do you?"

"It doesn't matter what you believe."

"Keep it around your neck. That ring represented feelings I don't have anymore. I'll buy another one later."

"If that's what you want," Julie whispered.

"I'll make the arrangements and get back to you."

Julie didn't have to wait long. Daniel called the following afternoon with more information. The wedding would be in one week. Daniel picked her up after work Tuesday night so they could apply for the marriage license. After the required three-day wait, they'd have a wedding—of sorts. Everything was cut-and-dried. Even as he relayed the details, Daniel had remained emotionless.

Julie's mother was shocked but pleased, and planned to fly in for the wedding. Unfortunately, she'd have to get back to her volunteer job the next day and Julie was relieved that her mother's stay would be cut short. She wasn't sure how long she could act the role of a happy bride.

The night before the wedding, with her mother sleeping in her bed, Julie tossed restlessly on the sofa. Just before six, she decided to give up and moved from the couch. She doubted she'd slept more than a couple of hours.

Standing at the window, she stared into the night, watching the dawn begin to overtake the darkness.

She bit her lip nervously. Today was her wedding day and in these last hours before the ceremony, she felt her freedom slipping through her fingers. Even now, Julie wasn't sure she was doing the right thing. Of one thing she was sure; right or wrong, she wouldn't walk out on Daniel a second time.

Several hours later, long after the last stars had faded with the morning sun, a car came to take Julie and her mother to the church. Clara Van Deen had insisted that her minister marry them. Neither Julie nor Daniel had any objections.

Daniel met them at the church. His eyes roamed over the long white dress Julie had chosen and something unreadable flickered across his face.

"Are you ready?" he asked casually, stirring her fear that she was making a terrible mistake. Julie swallowed hard and decided to ignore it.

The ceremony was short. Daniel responded methodically to the minister's instructions as if the words held no meaning for him. In contrast, Julie's voice wavered as she recited her vows.

Daniel glanced at her when she pledged her love, a glint of challenge in his gaze.

Julie's fingers trembled as he slipped a plain gold band on her finger. The simplicity of the ring suited her, but she was sure Daniel had chosen it in contrast to the beautiful diamond he'd given her the first time. Julie was confident the difference didn't stop there.

After the ceremony, Julie's mother hugged them both, her eyes shining with happiness. They rode to the hospital together and were allowed a short visit with Daniel's mother.

Clara Van Deen smiled as a joyful tear escaped from the corner of her eye.

"Trust me, Julie," she whispered. "Things will work out."

Julie nodded, smiling feebly as she kissed Clara's wrinkled brow.

From the hospital, Daniel and Julie drove her mother to the airport. Margaret Houser insisted on paying for everyone's lunch. If she noticed the stilted silence between the bride and groom, she said nothing.

Julie suddenly wished for a longer visit with her mother, but Daniel was obviously in a hurry and after an abrupt goodbye, he ushered her back to the car.

Watching him as he drove, Julie clutched the small bouquet of flowers her mother had given her. The unfamiliar gold band felt strange against her finger and she found herself toying with it.

At a red light, Daniel caught her staring at her hand. "Don't be so anxious to remove that wedding ring. It's not going anywhere anytime soon."

Julie glared at him. "Of course. You've made your feelings perfectly clear."

Neither spoke again until Daniel had parked at his condominium in Wichita's most prestigious downtown area. The doorman smiled as he held the door open for Julie.

"Good afternoon, Mr. Van Deen," he said, eyeing Julie and the two suitcases Daniel carried.

Daniel nodded and placed his hand under Julie's elbow, hurrying her toward the elevator. The doors parted at the press of the button and Julie was ushered inside. The strained silence continued as he unlocked the door of the condo, swinging it wide to allow Julie to enter first.

Julie hesitated, wondering what lay before her.

"You don't expect me to carry you over the threshold, do you?"

"Of course not," she replied shortly. She took a deep breath and entered her new home.

The condo was surprisingly spacious. The tiled entry led to a sunken living room carpeted in plush brown pile. Two picture windows overlooked the downtown area and Julie paused to admire the view from fifteen floors up.

Daniel moved around her and carried her suitcases to one of the bedrooms. He stopped outside the door. "This is your room," he said, interrupting her search for city landmarks.

Julie moved away from the window and followed the sound of his voice.

A glance inside the room confirmed her belief that this had been a guest room. Fitting, Julie thought, since she was little more than an unwelcome guest in Daniel's life.

"The rest of your things will be delivered sometime this afternoon," he informed her. "I have to get back to the office for a couple of hours."

Back to the office! Julie couldn't believe it. They'd barely been married three hours. She'd taken the day off work. He could've done the same.

"What am I supposed to do?" she asked. "Make myself at home in a strange house—alone?"

"Unpack," he replied flippantly.

"That'll take all of five minutes. Then what?"

"Don't tell me I have to stay home and babysit you for the next twenty years."

"Go ahead and leave," Julie said. "No need to hurry back on my account."

Daniel laughed mirthlessly as he headed out the door. "Don't worry, I won't."

As she'd told him, five minutes later, both suitcases were empty. After a quick tour of the condo, Julie returned to her room. She yawned, and her neck hurt from a sleepless night on the sofa, so she decided to take a nap. The bed was soft and welcoming; within minutes she fell into a deep, comfortable slumber.

She woke around four, feeling refreshed. Daniel had been gone for several hours. After leafing through a magazine, she considered going out for dinner, letting him come home to an empty apartment. It would serve him right. But no, being antagonistic wouldn't help their situation. She'd prepare dinner and try to make the best of things.

The kitchen was beautifully organized and well stocked—either Daniel enjoyed cooking or he had someone come in to cook for him. Julie's hand tightened against the counter. She couldn't deny that the thought of Daniel bringing another woman into this kitchen made her feel jealous.

She quickly prepared a fresh salad and dessert, and then thawed two large steaks in the microwave until they were ready to grill.

After a moment's deliberation, she chose to set the dining room table rather than the small one in the kitchen. This was, after all, their wedding day—although Daniel seemed to be doing his best to forget that.

Another suitcase and several boxes from her apartment were delivered shortly after five and Julie spent the next hour unpacking and arranging her things among Daniel's. She wasn't surprised to find that they shared similar tastes in literature and art. As she placed each book on the shelf, she frequently discovered that Daniel already owned a copy.

Julie didn't know why this astonished her. They'd discovered a number of similarities since their first meeting. Julie wondered if Daniel still played tennis. That was how they'd first met. The attraction had been immediate and intense. They'd fallen so deeply in love.

As dusk fell over the city, Julie lit the candles, creating a warm, romantic mood. She regretted the harsh parting words she'd exchanged with Daniel that afternoon. Maybe this dinner would show him that she was willing to work things out. She'd taken the first step. But the next one had to come from Daniel.

Minutes ticked into hours and at eleven Julie finally accepted that Daniel wouldn't be coming home for dinner. She wasn't sure if he'd be home at all.

After blowing out the candles and turning on the lights, she began to clear the table piece by piece, returning the china place settings to the rosewood cabinet.

When half the dishes were cleared, the door opened. Julie paused, clutching the expensive plate tightly to her stomach, her heart pounding wildly.

From across the room, Daniel's eyes met hers.

Julie smiled nervously and resumed her task, praying he wouldn't comment. She should have known better.

"A romantic dinner complete with candlelight? What's this, Julie? An invitation to your bed?"

Five

"No," she said, hoping her voice sounded light and carefree. "It wasn't that at all."

"Pity," he mumbled under his breath.

Julie had to bite her tongue to keep from asking where he'd been. That was exactly what he wanted her to do, but she refused to play his games.

"If you'll excuse me, I think I'll go to bed."

Daniel continued to stare at her from the tiled entryway. "I didn't know if you'd eaten or not."

Julie shook her head. "No, I thought I'd wait for you."

"I'm surprised you did."

She moved past him and down the hall to her room. Daniel had made it clear they'd make no pretense of a honeymoon and Julie was going back to work in the morning. As she undressed, she could hear Daniel's movements in the kitchen.

Tying the belt on her housecoat, Julie moved across the hall to the bathroom to brush her teeth. The appealing aroma of broiling steak reminded her that she hadn't eaten since lunch. She tried to focus on brushing. Not for anything would she go back into that kitchen.

In her room, she sat on the bed and opened the novel she'd been reading. The light tap at the door startled her.

"Your steak is ready." Daniel stuck his head in and smiled. "Medium rare, as I recall."

Julie opened her mouth to tell him exactly what he could do with the steak, then stopped herself. It had been a tiring day for both of them and the last thing they needed was an argument.

"I'll be there in a minute." Strangely pleased with this turn of events, Julie put on her slippers and joined him in the kitchen.

The table was set for two. Their steaks were served with grilled tomatoes and melted cheddar.

Julie opened the refrigerator and brought out the salad she'd made.

As she set the bowl on the table, Daniel said, "There were some briefs I needed to review for a court case in the morning."

Julie paused as she sat at the table, fork in hand. Daniel was telling her why he was late. She hadn't expected it, sure he'd wanted her to fret.

"Perhaps it would be best to let the other person know if one of us is going to be late," she said as her knife cut into the steak.

"Sounds fair," Daniel commented.

Julie smiled. The evening had gotten off to an uneasy start, but they were working things out.

"We should probably decide on some house rules," she suggested casually.

"Such as?"

"Since you did the cooking, I'll do the dishes."

"That seems reasonable." Daniel grinned approvingly.

He hadn't smiled at her—really smiled—since she'd returned. She'd almost forgotten how wonderful it felt.

Julie laid her knife on the plate and looked up. "That was wonderful. I don't remember you being such an excellent cook."

"I've managed to pick up a few skills," he said dryly.

Julie stood and carried their plates to the sink while Daniel poured them each a cup of coffee.

"Shall we drink this in the living room?" he asked.

"I'll be there in a minute. I want to get these in the dishwasher."

When Julie joined him, Daniel was standing at the window looking out at the sparkling lights of the city.

"My mother seemed better today, didn't she?"

Julie took her coffee cup from the end table and sat down. "Yes, she did. There was some color in her cheeks for the first time since she collapsed."

"It's going to be an uphill battle for her in the coming months."

"I know. I'll do anything I can to help her," Julie said, taking a sip of her coffee. Daniel remained at the window with his back to her.

"I think we should agree that no matter what happens between us, we won't take our squabbles to my mother."

"Of course not." Julie blinked. She was surprised that Daniel would think otherwise. "If we need to talk something over, the person I'll come to is you."

"Good." He moved to sit in the wing-back chair beside her. "Don't worry about the housework. The cleaning lady comes twice a week."

"What about the cooking?" She focused on the mug in her hands. "I hate to admit it, but I'm not much good in the kitchen. You're probably more adept—do you want to take turns?"

"If you'd like."

"It might be the easiest thing." She shrugged. How could they sit beside each another—husband and wife—and talk of trivialities? Julie didn't want her marriage to begin this way. Twice before the wedding, she'd tried to discuss their past and both times Daniel had cut her off. He obviously wanted to leave that period in their relationship behind them. Julie realized they'd have no future until they faced the hurts and misunderstandings of the past. But tonight wasn't the time.

"You look tired," Daniel commented.

"Sorry." Julie shook her head to clear her thoughts. "I guess I am."

"Let's turn in."

Together they carried their cups into the kitchen. Julie put them in the dishwasher and Daniel showed her how to start it. The soft hum of running water followed them into the hallway.

Daniel flipped off the light switch and the condo went dark. Julie's eyes adjusted to the moonlit room.

"Can you find your way?" Daniel asked.

"Sure," Julie said. Their eyes met in the darkness and everything went still. She couldn't see his expression well enough to know what he was thinking, but time seemed to slow.

When his hand reached out to caress her cheek, a warm sensation spread down her neck. She sighed, closed her eyes and placed her hand over his.

"Good night, Julie," he said tenderly, removing his hand. He walked her to her room, but then hesitated in the open doorway.

For a fleeting moment, the hurt that had driven them apart faded. Julie took a wishful step in his direction. This man was her husband. They were meant to be together.

"If you'd like, I'll cook breakfast in the morning," she offered, wanting an excuse to linger with him in the darkness.

He didn't answer, and Julie wondered if he'd heard her. "I thought you said you weren't much of a cook," he finally said.

"I can manage breakfast."

"Did you eat out often? Is the reason you can't cook because you dated so much?"

"No," she answered simply. "Not much at all."

Silvery moonlight filled the narrow hallway as Julie studied her husband, waiting for a reaction.

"I wish I could believe that," he said with a sigh, "but you're much too beautiful not to have men fawning over you." And with that, he abruptly walked away.

Julie's clock radio went off at six, filling the silent room with music. She lay in bed for several minutes, listening to a couple of songs before throwing back the covers and climbing out of bed.

Slipping into her housecoat, she hurried into the kitchen to put on a pot of coffee. The morning was glorious. The sun was shining and Julie stood at the window looking down on the city as it stirred to life.

When she turned around, she found Daniel waiting by the coffeepot, clutching a large mug.

"Good morning," she greeted him with a warm smile.

Daniel mumbled something unintelligible under his breath.

"What did you say?" she asked as she took his empty

mug out of his hand, and poured in what little coffee had drained through.

"Nothing," he said.

"No one told me you were such a grouch in the mornings," she teased. "I'll go get dressed and stay out of your way until you've had your coffee."

"That's probably a good idea."

Julie returned to her bedroom and dressed, choosing a new outfit—a gray-and-blue striped dress with a wide V neckline. Putting on a pair of pumps, she did her makeup and brushed her hair before re-entering the kitchen.

The bacon was sizzling in the pan when Daniel came in to pour himself a second cup of coffee.

"How do you want your eggs? Over easy?" She was surprised to see the scowl on his face. "Is something wrong?"

"That dress."

"It's new. Don't you like it?" She swallowed uncomfortably.

"It's a little revealing, don't you think?"

"Revealing?" Julie gasped. "In what way?"

Daniel grabbed the paper and sat down to read it. "The neckline."

"The neckline?" Julie's hand flew to the V-shaped front. She hadn't found it to be too low. "There's nothing wrong with this dress," she insisted.

"That's a matter of opinion," he said from behind the paper.

"How do you want your eggs?" Julie repeated, choosing to ignore his reaction to her dress.

The newspaper was a barrier between them. "I've lost my appetite," he muttered.

"So have I," she whispered, turning off the burner.

The office was only a few minutes away. Neither spoke

on the drive over. Julie kept her hands folded in her lap, her head rigid as she focused straight ahead. She hadn't changed her outfit, nor would she. Daniel was being unreasonable. A wry smile touched her mouth. And she'd expected him to like the new dress.

He pulled into the parking garage across the street and into his allotted space.

"I may be late tonight," he said.

Julie nodded without looking at him. "I thought I'd go to the hospital after work."

"Then I'll meet you there."

They sounded like robots, their voices clipped and emotionless.

Julie did a double take when she entered the office—Sherry was already at her desk.

"Are my eyes deceiving me?" Julie teased. "Sherry early? That's impossible."

Sherry's smile was weak. "Morning." She lowered her head and blew her nose in a tissue. "I guess it's a bit of a shock, isn't it?"

"What's wrong?" Julie asked.

"Wrong?" Sherry laughed. "What makes you think something's wrong?"

"Maybe it's the mountain of wet tissues, or perhaps the red eyes. But then I've always had a reputation for being a good sleuth."

Sherry made a gallant effort to smile.

"I guess I should've said something the first time you mentioned Daniel," Julie explained, realizing what this was probably about. "I didn't want to hurt you, Sherry. Not for anything. Daniel and I have known each other for several years."

Sherry glanced up tearfully. "It's not that. I was surprised to hear about you two, but that's not the problem."

Julie was confused. "Then why are you crying?"

"It's Andy." Sherry said, her voice wavering.

"Your ex-husband?"

Sherry tugged another tissue from the brightly colored box and nodded. "The divorce isn't final until the end of the month."

"And you're having second thoughts?" Julie's knowledge of Sherry's marriage was limited to the bits of information her friend had shared. As far as Julie could tell, they didn't have any one specific reason to separate. Both had been too involved in their jobs and they'd grown apart. The trial separation had led to the decision to file for the divorce. In the short time Julie had known Sherry, it had been obvious that Sherry wanted to prove how much fun she could have without her husband.

"I...I saw Andy last night."

"Did you two talk?" Julie asked. She didn't want to pry, but figured Sherry would feel better if she confided in someone.

"Talk!" Sherry hiccuped loudly. "There was a voluptuous blonde draped all over him."

"But Sherry, that shouldn't bother you. For heaven's sake, you've been out with a dozen different men just since I've known you."

"Yes, but that was different," Sherry said.

"How?"

"Andy didn't care if I saw someone else."

"How can you be so sure?" Julie asked. "Maybe he did care. But maybe he's decided the time has come for him to start dating again, too."

"Not Andy. He's always hated blondes."

"You're blonde," Julie pointed out.

"I know, but the woman he was with last night isn't like his usual type."

Julie couldn't question her further because Mr. Barrett entered the room just then, nodding a brief greeting as he hung his coat in the closet. He seemed about to say something when he noticed Sherry's red face. Swiftly, he retreated into his office, closing the door.

"Why don't we see if we can take our lunch hour together and talk some more," Julie suggested.

"I'd like that," Sherry said, dabbing at the last of her tears. "I meant to tell you earlier how nice you look today. Is that a new outfit?"

"Yes." Julie smiled. "Do you like it?"

"It's perfect on you."

"What about the neckline?" Julie tilted her head back and arched her shoulders.

"What about it?" Sherry asked.

"It's not too revealing?"

"Revealing?" Sherry echoed. "No way."

"That's what I thought."

Clara Van Deen was looking much improved when Julie arrived at the intensive care unit that afternoon. She took Julie's hand in hers as Julie approached the bed.

"How's my new daughter?"

"How's my new mother?"

Clara closed her eyes and when she opened them again, they were glistening with tears. "Better now that I've made up for some of the pain I caused you and Daniel."

"I'm glad to hear that," Julie said. "I love him, Clara."

"And Daniel loves you. Don't ever doubt that, Julie. I don't know much about his life anymore—I understand he saw lots of women—but, Julie, there was never anyone he truly loved. No one but you."

Julie squeezed the old woman's hand gently. "I'll be a good wife to him."

"I don't doubt that for a minute." Clara's smile was weak, but infinitely happy.

When Daniel got there thirty minutes later, Julie was in the waiting room leafing through a dog-eared magazine she'd already read twice. She glanced up to see that his gaze had fallen on her neckline and the fullness of her breasts, but his expression was unreadable.

"Your mother seems better," Julie said.

Daniel nodded. "I'm looking forward to visiting with her."

Julie's eyes were drawn to her husband. His rugged appeal gave the impression that he worked outside. His face was quite tanned for early spring and Julie suspected he was exercising regularly. She wondered if he still played tennis.

"I talked to the doctor this afternoon," Daniel said as he rubbed his hand along the back of his neck.

"And?" Julie uncrossed her legs, setting the magazine aside.

"He said she's improved enough for him to consider open-heart surgery."

"When?" Julie breathed.

"A month from now."

"That's wonderful!" If the surgery was a success, the possibility of Daniel's mother returning to a normal life would be greatly increased.

"Is it?" Daniel responded almost flippantly. "Even if she gains enough strength for the surgery, her chances of survival are only fifty-fifty."

"But what would they be without it?"

Daniel wandered to the far side of the room, then pivoted sharply. "Far less than that."

Julie understood and shared his concern, but she felt that the chance of a longer, healthier life for his mother was worth the risk. "Everything's going to be fine," she assured him.

"How do you know that?"

"I don't," Julie admitted. "But your mother's content. Her spirits are high and she has the will to live. A positive attitude is bound to help." It was on the tip of her tongue to reveal that on the day Clara had collapsed, she'd mentioned how much she longed for grandchildren. Julie believed sheer willpower would see her mother-in-law through this surgery.

Daniel's expression tightened as he studied her.

The nurse arrived and told Daniel he could go in to see his mother.

Later, when they'd driven home, Julie noticed a spark of amusement in Daniel's eyes, an expression that was still there as she set the table for dinner.

"What's so funny?" she finally asked.

"What makes you think anything's funny?"

Julie pretended an interest in the green salad she was tossing. "Every time I look up, you're trying to keep from laughing."

"Something my mother said, that's all," Daniel told her.

"About me?" Julie asked stiffly, hoping she wasn't the brunt of some joke.

"Indirectly."

They ate in near silence. Not an intentional silence, at least not on Julie's part, but there was very little to talk about, since Daniel hadn't allowed her into his life. Julie was confident that he'd open up in time, but the one thing they desperately needed to talk about, Daniel refused to discuss.

"Are you still playing tennis?" Julie asked as she cleared the table.

"Often enough."

Julie noted that he didn't ask if she still played. They'd met on the courts and had regularly played as a doubles team. Julie still enjoyed the game, but didn't know how to volunteer that fact without making it look as if she was seeking an invitation—which, of course, she was.

"I'll do the dishes later." Daniel broke into her unhappy thoughts. "There are a few papers I want to go over tonight."

"Do you bring work home a lot?" Julie hadn't meant to sound so accusatory.

"Hardly at all," Daniel replied defensively.

She offered to do the dishes for him so he could work, but Daniel turned her down. "When I say I'm going to do something, I do it," he said pointedly.

Julie gripped the edge of the oak table. "In other words, you don't walk out five days before a wedding. That's what you're saying—isn't it, Daniel?"

"That's exactly what I'm saying," he snapped.

Julie stood and pushed her chair back from the table. Without a word, she left the kitchen, reached for her jacket and headed for the door.

"Where are you going?" Daniel demanded.

"Out," she replied and closed the door behind her. Half hoping Daniel would come after her, Julie lingered in the hall, but he didn't follow. She should have known.

Without her purse and nowhere to go, Julie was back in an hour after taking a brisk walk.

When she returned, Daniel was in his office, or so she assumed. The two pans from their meal were washed and stacked on the kitchen counter. Julie dried them and put them away. When she'd finished she glanced up to see that Daniel was standing in the doorway of the office, watching her.

"You came back."

"What's the matter?" she asked. "Were you hoping I wouldn't?"

A muscle twitched in his jaw as he broke the pencil he was holding. He pivoted and returned to his office.

Julie closed her eyes and took several calming breaths. This tension between them was taking its toll. She couldn't live like this. When she was younger, she'd avoided confrontation and had paid dearly for it, but she wasn't the same Julie now as she'd been then. She didn't avoid conflict these days, but she didn't instigate it either.

Daniel remained in his office with the door shut, while Julie sat alone in the living room reading. She felt drowsy, but shook herself awake, determined to be up when Daniel came out. She wasn't going to run away, not anymore. It was important that he recognize that.

But as her eyelids became heavier, she was afraid she couldn't fight off sleep anymore. She closed her book, switched the light to its lowest setting and leaned her head against the back of the chair, finally surrendering.

"Julie." Daniel's whisper woke her. "You'll get a crick in your neck."

She opened her eyes and stretched. The soft glow from the lamp was the only light in the house. Daniel stood above her, his shirt open. He studied her carefully and Julie yearned to reach out to him, slide her arms around his neck and gently place her mouth on his. He hadn't kissed her, had avoided touching her, but Julie felt that if he walked away from her now, she couldn't bear it.

"Julie," he whispered.

Surely, he could see the hunger she was feeling for his touch, her need to be loved, forgiven and trusted by him again.

He helped her to her feet, his manner impersonal.

"Daniel," she pleaded softly.

Without a word, he wrapped his arms around her, his gaze drawn to her lips as he slowly closed the distance between them.

Julie sighed as she slid her hands over his shoulders and linked her fingers at the base of his neck. "Oh, Daniel," she whispered, "it's been so long."

He held her against him, his mouth moving sweetly over hers as he brought her closer.

Julie thrilled to the urgency of his mouth as he kissed her. He buried his face in the curve of her neck as Julie drove her hands through his thick hair.

Daniel pulled away and looked into her eyes. Julie smiled and brushed her mouth over his, kissing the tiny cleft in his chin. That was something he'd always loved and she wanted him to know she hadn't forgotten.

His body stiffened against hers as he tugged his arms free. "Good night, Julie," he murmured before turning and walking away. He hadn't forgotten anything, either.

How many times would he walk away from her before they were even, before she'd been punished enough for the way she'd left him? Standing alone in the darkened room, Julie had no answer. Defeated, she retired to her room, hoping to find some peace in sleep.

The next day, they continued their new routine. They rode to work together in silence, and from there they went to the hospital, taking turns visiting his mother. Daniel cooked dinner while Julie changed out of her work clothes.

"I'm going to the library," she announced as she set their plates in the dishwasher.

"How long will you be?" Daniel asked without looking up from the mail he was sorting through.

"About an hour." Anything was better than sitting in a silent house again while Daniel closed himself off in his office.

He shrugged, but said nothing.

"Would..." Julie hesitated. "Would you like to come?"

"I've got things to do around here," he replied.

Julie let herself out the front door, her heart aching. The first night, she'd accused Daniel of playing games. Now she was the one escaping, hoping that he'd somehow show that he wanted her to stay. He didn't.

Six

Saturday morning, Daniel left the condo before Julie climbed out of bed. Lying awake with her bedroom door partially open, Julie listened to his movements as he walked down the hall. She expected him to go into the kitchen but was surprised to hear the front door click a few moments later.

Julie slipped out of bed and found a pot of coffee on the kitchen counter along with a note. The message read: *Playing tennis all day.*

All day, Julie mused resentfully. They'd talked about tennis earlier in the week. There'd been ample opportunity for him to include her in today's outing had he wished to.

After brewing a fresh pot of coffee, Julie sat at the round oak table, mug in hand. She'd known when she agreed to marry Daniel that there were several factors working against them. Some days, Julie was convinced that he'd never forgive her for leaving. But at other times, she could feel him studying her, apparently still interested. He hadn't touched her since the other night. Julie could tell he regretted that one slip and was taking measures to ensure that it wouldn't happen again.

She cooked a light breakfast, then dressed in jeans and a sweatshirt. The last of her things had arrived from the apartment. Only a few of her everyday items were necessary, since Daniel's condo was fully furnished.

Stacking the cardboard boxes in the bottom of her closet, Julie located the one full of mementos from her relationship with Daniel. Now that they were married, she could set them out freely. If she left their engagement photo out in the open, it might prompt him to discuss the things he chose to ignore.

Encouraged by the thought, she set the gold-framed picture on top of the television and stepped back to examine it. As always, she was struck by how happy they looked and vowed that one day they'd be that happy again.

She placed a few other things around the room and then stood back to admire her efforts. The condo now reflected who they'd been as a loving, happy couple. Daniel couldn't help being affected by it. Undoubtedly, he'd be surprised that she'd kept all these things, but she wanted him to understand that although she'd left, she'd never stopped loving him.

After a shower, Julie had lunch and decided to drop in at the hospital to visit Clara.

"Good afternoon," Julie said, leaning over to lightly kiss Clara's cheek. "How are you feeling today?"

"Much better."

She looked well, and Julie felt encouraged.

"Where's Daniel?" Clara asked.

"He's playing tennis." Julie hoped that her mother-in-law wouldn't ask for details because Julie wouldn't know what to say. She hoped to paint an optimistic picture of their marriage, but she wasn't willing to lie.

"That's right," Clara said. "Daniel mentioned something

about playing in a tournament this weekend. I'm surprised you aren't at the club with him. As I recall, you two made an excellent team."

So he'd told his mother but hadn't bothered to say anything to her. Maybe he had another partner and didn't want Julie interfering with his plans. The thought made her jealous, but she squashed the feeling before her mother-in-law could read her expression.

"You still play, don't you?" Clara asked.

"I'm a bit rusty," Julie admitted. The Country Club— Julie could vividly recall how uncomfortable she'd been around those people. Daniel had taken her there several times for dinner or tennis, but Julie hadn't been able to overcome her insecurity.

"I thought you'd want to be with him," Clara continued, studying Julie carefully.

"I'm meeting him later," Julie said. It wasn't exactly a lie. She would show up at the Country Club. The time had come for her to face some of the other ghosts of her past.

"There was no need to disrupt your day to come and visit me," Clara said. "I already know how much you care. Whether I live or die is of no consequence to me. All I want before I go is the assurance that the two of you are happy." The white-haired woman regarded Julie seriously. "I wouldn't, however, mind a grandchild or two." She smiled. "Daniel seemed quite amused when I mentioned how much I was looking forward to grandchildren."

So that was what he'd been so smug about the other night. "I think he feels we should wait," Julie improvised.

"His words exactly. But try to convince him, Julie. I don't have all the time in the world. And he's at the age when he should be thinking of starting a family."

"I'll bring it up," Julie promised. "But remember we've only been married a little while."

Clara closed her eyes. "It seems so much longer. In my muddled mind, it's difficult to remember you were gone all those years."

"My heart was here," Julie said softly.

"Would you read to me, dear?" Clara asked, handing over a book from her nightstand.

"I'd be happy to."

Julie read until she was certain Clara was asleep, then she slipped quietly from the room. She was set on facing Daniel at the Country Club, but her determination began to waver. Her unexpected arrival could be uncomfortable for everyone involved. No, she reasoned. As his wife she had a right to see her husband. Resolutely, she left the hospital, got into her car and headed for the outskirts of town.

Julie was lucky to find a parking space in the crowded lot. The tennis courts and surrounding areas were jammed with spectators. Julie signed in as Daniel's wife and was grateful no one questioned her.

It only took her a few minutes to find him. He was on the courts in what she learned was the men's singles semi-final. She sat in the bleachers, silently engrossed in the competition, proud when Daniel won. The championship game followed fifteen minutes later. It was a tense match and Daniel's composure astonished her. He lost the title, but shook hands with his opponent, smiling as he exited the court.

The crowd gathered around the winner as the stands emptied. Julie made her way to her husband.

Daniel was wiping his face with a hand towel.

"Nice game," she said from behind him.

He didn't pause or give any indication that he was surprised as he turned toward her. "How'd you know where to find me?"

"Well, your note. And then your mother mentioned the tournament, so I thought I'd stop by to cheer you on."

"I saw you in the stands," he said.

She noticed that he didn't indicate one way or the other how he felt about her being there. "You were good. Your game's improved."

"I've played better," he said, packing away his racket.

"Good game, Van Deen" a deep baritone voice said from behind them.

Daniel's posture stiffened. "Thanks." He slung the towel around his neck.

Julie didn't recognize the tall, athletic man who'd joined them.

"I see you brought your own cheering section," the man said.

Daniel wrapped an arm around Julie's waist, bringing her to his side. "Patterson, meet my wife, Julie. Julie, this is my friend and associate, Jim Patterson."

"Your wife!" Jim exclaimed. "When did that happen?"

"Recently," Daniel said.

Jim chuckled and rubbed the side of his jaw, bemused. "It must've been recent. Does Kali know?"

At the mention of another woman's name, Julie eyed her husband speculatively. She'd briefly wondered if there was anyone Daniel was seeing seriously, but figured Sherry would have known if he'd been involved with someone else. Clearly, Jim knew more than her coworker.

"I haven't talked to Kali yet," Daniel replied.

"This calls for a celebration," Jim said, obviously trying to cover the awkward moment. "Let me buy you two a drink."

"Not today," Daniel answered. "Unfortunately, Julie has an appointment she needs to get to." His arm slid from around her waist to her lower back. "I'll see you to your car, honey." He steered her toward the parking area.

Julie looked back over her shoulder. "It's a pleasure to have met you… Mr. Patterson."

"We'll have that drink another time," Jim promised with a brief salute.

Once they were alone, Julie shook Daniel's hand loose. "What was that all about? And who's Kali?"

He clenched his jaw. "No one you need to concern yourself with."

"And why couldn't we stay for a drink?" she sputtered. "It's time I met your friends. I'm your wife."

"Don't remind me."

She looked away, refusing to let him see how badly his words had hurt her.

Daniel jammed his hands into his pockets. He looked as if he was about to say something more, but Julie didn't wait to find out. She turned and walked briskly to her car. She couldn't get out of that parking lot fast enough.

Unwilling to return to the empty condo, she drove around until the hurt and anger had faded. So there'd been another woman. She could accept that as long as this Kali remained in the past. She'd need to be told, of course, that Daniel had married or there'd be trouble down the road.

Julie wasn't so naive as to think that Daniel had lived like a monk during the time she was gone. But it still hurt more than she thought possible. What worried her most was his reluctance to tell her anything about Kali.

When she got home two hours later, Daniel was sitting the living room.

"Julie." He jumped up and approached her, running a hand through his hair. "Where were you?"

"I went for a drive. I needed time to think."

He scowled and nodded.

She glanced at her watch. "I didn't realize it was so late. It's my turn to cook, isn't it? I'll start something right away. You must be starving."

The sound of his voice followed her as she headed for the kitchen. "I thought I'd take you out tonight."

Julie froze. "Take me out?"

"As you said earlier, it's time you and I were seen together."

Julie breathed a sigh of relief. This dinner invitation was his way of telling her he was sorry for what had happened that afternoon. It wasn't an eloquent apology, but it was encouraging.

"Well?" Hands deep in his pockets, he studied her.

She replied with a slow, sensual smile. "I'd like that."

"Wear something elegant."

Her smile faltered. "I'm afraid I may not have anything appropriate. Would you mind if we went somewhere less formal?"

"As I recall, you liked fancy places."

"I was twenty-one," she explained. "I never really liked it, but I couldn't tell you that. I was afraid if you knew how shy I really was…"

A flicker of surprise touched Daniel's features. "Our relationship was riddled with misunderstandings, wasn't it? Why didn't you tell me how you felt?"

"I was so crazy about you, I was ready to be anything you wanted."

"Everything but my wife," he said, his expression impassive.

"I couldn't," she said. "Not then." She left the kitchen and moved into her bedroom. Leaning against the door, she closed her eyes. Surely, Daniel must realize that if they'd gone through with the wedding three years ago their marriage would have been doomed. Julie knew that it wasn't any more secure now and the thought saddened her.

She changed into a pale blue dress and a white jacket. A glance in the mirror confirmed that even the most critical eye would find no fault with the neckline. She completed the outfit with white high-heeled sandals and a single strand of pearls which Daniel had given her. She doubted he'd remember, though. He'd given her so many beautiful things.

She went into the living room, where Daniel was waiting. He wore dark slacks with a blue shirt under a sports coat.

"I made a phone call and was able to get last-minute tickets for the dinner theater," he said as he pulled out of the parking garage.

Julie nodded. "That sounds wonderful. Thank you. What's playing?"

"Never Too Late," he said, casting an amused glance at Julie.

"Seems appropriate," she said, returning his smile. She prayed it wasn't too late for them.

When his hand reached for hers, Julie felt a warm sensation radiate up her arm from his touch. It had always been like that. Daniel was capable of stirring emotions in her that she'd only dreamed existed.

Dinner was delicious and the comedy had both of them laughing. For those few hours, they managed to set aside their difficulties and were husband and wife without the past intruding.

"Would you like to go someplace for a drink?" Daniel asked on their way out of the dinner theater.

"We could if you like," she said. "But I think I'd prefer a cup of coffee in our own kitchen so I can prop up my feet. I shouldn't have worn these shoes."

"If you promise to wear a more sensible pair the next time I take you to dinner, then I'll give you a foot rub," Daniel admonished with a lazy smile.

"You're on." It felt good to joke with him. Tonight it had been so easy to pretend they were a loving husband and wife enjoying an evening out together.

Back at the condo, Julie made them cappuccinos, while Daniel put on a CD. Mellow music filled the space, a beautiful love ballad.

She carried the cups into the living room and sat on the opposite end of the sofa from Daniel. "Here." She swung her feet onto his lap. "Work your magic."

While she sipped from the cup of creamy coffee, Daniel gently massaged her feet.

"Why do you wear those silly things?" he asked. "You've got a blister on your heel."

"I know," Julie said, "but they're the only decent pair of dress shoes I have."

"Is that a hint for me to hand over my credit card?"

Julie swung her feet onto the floor. "No," she answered evenly. It was difficult to tell if he was teasing or not. She studied his face, but he hid his emotions well.

"A husband enjoys buying his wife gifts. You certainly had no difficulty accepting things from me in the past. You kept them, too, if the pearls are any indication."

"I kept every reminder of you I could," she whispered. She looked at the television and stiffened when she saw that the framed engagement photograph was missing.

"What happened to the picture?" She got to her feet. "I put it here this morning and now it's gone."

"I put it away," Daniel said.

"Away?" she echoed in disbelief. "What do you mean, *away?*"

Daniel stood up and moved to the opposite side of the living room. "It's in your bedroom."

"But why?" she asked, watching his reaction.

"Because I was angry and I took it out on the photo."

Julie went pale. "You…didn't destroy it, did you?"

"No, but I was tempted. I don't want reminders of that time in my life."

"I see," Julie said, trying to remain calm. She refused to give in to the tears. For a minute she thought he would explain further, but he just walked into his office and closed the door.

Julie was shaking so badly the cappuccino sloshed over the rim of her cup and into the saucer as she carried it to the kitchen. After rinsing everything in the sink, she returned to the living room and removed the other mementos she'd placed there. Those items, however small, meant a great deal to her. She couldn't bear to have Daniel reject them as he had the photograph.

That night, she woke from a fitful slumber around three. Just when it looked like she was making progress with Daniel, something would happen and she'd realize how far they still had to go.

She got out of bed and wandered to the kitchen for a glass of milk. She stood at the picture window, looking down on the silent, sleeping city below. She sensed more than heard Daniel coming up behind her. Julie remained where she was.

"You couldn't sleep?"

"No." The word tumbled from her mouth as tears filled her eyes.

His hand clasped her shoulder and he pressed his face into her hair. "Julie, I'm sorry about the picture. The minute I saw how much it meant to you, I regretted taking it down. To be honest, I wasn't sure why'd you put it out. I thought you wanted to torment me."

"Torment you?" She turned, her gaze seeking his in the moonlight.

He took the glass of milk from her, set it aside and brought her into the warm circle of his arms. His chin rested on her head as his hands roamed soothingly up and down her back.

It felt so right to be in his arms again, almost as if she'd never left.

With one finger under her chin, he lifted her mouth to his. Julie stood on tiptoe and fit her body to his, feeling Daniel resist momentarily as she melted against him.

"I'm sorry, Julie," he whispered against her lips.

"I know," she said, kissing him once more. Daniel moaned and hungrily kissed her back, holding her so close it was difficult to breathe.

"I won't make you cry again," he promised.

Julie sighed longingly and pressed her face to his shoulder. Nestled in the comfort of his embrace, she tried to stifle a yawn.

"Come on, sleepyhead," he whispered and kissed her temple. "I'll tuck you in."

Daniel led her back to the bedroom, his arm around her waist. Julie's heart was pounding as he helped her into the bed. He wanted her, Julie was sure of it. She was his wife and he longed to take her in his arms and love her as a husband should. Yet he kept his distance, his face revealing the conflict he felt.

"Good night," he whispered, finally turning away.

"Good night," she repeated, suppressing her own frustration.

Daniel lingered in the doorway and Julie leaned up on her elbows. "Daniel?"

"Yes?" He turned back eagerly.

"Thank you for tonight. I enjoyed the show."

"I did, too," he said softly. "We'll do it again soon. Next time I'll take you to Gatsby's."

"Really?"

"If you'd like, we could take up tennis again," he suggested.

"I would like that," she responded happily. "Very much."

"Tomorrow?"

"That would be lovely."

To his credit, Daniel did play a set of tennis with her the following morning. But he glanced repeatedly at his watch, distracted from their game. He beat her easily, but then it'd been a long time since Julie had played anyone who challenged her the way Daniel did. He seemed out of sorts by the time they finished. Julie couldn't understand his attitude. And she'd been hoping to meet more of his friends, but Daniel introduced her to no one.

"Half the morning's gone," he commented as they left the court. Again, he glanced at his watch impatiently. "I've got several things I need to do this afternoon."

Julie remained tight-lipped as they returned to the condo. Daniel had been the one to suggest the game, not her. Almost immediately, he closed himself in his office. When lunch was ready half an hour later, Julie entered to find him poring over papers and checking the internet. He barely noticed she was there.

"Would you prefer to eat in here or the kitchen?"

Daniel looked up. "Here," he said.

Julie brought in a tray with tomato soup and two grilled cheese sandwiches.

"Thanks," he muttered.

Julie ate silently while leafing through the Sunday paper. Later in the afternoon, she did the weekly shopping and ran a few other errands. On her way back home, she dropped by the hospital. Clara was being transferred out of intensive care the next morning and Julie promised to stop in for a visit the following evening on her way home from work.

After leaving the hospital, Julie picked up some hamburgers at a drive-thru for dinner. To her surprise, Daniel was still in his office when she returned. "You're still at it?" she asked as she entered the room.

He looked up and nodded. "This case is more involved than I thought."

"I brought you some dinner."

"Thanks," he said. "I could use a break. What've you made?"

Julie glanced at him guiltily. "Well, I didn't exactly cook..." She held up the paper take-out bag.

"Julie," Daniel groaned. "Sometime in the next twenty years, you're going to have to learn to cook."

That meant they'd still be together in twenty years, she mused contentedly.

Seven

"Married life doesn't seem to agree with you," Sherry commented as she watched Julie work.

"What do you mean?" Julie asked. Another week had passed and just when she thought the tension was lessening between her and Daniel, something would happen to set them back. They hardly spoke in the mornings—not even on their drive to work. In the evenings they visited his mother, came home and ate dinner. Immediately afterward, he'd hole himself up in his office, and sometimes Julie wondered if he forgot she was there. He treated her more like a roommate than a wife.

"Maybe I should keep my mouth shut," Sherry continued, "but you don't have the look of a happy bride."

Julie bit her lip as she opened a file and stared blankly at the pages inside. "I don't feel much like a bride."

"Why not?"

A tear traced its way down Julie's cheek. "Daniel's so busy right now. I hardly ever see him."

Sherry rolled her chair close to Julie's desk and handed her a tissue. "Believe me," she said sympathetically, "I know the feeling. That's how all of my problems with

Andy started. He worked such long hours that we didn't have time to be a couple anymore. He was so involved with his job that eventually we drifted apart. It reached the point where I'd be gone a week before he even knew I was missing."

Julie felt comforted to know she wasn't alone.

Ten minutes later, Mr. Barrett came out of his office. "I was wondering..." he started. "Would you two like to take an extra half hour for lunch today? It's been a hectic week."

Julie and Sherry exchanged surprised glances. "Thank you," Sherry said. "We'd love to."

The long lunch with Sherry proved to be just what Julie needed to raise her spirits.

"You know," Sherry said between bites of her chicken and cashew salad, "if I had it to do all over, I'd make it so Andy never wanted to leave the house again."

Julie stirred her clam chowder without much interest. Her appetite had been nonexistent lately. "What do you mean?"

"Think about it." Sherry leaned against the table, her eyes shining mischievously. "There are ways for a woman to keep her husband home at night."

Julie simply nodded, her thoughts spinning.

As the day progressed, Julie gave more thought to Daniel's actions. In the beginning he'd been bitter, but as the weeks progressed, his hostility was fading. He'd promised after taking down their engagement photo that he wouldn't hurt her again. And he hadn't. If anything, he was all the more gentle—and the other night, she'd found him holding the photo, studying their young, happy faces. Julie had held her breath, worried he'd look at the picture and remember the pain and embarrassment she'd caused. Instead his gaze had held an odd tenderness. She'd been puzzled when he then retreated into his office. If he'd forgiven her, if he loved her and wanted her, wouldn't he come to her? Julie was beginning to hate that guest bedroom. She didn't belong there; she was his wife, and she longed to fill that role completely.

In the weeks since their wedding, physical contact between them had been brief, but she'd seen the desire in his eyes. He wanted her. He spent the evenings avoiding her for fear of what would happen otherwise. His pride was punishing them both.

A smile touched Julie's lips as she recalled a pearly-white satin nightgown she'd recently admired in a department store window. Perhaps she should do as Sherry suggested and lure her husband to bed without involving pride or egos. The more she thought about it, the more confident she became.

That evening, Julie and Daniel drove to visit Mrs. Van Deen in the hospital.

"It's so good to see you," she murmured in a cheerful tone.

"Hi, Mom." Daniel kissed her cheek and held Julie close by his side.

"Julie, you're looking lovely. That color agrees with you."

Daniel looked at his wife as if seeing her for the first time that day. His eyes softened as he noted the way the pink dress accented her figure. "It certainly does," he agreed.

"How are you feeling?" Julie asked, still blushing from Daniel playing the role of the loving husband.

"Better," Clara said with a sigh. "The doctor said he'd never seen anyone make a swifter recovery. I told him I have something to live for now. My son has the wife he's always wanted and I'll soon have the grandchildren I've dreamed of."

Daniel's grip tightened around Julie's middle and she had to suck in a breath to keep from crying out. Her hand moved over his to silently let him know he was hurting her. Immediately, his grip slackened.

"My grandchild will have the bluest eyes," Clara continued, oblivious to the tension in the room. "My husband's eyes were blue. Deeper than the sea. I wish you'd known him, Julie. He would have loved you just as I do. He was a good man."

"I'm sure he was," Julie said.

"A lot like Daniel." Clara gestured toward her son.

Julie glanced up at him as Daniel's mother continued reminiscing about the late August Van Deen.

When Julie and Daniel returned home that evening, Julie breathed a long sigh.

"What was that about?" Daniel asked.

"It's nothing," Julie said. "I was just hoping that our lives will be as rich and rewarding as your parents' were."

Daniel smiled. "They did have a wonderful life together."

Daniel went to drop his briefcase in his office. It was nearly seven and they hadn't eaten dinner.

Julie put some noodles on to cook then headed for her room to change clothes, donning a pair of navy-blue cords and a thin sweater that clung to her curves. She refreshed her makeup and dabbed on Daniel's favorite perfume for good measure, then returned to finish preparing dinner.

Daniel looked surprised as he joined her in the kitchen. He studied her for a moment, noting the change in outfit.

"I didn't want to spill anything on my dress," Julie told him, hiding a smile.

He answered with a short nod, but couldn't seem to keep his eyes off her as she deftly moved around the tiny kitchen.

He didn't talk much during dinner, but that wasn't unusual. Perhaps Julie was reading too much into his actions. After so many years of living alone, he was probably used to keeping his thoughts to himself.

With seduction plots brewing in her head, every bite of her meal seemed to stick in her throat. After a few minutes, she stood and scraped half her dinner down the garbage disposal before placing her plate in the dishwasher.

"I thought I was doing dishes," Daniel said, looking up from the table.

"There aren't many," Julie said dismissively.

"Hey, we made a deal. When you cook, I wash the dishes," he said. "Now scoot."

Having been ousted from the kitchen, Julie sat to watch some TV, but her mind wasn't focused.

Daniel worked away in the kitchen, but Julie felt his eyes occasionally rest on her. A few times she'd glanced up and smiled at him.

"A penny for your thoughts," he said, handing her a hot cup of coffee.

Julie swallowed a laugh. "You wouldn't want to know," she teased. "You'd run in the opposite direction."

"That sounds interesting."

"I promise you it is."

Daniel surprised her by sitting in the wing-backed chair beside her. "Julie." He took the remote control and muted the television. "Can we talk a minute?"

"Sure." She turned toward him expectantly.

"I haven't been the best of company lately," he started.

"There's no need to apologize," Julie told him. "I understand."

"You do?"

"You must be exhausted. Heaven only knows when you sleep. You've been working yourself half to death this last month." Crossing her legs, Julie leaned back into the couch. "And then this evening your mother started talking about grandchildren and neither one of us has the courage to tell her we aren't sharing a bed." Nervously, she glanced down at the steaming coffee. It was on the tip of her tongue to admit how much she wanted that to change, how much she longed to be with him and start a family together.

"Julie, listen."

Just then, the phone rang, distracting them both.

"Hold that thought," Julie said, reaching for the receiver. Whoever it was, she'd get rid of him in a hurry. For the first time, Julie felt like they were making strides in their marriage. "Hello," she answered.

There was silence on the other end.

"Hello?" Julie repeated.

"Who's this?" a husky female voice replied.

"Julie Van Deen," she answered. "Who's this?"

"So it's true," the woman said, clearly shocked.

"Who am I speaking to?" Julie asked, already certain it had to be the woman Jim Patterson had mentioned at the club the other day. Julie had bitten back many questions about her, but now they were resurfacing.

"Kali Morgan," the woman answered.

A chill raced up Julie's spine. "Would you like to talk to Daniel?"

Kali paused. "No. Just…just give him my best…to you both."

"Thank you," Julie murmured. Confused, she hung up the phone.

Daniel was looking at her expectantly. "Who was it?"

"An old friend of yours," she said weakly.

"Who?"

"Someone who clearly didn't know you had a wife."

"Kali." The word was a statement, not a question.

"You didn't tell her about us, did you?"

Daniel stood, putting some distance between them. His voice was unsure, worried. "What did Kali say?"

Julie searched his expression. The man who stared back had become a stranger. Daniel didn't seem to find it necessary to tell Kali that he got married. Maybe he believed that he'd go back to his old life eventually, keep his options open in case his mother didn't survive. He could quickly annul their marriage. Or maybe he was just looking for ways to hurt her as she'd hurt him. If so, he'd succeeded.

Daniel took a slow step toward her. "Julie, please don't look at me like that."

She felt her chest tighten as she got up and moved down the hall to her room. The bag containing the nightgown she'd bought rested on her bed. She stared at it in disbelief. Only minutes before she'd intended to seduce her husband.

Daniel appeared in the doorway. "Julie, be reasonable. Surely, you didn't think I've lived the last few years like a priest."

Everything went incredibly still. "For three years, my heart grieved for you until I couldn't take it anymore... and I came back because...because facing your bitterness was easier than trying to forget you."

"Julie." His voice took on a soft, pleading quality. He paused as if desperately searching for the right words.

"Kali and I had been dating for several months," he explained. "But that's in the past. I haven't touched her since the day I saw you in the elevator."

"Touched her," Julie repeated shakily. "Is that supposed to reassure me? You haven't touched me either!" She felt her stomach heave and she rushed into the bathroom.

Daniel followed her. Julie stood in front of the sink and pressed a cool rag to her face.

"What did you expect me to do?" he shouted. "You walked out on me!"

Julie turned sharply to face him. "You didn't tell her we were married!" She hiccuped on a sob. "And…and all these years I've loved you."

"Don't tell me there hasn't been anyone in—"

"No," she shouted. "I seldom dated. You were the only man I ever loved. The only man I ever could love." She wept into the washcloth.

"Julie." He moved to stand behind her, a hand on each shoulder.

"Don't touch me," she commanded and shrugged her upper torso to shake him off. "Your tastes have changed, haven't they, Daniel? You must find me incredibly stupid to think you still care."

She started to leave but he pulled her into his arms. "You're going to listen to me, Julie. Perhaps for the first time since we met, we're going to have an honest discussion."

Julie was in no mood to be reasonable. "No," she cried, pushing past him to get back to her room. Grabbing the package from her bed, she shoved it in his arms. "Here. Once I'm gone, you can give this to one of your other women." With that she slammed the bedroom door.

* * *

Sherry was at her desk when Julie got to work the following day.

"Morning," Julie greeted her, doing her best to disguise her misery. She knew she looked terrible. Makeup had been unable to camouflage the effects of her sleepless night. For the first time since getting married, Daniel had left for work without Julie.

"Morning," Sherry replied without looking up. It was obvious she'd been crying again.

"Did something happen?" Julie pried.

Wiping her face with the back of her hand, Sherry sat up and sniffled. "After our talk yesterday, I got to thinking about how much I miss Andy...so I saw him last night."

"Was he with another woman again?"

"No, this time he was with me," Sherry said. "I...I told him I wasn't positive I wanted the divorce and that I thought we should talk things over more thoroughly before we take such a serious step."

"I think that's wise." Julie recognized how difficult it must have been for Sherry to contact her husband and suggest that they meet. She and Daniel weren't the only ones with an overabundance of pride.

"We sat and talked for ages and, well, Andy ended up spending the night." Sherry continued, her fingers nervously toying with a tissue. "Then this morning when I woke up, Andy was gone. No note. Nothing. He regrets everything—I know he does. I feel so cheap and used and..." She paused and blew into the tissue.

"Sherry." Julie moved to gently pat her on the back. Julie definitely felt her friend's pain. Like a pair of idealistic fools, they'd hoped everything would work out because they loved their husbands. "I'm sure there's a perfectly logical explanation for why Andy left." Julie tried to sound optimistic.

"I feel like a one-night stand."

"But you are married," Julie said.

"Yes, but not for very much longer."

"Things have a way of working out for the best," Julie assured her, hoping it was true.

Sherry attempted a smile. "How did everything go for you?"

"Fine," Julie lied but, at Sherry's narrowed look, amended, "Terrible."

The office door opened and Julie and Sherry lowered their heads, pretending to be absorbed in their work. Mr. Barrett passed through the room with his usual morning greeting.

"He must think we've gone off the deep end," Sherry whispered once he was in his office with the door closed.

"Maybe we have."

They worked companionably, taking turns answering the phone. When she had a free moment, Sherry placed her purse on the desk and took out her makeup case. "Count your blessings, Julie. You're much too levelheaded to do some of the dumb things I've done."

"Maybe you should reach out to him?" Julie suggested.

"I couldn't...not after what happened."

"I'm sure he'd be willing to talk, especially after last night," Julie insisted.

"I wish that was true," Sherry said. "But somehow, I doubt it."

Daniel was already in his office when Julie got home that evening. At their usual visit, Clara had mentioned that her son had been by earlier. Her mother-in-law had noticeably studied the dark shadows under Julie's eyes, but didn't comment. Julie was grateful. Answering Clara's questions would have been her undoing.

Hanging up her jacket in the closet, Julie headed for the kitchen. A package of veal cutlets rested on the countertop. Julie sighed as she reached for the frying pan.

"I thought it was my turn to cook," Daniel said from behind her.

"All right," she muttered. "But I'm not very hungry. In fact, I think I'll lie down for a while."

He took so long to answer that Julie feared another confrontation.

"Okay," he said at last. "I'll call you when dinner's ready."

"Fine." They were treating each other like strangers.

Julie moved into the room and sat dejectedly on the side of her mattress. A month into their marriage and she was little more than an unwelcome guest in Daniel's life. She leaned back and closed her eyes.

It seemed only minutes later when Daniel knocked lightly against the open door. "Dinner's ready."

Julie toyed with the idea of telling him she wasn't feeling well. But Daniel would easily see through that excuse. It was better to face him. Things couldn't possibly get much worse.

The table was already set when Julie pulled out a chair to join Daniel.

"Your mother looked better tonight," she said.

Daniel deposited a spoonful of wild rice on his plate before answering. "She asked about you. I didn't know if you'd be stopping in to see her or not."

"I did," she told him.

"So I surmised."

Five minutes passed and neither spoke. Julie looked out the window and noted the thick gray clouds rolling in.

Daniel noticed them, too. "It looks like rain."

Julie nodded. Another awkward silence filled the kitchen until Julie stood and started to load the dishwasher.

"I'll do that," Daniel volunteered.

"It's my turn."

"You're beat."

"No more than you," Julie countered, stubbornly filling the sink with hot tap water.

The dishes took all of ten minutes. The hum of the dishwasher followed her into the hallway. The thought of spending another night in front of the television was intolerable. But going out was equally unappealing. Daniel had disappeared inside his office and Julie doubted she'd be seeing him again that evening, which was just as well.

Deciding to read, she returned to her room. Once she was settled on her bed, a flash of satin caught her attention. Setting her book aside, she discovered that the nightgown she'd shoved at Daniel was hanging in her closet. She ran her fingers over the silky smoothness, suddenly feeling emotional. She'd so wanted things to be different.

"Julie," Daniel called through the closed door. "Are you all right?"

"I'm wonderful," she said sarcastically. "Just leave me alone."

For a moment, nothing happened. Then the door was shoved open.

Julie gasped as Daniel marched into her room and hoisted her in his arms.

"Put me down," she cried.

"You're my wife, Julie Van Deen. And I'm tired of these games." He marched down the hallway to his bedroom and slammed the door closed with his foot.

Eight

"You didn't even tell Kali you were married!" she shouted.

"I couldn't," he shouted right back. "She was in England on a business trip."

Julie's anger died a swift and sudden death. She went completely still.

"I don't know what's going on in that head of yours," Daniel continued. "For heaven's sake—we're married. What's Kali got to do with us now?"

"Nothing," Julie whispered, laughing softly. "Nothing at all."

"What's so amusing?" he barked. He sank onto the edge of his bed, his hold on her loosening as she rested in his lap.

"You wouldn't understand," she murmured, linking her arms around his neck. "I thought you were planning… Never mind." Gently, she kissed him.

"Julie," he breathed, his arms tightening around her.

"Are you really tired of playing games?" she asked, teasing him with a series of short, playful kisses along his jaw.

"Yes," he said, gripping the back of her head and directing her lips to his. "Oh, yes."

His hands began undoing the tiny buttons of her blouse. Frustrated with the small pearl-shaped fastenings, he abandoned the effort and broke the kiss long enough to try to pull the blouse over her head.

Winded, Julie stopped him. "We've waited a whole month. Another thirty seconds shouldn't matter."

As she freed her blouse, Daniel softly cupped her breasts and buried his face in the hollow of her throat. "I couldn't live another month like that," he told her. "I couldn't sleep knowing you were just down the hall. Every time I closed my eyes, all I could see was you."

"I've wanted you so badly," she said, sliding her hands up and down his shoulders.

Hungrily, he kissed her again. "You're my wife, Julie, the way you were always meant to be."

"Wake up, sleepyhead," Daniel whispered lovingly in her ear. "It's morning."

"Already?" Julie groaned, resting her head in the crook of his arm. Her eyes refused to open.

"How are you this morning?" Daniel asked, kissing the crown of her head.

"Very happy." Julie smiled.

"Me, too. I never stopped loving you, Julie. I tried. Believe me, I tried every way I could to forget you. For a time I convinced myself I hated you. But the day I saw you in the elevator, I knew I'd been fooling myself. One look and I realized I'd never love another woman the way I love you."

Raising her head, Julie rolled onto her stomach and kissed him.

The hunger of his response surprised her. Quickly, he

spun them sideways so that Julie was on her back, looking up at him.

"Daniel," she protested lightly. "We'll be late for work."

"Yes, we will," he agreed. "Very late."

An hour later, while Julie dressed, Daniel cooked breakfast, humming as he worked.

"You're in a good mood this morning," she teased, sliding her arms around his middle.

Daniel chuckled. "And with good reason." He pulled her into his arms, kissing her soundly. "I love you."

She smiled. "I know."

"I think it's time we took that diamond ring hanging around your neck and put it on your finger, where it belongs," he said. He helped her remove the chain and slid the solitaire diamond onto her finger with a solemnness that told her how seriously he took his vows. "I wanted you the minute the minister pronounced us husband and wife," he admitted sheepishly. "I had to get out of the house that day because I knew what would happen if I stayed."

"And I thought—"

"I know what you thought," he said. "It was exactly what I needed you to believe. My ego had suffered enough for one day. I couldn't tolerate it if you knew how badly I wanted you."

The workdays flew by and after a wonderful weekend together, Julie and Daniel spent a quiet Sunday with his mother at the hospital. Clara Van Deen's heart surgery was scheduled for the following Tuesday and both Julie and Daniel wanted to spend as much time with her as possible.

"Have you told Julie about her surprise yet?" Clara

asked as Daniel wheeled his mother into the sunny hospital courtyard.

"Surprise?" Julie's face lit up. "What surprise?"

"Oh, dear." Mrs. Van Deen glanced over her shoulder at her son. "I didn't let the cat out of the bag, did I?"

Leaning forward, Daniel kissed his mother's cheek. "Only a little," he whispered reassuringly. "I was waiting until later."

"Later?" Julie spoke again. "What's happening later? Daniel, you know how much I hate secrets."

"This one you'll enjoy," he promised. He laughed at her puzzled expression and slid a hand around her waist. "I won't make you wait any longer than this afternoon," he said. The mischievous look in his eyes was enough to make her feel light-headed.

After an hour in the fresh air, Clara Van Deen announced that it was time for her to go back inside.

Daniel stood and started to wheel her inside. "We shouldn't have kept you out so long."

"Nonsense," Clara protested. "I've been wanting to feel the sun for days."

Within half an hour Clara was fast asleep. Standing on opposite sides of the hospital bed with the railing raised, Daniel whispered, "Are you ready for your surprise now?"

Julie nodded eagerly. Now that she thought about it, he had been acting suspicious. Several times he'd looked as if he wanted to tell her something, but then stopped himself.

Holding hands, they strolled out to the parking lot. Daniel opened the car door for her and stole a lingering kiss when no one was looking.

"Are you going to give me any hints?" Julie asked excitedly.

"Not a one," he teased. "You'll just have to be patient."

Daniel took the freeway that led past the densely populated suburbs and out of town. Finally, he exited, turning down a winding road in the countryside.

"For heaven's sake, Daniel, where are you taking me? Timbuktu?"

He chuckled. "Wait and see."

Julie felt so lucky to be with him. Finally. Everything was so perfect. So right.

When he pulled the car into the long driveway of a newly built two-story house, Julie was awestruck.

"What do you think?" he asked, one brow raised inquisitively.

"What do I think?" she repeated. "You mean this... house...is my surprise?"

"We're signing the final papers on Monday morning. There are several things you'll have to decide. The builder needs to know what color you want for the kitchen counters, and you need to pick the design of the tile for the bathrooms. From what I understand, there are several swatches of carpet for you to look at while we're here."

Julie nodded, not knowing what to say. She couldn't understand why Daniel wanted a place so far from the city. It would mean a long daily drive both ways in heavy traffic. Julie loved the city. Daniel knew that.

"Come inside and I'll give you the grand tour." He climbed out of the car, walked around to her side and extended his hand. "You're going to love this place."

Julie wasn't convinced. Why would he pick out something as important as a house without consulting her? Daniel took out the key and opened the front door, pushing it aside so she could enter before him. At first, she was overwhelmed by the magnificence of the home. The sunken living room contained a massive floor-to-ceiling brick fireplace. The crystal chandelier in the formal dining room looked like something out of a Hollywood movie. No expense had been spared. But the kitchen was compact and the only real eating space was in the formal dining room. It also didn't appear to have a family room.

"What do you think?" Daniel asked eagerly.

"Nice." Julie couldn't think of anything else to say. It was a beautiful home, that she couldn't deny, but it wasn't something she would have chosen. In many ways, it was exactly what she wouldn't want.

"The swimming pool is this way." He led her through the sliding glass doors off the kitchen to a deck. A kidney-shaped pool was just beyond. Although the cement structure was empty, Julie could picture aqua-blue water gently lapping against the tiled side.

"Nice," she repeated when he glanced expectantly toward her.

"If you think this is impressive, wait until you see the master bedroom." Daniel took her hand and pulled her through the hallway.

The room was so large that Julie blinked twice. Fireplace, walk-in closets, soaker tub in the private bath. It was perfect. Just not for Julie.

"What about the other bedrooms?" she asked.

"Upstairs."

Like a robot Julie followed him up the open stairway. The first bedroom they came to was a decent size and had a bath. The second room was smaller. Julie assumed it would be Daniel's office. The third room looked as if it could be an art room with huge glass windows that overlooked the front of the house.

Julie made the appropriate comments, but felt as if she was being suffocated. She didn't know how much more of this she could take. Abruptly, she turned and walked down the stairs.

"Julie." Daniel followed her out the front door. "What's the matter?"

Shaking her head, Julie tried to control what she was feeling. That Daniel would look for and buy a house without consulting her felt all too familiar—and not in a good way. She wasn't a naive young girl anymore. His mother had picked out their first home as a wedding present without consulting Julie. And now Daniel was doing the same.

"You don't like it, do you?" A hint of challenge was evident in his voice.

"That's not it," she admitted. She was angry with Daniel, but equally upset with herself. Most women would love a home like this. Unfortunately, she wasn't one of them.

"All right," Daniel breathed, scrutinizing her. "What don't you like? I'm sure whatever it is can be changed."

"Changed?" she flared back. "Can you change the location? I love Wichita. I want to live in the city. I thought you did, too. What suddenly made the country so appealing?"

"Peace, solitude—"

"What about the hour's commute in traffic every day?"

"I'll get used to it," he said, attempting to reason.

She crossed her arms. "Sure you will."

Frustrated, he mirrored her closed off pose. "Is there anything else?"

Julie swallowed hard. "Three years ago I didn't say anything when your mother bought us a house. I let everything build up inside until it exploded and I fled. I can't do that anymore. This is a beautiful house, but it's not for us. Someday I'd like to have children. This isn't a family home. It's for a retired couple, or a family with teenagers."

Daniel frowned; his forehead was lined with disappointment.

"I...I appreciate what you're trying to do, but—"

"Be honest, Julie. You don't appreciate anything about this." He held the car door open for her and shut it once she was inside.

She waited until he was in the driver's seat. "Daniel." His name rushed out in a low breath. "I'm sorry I seem so ungrateful. But something as important as a home should be chosen by both of us. I realize you were saving this as a surprise and I'm sorry if I ruined that."

Either he didn't hear her or he chose to ignore her. The tires squealed as he pulled out of the driveway and onto the road.

On the drive home, Julie sat in miserable silence. Moving into that house feeling the way she did wouldn't have been right. She'd come too far to allow something like this to happen a second time.

When they arrived back at the condo, Daniel went directly into his office to make a series of phone calls while Julie tried to understand what had motivated him. Only that afternoon, Julie had doubted that anything could destroy their utopia. Now she saw how fleeting their happiness was.

Julie was cooking dinner when Daniel joined her. She kept her back to him, needlessly turning the slices of beef every few seconds. "I wish you hadn't closed yourself off in your office," she began. "I thought we were beyond that. It's important that we talk this out."

He didn't answer.

She turned to find him sitting at the table, reading the newspaper. "Are you giving me the silent treatment?"

He lowered the page. "No."

"Then let's talk," she continued, but his attention had returned to the paper. "If...if that house means so much to you then I'll adjust." Making a concession like this was one of the most difficult things Julie had ever done. But her marriage was worth more than her pride.

Apparently engrossed in his paper, Daniel didn't speak for several long minutes. "You're right. I should have consulted you first."

"Then why are you so angry?" she asked.

He set the paper aside. "I don't know," he admitted honestly. "When you left, my mother claimed you were ungrateful for everything we'd done for you. I'm beginning to understand what she meant. I bought that house for you, Julie, and for our life together."

"What a horrible thing to drag up now. You're being completely unfair."

"Was it fair when you walked out on me three years ago? Don't talk to me about fair."

Julie couldn't believe what she was hearing. Clearly unconcerned about the damage he was causing, Daniel raised the newspaper and continued reading.

A full minute passed before Julie could move. She turned off the stove and walked out of the kitchen.

Daniel claimed to have forgiven her, but he hadn't. Not in his heart.

"Julie." He followed her into the living room. "I didn't mean that."

"I doubt that," she said. "I believe you meant every word."

"Maybe I did," he said.

The next thing Julie heard was the front door closing softly.

* * *

Julie left early the following morning, not waiting for Daniel. She was already at her desk when Sherry arrived.

"You're so punctual," Sherry commented as she sat in her rollback chair and stowed her purse in the bottom drawer.

"I try to be," Julie said, not looking up from her paperwork.

"I'm going to run down and grab a maple bar for breakfast. Do you want one?"

"Sure," Julie agreed rather than explain why she wasn't hungry. She was handing over enough money to cover it when the office door opened.

Standing on the other side was Daniel. A muscle twitched in his jaw as he glared at Julie. She could see his anger and the effort he made to control it.

Sherry looked from one to the other. "If you'll excuse me, I'll run downstairs."

Julie smiled a silent thank-you. Sherry winked and edged her way past Daniel.

"Don't do that to me again," he commanded.

"I needed some time alone," Julie explained. "I thought you'd understand... You felt the same way yesterday."

"That was different," he snapped.

"If you can disappear until the wee hours of the morning then I have a right to leave for work unannounced."

The phone rang and she swiveled around to answer it, presenting Daniel with a clear view of her back. Halfway through the call, she sensed he'd left and the tension in her shoulders relaxed.

Sherry returned by the time Julie was off the phone. Julie could tell she was full of questions, but Julie didn't feel up to explaining and thankfully, Sherry seemed to pick up on that fact.

"You have tomorrow off, don't you?" Sherry asked, changing the subject.

Julie had nearly forgotten. "Yes. Daniel's mother is going in for heart surgery."

With Daniel under so much stress, he didn't need a war between them. Tonight, she'd insist they put an end to this.

The day dragged by but her visit with Clara that evening went well. Although Julie stopped by immediately after work, she learned that Daniel had already come and gone and they'd only missed each other by a matter of minutes.

Julie stayed for a longer visit than usual. They chatted together, and talked about gardening, which Clara enjoyed. The nurse arrived and gave the older woman a shot to help her relax. Julie waited until she was confident Clara was sleeping comfortably.

Daniel wasn't home when she came through the front door. Julie felt as if she were carrying the weight of the world on her shoulders. Briefly, she wondered if he'd gone to Kali. No. He wouldn't. She couldn't believe he'd do something like that.

She forced herself to cook dinner, but had no appetite and only picked at the cutlet and salad. After washing her dishes, she turned on the television. Every five minutes, her eyes drifted to the wall clock. Where was Daniel? His mother was having major heart surgery in the morning. This was a time when they needed each other more than ever. Julie turned off the television and went to bed.

Shadows flickered against the dark bedroom walls as Julie lay staring at the ceiling. The front door clicked softly and Julie sat upright. A quick look at the clock confirmed it was after midnight.

Daniel paused in the open doorway of their room. He loosened his tie as his eyes locked with hers. He took off his coat and carelessly tossed it over the back of a chair. The space between them seemed impossibly wide.

Frantically, her mind searched for the right words. She should have been rehearsing what to say.

She reached out to him and for one heart-stopping moment, thought he might reject her. She watched as he stiffened, hesitant. With a low groan he crossed the room and fell into her arms.

"I'm sorry," she whispered. "Oh, Daniel, I'm so sorry. We need each other now more than ever. Let's forget the house." She hugged him tightly, wanting to laugh away the hurt they'd each foolishly inflicted.

"Julie," he said in a husky voice. The anger was gone. He buried his face in her neck and inhaled deeply. "I need you."

"Yes," she breathed, weaving her hands through his hair. "I love you." She drew his mouth to hers.

An hour later, her head lay nestled against the cushion of his chest, and Julie lovingly ran her fingers over his bare skin. "We can't settle all our arguments this way."

Daniel chuckled and ran his hand down the length of her spine. "I think it has its advantages."

"I feel terrible about our fight. The way I handled everything was wrong. You wanted to surprise me and—"

"No." He gave her a squeeze. "You were right. Anything as important as a house should be a mutual decision. When I got over being angry, I saw how unreasonable I'd been."

"It reminded me too much of what had happened before." She shrugged, unsure of dragging the past into this moment. "Do you really want to live in the country?"

The pause was long enough that she raised her head. "Not if you don't," he answered.

"My home is with you." She snuggled closer to his warm body. She could still sense that something was troubling Daniel, something more than his mother's pending surgery. Whatever it was had to do with their marriage. Julie didn't know what, but she had a feeling she would soon.

Nine

Daniel paced the waiting room as Julie sat in a vinyl-cushioned chair, attempting to read. Repeatedly, her concentration wandered from the magazine to her wristwatch.

"What time is it?" Daniel inquired with a worried frown.

What he was really asking, Julie knew, was how much longer it would be. The doctor had informed them the surgery would take at least five hours—possibly longer.

"I'm sure it'll be anytime now," Julie said. They'd been in the waiting room most of the day. A nurse came at noon and suggested they break for lunch, but Julie couldn't have forced anything down and apparently Daniel felt the same way.

Her husband took the seat beside her and reached for her hand. "Have I told you how much I love you?"

Before Julie could answer, the doctor, clad in a green surgical gown, walked into the room. His brow was moist and he looked as exhausted as she felt.

Julie and Daniel stood, Daniel holding on to her hand with such force that her diamond cut into her fingers.

"Your mother did amazingly well," the doctor announced. "Her chances at a full recovery are excellent."

Julie smiled brightly at her husband as relief washed over her.

"Can we see her?" Daniel asked.

Julie knew him well enough to know that he wanted visual confirmation of his mother's condition.

"Yes, but only for a few minutes. You can both go in. She'll be in intensive care for a few days, then, if everything goes well, she'll be moved to a room on the surgical floor."

Julie appreciated the support the doctors and staff had given throughout this whole ordeal.

"Thank you, Doctor." Julie stepped forward to shake his hand. "Thank you very much."

Julie and Daniel were led into the intensive care area. When Julie saw Clara, her appearance came as a shock. She was deathly pale and surrounded by tubes and machines.

"How are you feeling?" Daniel leaned forward to hug her.

"I'm fine," she assured him. She tried to lift one hand, but it was taped to a board to hold the IV in place.

Daniel laid his hand over his mother's and gave it a squeeze.

"I'm afraid I'm going to have to ask you to leave," a nurse requested a few minutes later. "You're welcome to come back tomorrow, but for now, Mrs. Van Deen needs to rest."

Julie thanked the nurse and they said their goodbyes, promising to return the next day.

The air outside the hospital smelled fresh and clean. Julie paused to take several deep breaths before getting in the car.

She was exhausted. With her head resting against the back of the seat, she closed her eyes as Daniel drove them home.

"Julie." A voice spoke softly in her ear. "Wake up."

She yawned and opened her eyes. "I didn't realize I was so tired."

"We didn't get much sleep last night," he reminded her. "And the way I feel right now, we may not tonight, either."

Daniel led her directly into the bedroom and pulled back the covers. "I want you to take a nice long nap and when you're rested, my mother has ordered us to have a night on the town."

"A night on the town?" She didn't think she'd have the energy.

"Mom and I had a long talk yesterday and she feels that we deserve a night out."

Julie opened her mouth to protest.

"No arguing," Daniel said sternly. "She insisted."

Daniel tucked her in and kissed her lightly on the forehead.

"Aren't you going to rest?" Julie asked.

"Honey, if I crawl in that bed with you, it won't be to sleep." He laughed and brushed the hair from her temple. "Actually, I've got some work to do. That should take an hour or two. Just enough time for you to catch up on some sleep."

Julie relaxed against the fluffy pillow and pulled the blanket over her shoulder. Her mind drifted easily into happy, serene thoughts as sleep overcame her.

The next thing Julie knew, Daniel was beside her, holding her close.

"Is it time to get ready for dinner?" she muttered, reveling in the warmth of the bed.

"I think breakfast is more in order."

"Breakfast?" She sat up. "I couldn't have slept through the night." She looked around, confused.

"I could have paraded a marching band through here yesterday evening and you wouldn't have budged."

Julie leaned back against the oak headboard. "I can't believe I slept like that. I was dead to the world for fifteen hours or more."

"I imagine you're starved."

Strangely, she didn't feel hungry, but once she ate some breakfast, she realized how famished she'd actually been.

"I'm sorry I ruined your night," she said, swallowing the last of her toast.

Daniel looked up from his plate and smiled. He reached over to trace the delicate line of her jaw. "You didn't ruin anything," he said. "Do you know how incredibly beautiful you are when you're sleeping? I could have watched you for hours. In fact I kinda did."

Somewhat embarrassed, Julie shook her head.

"I lay awake last night, and I realized I'm the luckiest man in the world."

"Yesterday was a good day to think that. Your mother survived the surgery, and we've been given a second chance."

"Yes, we have," Daniel agreed, his mouth seeking hers.

"What did you and Daniel decide on regarding this house business?" Sherry asked later that week over lunch.

Julie shrugged, setting aside her turkey sandwich. "It's on hold. We've more or less decided to wait until we have a reason to move."

"Do you want to start a family right away?"

"Yes." And no. Things weren't perfect. The incident with the house had proven that. Daniel loved her, but Julie was convinced he didn't completely trust her. It was almost as if he was waiting for her to pack her bags and walk out on him again. Julie realized that only time would persuade him otherwise. She wanted a secure marriage before they had children.

After lunch, the two women returned to work. The phone was ringing when they entered the office.

"I'll get it," Sherry volunteered, reaching for the receiver.

Julie didn't pay much attention to the ensuing conversation until Sherry laughed and handed the phone to her. "It's for you. Personal."

"Daniel?"

"Nope. Jim Patterson."

Julie hadn't encountered Jim since the day of the tennis match. "Hello, Jim," she greeted him, curious as to why he'd be contacting her.

"Julie. Sorry to call you at the office, but I didn't want Daniel to answer and I didn't have your cell number."

"It's no problem. What can I do for you?"

"The Country Club has voted Daniel Man of the Year. We'd like to keep it a secret until the big night so don't let on that you know."

"I won't breathe a word," she promised. "Daniel will be so pleased."

"Each year we do a skit that tells the life story of the recipient. You know, *This Is Your Life* type of thing. Of course we tend to ham it up a bit."

Julie giggled, imagining the types of jokes they must come up with.

"I was wondering if you and I could get together and go over some of the details of Daniel's life. I'd ask his mother, but apparently she's in the hospital."

"I'd be happy to do that," Julie said.

They agreed on a time and Julie was beaming with pride when she hung up the phone.

Daniel turned up at her office at quitting time. Usually, she walked down the one flight of stairs to his suite and waited for him. But she was running behind, having stayed late to sign final escrow papers with a young couple. Julie was still with the Daleys when Daniel walked through the door.

Julie smiled at her husband and gestured for him to take a seat. "I'll be done in a minute," she told him.

"I didn't realize it was so late," Mrs. Daley said, glancing up from her wristwatch. "We've got to pick up our son from day care. Is there much else to sign?"

Julie scanned the documents. "No, you're both free to go as soon as you hand over the certified check."

"I've got that here." Mr. Daley reached into his jacket pocket.

Once everything was settled, Mr. Daley shook Julie's hand and thanked her again for her help. This was the best part of her job. The Daleys were buying their first home—a dream they'd saved toward for years.

After they were gone, Julie quickly sorted through the remaining paperwork.

"Why couldn't Sherry have stayed?" Daniel asked stiffly.

"Because I volunteered," she answered on the tail end of a yawn. She lightly shook her head from side to side. "I don't know what's the matter with me lately. I've been so tired."

Daniel set his briefcase down and claimed the chair recently vacated by Mr. Daley. "I don't understand why you continue to work. There's no need. I make a decent living."

"I'd be bored if I didn't work." Julie immediately shelved the idea, surprised he'd even suggest it.

"You might have time to learn how to cook."

"Are you complaining about my meals?" she joked, knowing he had every right to. As long as she stuck to the basics, she was fine, but their menu was limited to only a handful of dishes and Daniel wasn't too fond of the lack of variety.

"I'm not actually complaining," he began, treading carefully. "But I want you to give some serious thought to quitting your job. I don't like you having to work so hard."

"It's not hard," she protested. "Besides, I enjoy it. Sherry and I make a great team."

"Whatever you want." Daniel clearly wasn't pleased and Julie couldn't understand why.

Only a week after surgery, Clara Van Deen was sitting up in bed looking healthier than Julie could remember since returning to Wichita.

"I can't tell you how grateful I'll be to go home," she said. "Everyone's been wonderful here. I can't complain, but I do so miss my garden."

"And your garden misses you," Julie said with a wink to her husband.

"That's right." Daniel shook his head. "Weeds up to my knees."

Clara grimaced. "I can't bear to think what weeks of neglect have done to my precious yard."

Unable to continue the game any longer, Julie patted her mother-in-law's hand reassuringly. "Your garden looks lovely. Now, don't you fret."

"Thanks to Julie," Daniel inserted. "She spent a good

portion of the weekend in that garden on her hands and knees."

"I should have been thinking of ways to keep my husband's mouth shut," Julie said with a sigh. "It was supposed to be a surprise."

Clara looked touched. "Did you really?"

"She has the blisters to prove it," Daniel said.

Clara smiled her thanks. "Say, Julie, isn't today the day you were meeting with—"

"No," Julie interjected before her mother-in-law could say anything more. After Jim had contacted her about Daniel's award, Julie had shared the good news with Clara. Apparently, she'd forgotten it was supposed to be a surprise.

"What's this about Julie meeting someone?" Daniel asked.

"Nothing," Julie replied.

"It's a surprise," Clara explained. "I nearly let the cat out of the bag the second time. Forgive me, Julie."

"There's nothing to forgive."

"Will someone tell me what's going on?"

"My lips are sealed," Julie teased.

"Mine, too." Clara shared a conspiratorial wink with her daughter-in-law.

"At least let me know whom you're meeting with," Daniel pleaded as they walked to the car.

"Never."

"I could torture it out of you," he whispered seductively.

"I'll look forward to that." She slid an arm around his waist and smiled up at him. He looked so handsome that she couldn't resist stealing a kiss.

"What was that for?"

"Because I love you."

A brief look of doubt passed over his features. One so fleeting that Julie was almost sure she'd imagined it. But she hadn't. After everything that had transpired between them, her husband didn't fully believe she loved him. Time, she told herself, he only needed time. As the years passed, he'd learn.

On the ride home, Julie thought about how they'd traveled this same route so many times over the past six weeks that sights along the way began to blend into one another.

She sat upright. "Daniel?"

"Hmm?"

"Take a right here," she directed.

"Why?"

"There's a house on the corner that's for sale." They must have passed the place a thousand times. Julie had noted the Realtor's sign, but hadn't given it a second thought. Now something about the house reached out to her.

Daniel made a sharp right-hand turn and eased to a stop in front of the two-story Colonial home. The paint was peeling from the white exterior and several of the green shutters were hanging by a single hinge. "Julie," he groaned, "it doesn't even look like anyone lives there."

Julie glanced around and noticed the other homes in the neighborhood. They looked well maintained. "All this place needs is a bit of tender loving care."

"It's the neighborhood eyesore," Daniel said impatiently.

"I'd like to see the inside. Can we contact the Realtor?" Already she was writing down the phone number.

"Julie, you can't be serious."

"But I am."

That evening they met the Realtor, Ryan Derek. "I'm

afraid this place has been vacant for several months," he told them.

"What did I tell you?" Daniel whispered in her ear. "This isn't what we're looking for—"

"No," Julie interrupted as she climbed out of the car. "But I still like it. I like it very much."

"Julie," Daniel moaned as he joined her on the cracked walkway that led to the neglected house.

Ryan Derek hesitated and Julie sensed that his opinion of the place was similar to Daniel's.

"Can we go inside?" Julie asked.

"Yes, of course."

The moment Julie walked through the door she knew. "Daniel," she breathed, her hand reaching for her husband. "This is it. This is the house."

"But, Julie, you haven't even looked around."

"I don't need to. I can feel it."

The entryway was small and led to an open staircase with a mahogany banister that rounded at the top of the steps. To her right was a huge living room and to her left, a smaller room that would make a great library or office. Dust covered everything and a musty smell permeated the house. The hardwood floors were dented and badly in need of repair.

The formal dining room had built-in china cabinets and a window seat. The kitchen was huge with a large eating area. The main level had two bedrooms and the upstairs held three more. The full basement had plenty of room for storage.

"It doesn't have a family room," Daniel commented after their tour. "That's something you insisted on with the other house."

"This house doesn't need one," Julie insisted. She hoped

that Daniel could see the potential of this house. "It's perfect. Right down to the fenced backyard, patio and tree house."

"Perhaps you'd see a few more houses before you decide," Ryan interjected.

Julie shook her head. "That won't be necessary."

She understood Daniel's doubts. This house would require some expensive repairs, but the asking price was reasonable.

"I feel you should be aware of several things." Ryan Derek's voice seemed to fade into the background as Julie moved from one room to the next, imagining how she would decorate. Two bedrooms downstairs were ideal. She could use one as a sewing area. The only problem she could foresee was having the washer and dryer in the basement. But the back porch was large enough to move the appliances out there. Of course, that would require some minor remodeling.

"Julie." Daniel caught up to her. "I think we should go home and think this over before we make our final decision."

"What's there to decide? If we don't go for it now, someone else will."

"That's not likely, Mrs. Van Deen," Ryan interrupted. "This place has been on the market for six months."

On the drive back to the Realtor's office it was all Julie could do to keep her mouth shut. Before she and Daniel climbed into their own car, Daniel and Ryan Derek scheduled another time for them to look at other houses.

"Why'd you do that?" she demanded when Daniel climbed into the driver's seat.

"Do what?"

"Set up another appointment."

"To look at houses—"

"But I've found the one I want," she declared. "Daniel, I love that house. We could look for another ten years and we wouldn't find anything more perfect."

"That house would be a nightmare. The repair costs alone would be more than the value. The roof needs to be replaced. There's dry rot in the basement."

"I don't care," Julie stated emphatically.

"I'm not going to fight with you about it. If we're going to buy a house then it has to be one we both agree on."

Julie had no argument. That house was everything Julie wanted. Hot tears blurred her vision. Something was definitely off with her lately. She couldn't believe she'd cry over something as silly as a house.

With Mrs. Batten's help, Julie ensured that Clara Van Deen's house was spotless the day she arrived home from the hospital.

The smile on her mother-in-law's face was reward enough for the long hours Julie'd spent caring for her much-loved garden.

Mrs. Batten cooked a dinner of roast, potatoes and fresh strawberry shortcake, which had long been a family favorite.

"Is everything all right with you, dear?" Clara asked as they sat on the patio together in the late-afternoon sun.

The question surprised Julie. "Of course. What could possibly be wrong?"

Clara took a sip of tea. "I'm not sure, but you haven't been yourself the last couple of weeks. Has the house hunt got you down?"

"Not really." Julie straightened in the wrought-iron

chair. "Daniel and I have more or less agreed to wait. There's no rush."

"But there was one house you liked?"

"We agreed to disagree." Julie changed the subject as quickly as possible. "Have you noticed how pink the camellias are?"

Deep in thought, Clara didn't answer. Daniel's expression was similar when he arrived at the condo an hour later.

Julie could tell something was wrong. "Is everything all right?"

"I thought we agreed not to take our disagreements to my mother."

Julie immediately understood. Clara had spoken to Daniel about the house. "We did," she admitted stiffly.

"My mother had a talk with me earlier."

"I know what it sounds like," Julie cut in, "but please believe me when I tell you that I only mentioned it. I tried to change the subject."

Julie watched as her husband's mouth thinned with impatience.

"I think I should have a talk with your mother," she continued. "She's going to have to learn that although we love her dearly, she can't get involved in our lives to the point where she takes sides on an issue. Okay?"

"Definitely."

Julie crossed the room, her arms cradling her middle protectively. They were walking on thin ice. Each desperately wished to maintain the fragile balance of their relationship.

Daniel cleared his throat and moved to stand behind her. "I can see that this house issue could grow into a major problem."

Julie shook her head. "I won't let it. It doesn't matter where we live, as long as we're together."

He gathered her in his arms. "I've been giving that house considerable thought."

"And?"

"I think we should be able to come up with a compromise."

"A compromise?"

"Yes." He pulled away slightly, his hands still linked at the small of her back. "We can buy that house if you agree to quit your job."

Ten

"Quit my job?" Julie repeated incredulously. "You've got to be joking."

"That house is going to need extensive remodeling. Someone has to be there to supervise the work."

"It isn't remodeling the house needs, it's repairs, most of which will have to be done before we move in." Julie walked to the far side of the room. "The house isn't the real reason you want me to quit—is it?"

"I want you to be my wife."

"And I'm not now?" she responded. "I enjoy my job. The problem is, you think I'm going to walk out on you again. It's almost as if you're waiting for it to happen."

"That's ridiculous."

"Is it?" she asked. "First you wanted a house that just happened to be an hour out of town. And now you want me to quit. Are you trying to close me off from the rest of the world?"

"I saw you with Jim Patterson last week," Daniel blurted out. "Will you tell me why you two found it necessary to have lunch together?"

"I can't," Julie replied defensively. "But I'm asking you

Debbie Macomber

to trust me. Surely, you don't believe Jim and I are involved in any way?"

"I've tried. A hundred times I've told myself that you must love me. You wouldn't have come back if you didn't."

"Of course I love you," she cried. "What makes you think I would even look at another man?"

Daniel lowered his gaze. "Sometimes I hate myself." The admission came with a bitter laugh.

"You don't trust me."

His expression confirmed her suspicions.

"I love you so much. I could never leave you," she said. "What will it take to convince you of that?"

Daniel couldn't meet her eyes. "I don't know. When I first saw you with Jim, I felt sick inside, then angry. Even though I'd heard you joke with my mother about some mystery meeting, I couldn't believe I'd see my wife and a good friend together. For two days I worried I'd wake up and find you gone."

"You actually thought I'd run away with Jim Patterson?"

"Why not? You ran away from me before."

"I haven't even thought about anyone else since I moved to Wichita."

"Why won't you tell me why you met him?" Daniel asked.

"I need you to trust me."

"I'm trying. Heaven knows I want to, but I don't know if I can."

"You don't look as if you slept at all last night," Sherry said when Julie walked into work the following morning.

"I didn't."

"Why not?"

When they'd gone to bed the night before, Daniel had

stayed on his side of the mattress. He could have been on the other side of the world for all the warmth they shared.

"It's a long story," Julie answered. She got herself settled at her desk. "What would you say if I told you Daniel wants me to quit my job?"

"Does he?"

"Let's make this a hypothetical question." Julie wondered if, without knowing the background of her relationship with Daniel, Sherry would read the same meaning into his actions.

"Well, first he wanted to move to the boondocks," Sherry said thoughtfully, rolling her chair the short distance between their two desks. "And now he wants you home all day. My guess is that he's insecure about something. But I can't imagine why. It's obvious how much you love him."

"I wish Daniel realized that."

"You're not going to quit, are you? You've helped me so much with Andy. I'd really miss your friendship."

"No, I'm not quitting." Julie refused to give in to Daniel's insecurities. "Enough about my problems. How *is* everything between you and Andy?"

Sherry lowered her gaze. "Who would have thought wooing my husband would be so difficult?"

The phone rang and Sherry looked up. Suddenly pale, she motioned for Julie to answer as she rushed into the bathroom. Not for the first time in the past couple of weeks, Julie suspected her friend was pregnant.

Julie was off the phone by the time Sherry returned. "Are you going to tell me or are you going to make me ask?"

"How'd you know?"

"Never mind that. Does Andy know?"

She began to cry. "No." She sniffed. "If we do get back together, I want it to be because he loves me. Not because of the baby."

"The divorce proceedings were halted, weren't they?"

Sherry nodded. "But only because Andy and I felt we needed time to think things through. We're not living together."

"You won't be able to keep this secret for long," Julie advised.

"I know. That's why I've given him three weeks to decide what he wants. If I'm going to lose him, then I'd prefer to face that now and be done with it."

"How does Andy feel about having an ultimatum?"

Sherry looked ashamed. "Andy doesn't know."

"Oh, Sherry," Julie groaned.

A tear slid down her friend's cheek. "I realize that sounds crazy, but I firmly believe I'm doing the right thing. If Andy found out about the baby and we reconciled then I'd never be sure. This way I can be sure that Andy really loves me and wants to make this marriage work."

The phone rang again and the pair were quickly thrown into their work.

That night, Julie taught herself to cook Daniel's favorite dinner.

"Did I miss something?" he teased, smelling the air as he entered the kitchen.

"Miss something?"

"It's not my birthday, is it? I've got it! You overdrew the checking account. Right?"

"Just because I made Stroganoff doesn't mean I'm up to something," Julie said.

"In my short experience as a husband, my immediate reaction is…you are!"

"Well, you're wrong. I've taken all your complaints to heart and bought a cookbook. I can't have my husband fainting away from lack of proper nourishment."

"Would you like me to demonstrate how weak I am?" he asked, slipping his hands under her shirt.

"Daniel, not now."

"Why not?" he moaned against her neck.

"Dinner will burn."

"That's never bothered you before."

"I thought you were hungry."

"I am. Come to bed and I'll show you how hungry I am."

Julie switched off the stove and fell into her husband's arms, relishing in the urgency of his kiss.

Dusk had settled over the city as they lay in bed an hour later. Daniel's hand caressed her bare shoulder. "I'll be happy when you're pregnant," he whispered.

"Why?" Julie asked.

"I thought you wanted a family."

"I do." But not before they were more secure in their marriage.

"Then why ask?"

"I want to know why you want a baby." Her greatest fear was that Daniel would see a child as a means of binding her to him.

"For all the reasons a man usually wants to be a father." He tossed aside the blankets and sat on the edge of the mattress. "And as I recall, we agreed that when you were pregnant, you'd quit your job."

Julie reached for her robe at the foot of the bed. She didn't know why he'd start an argument after they'd just made love. "I think you should know I've made an appointment with the doctor."

Daniel eyed her carefully. "So you think you might be pregnant."

"No," Julie said. "I want to make darn sure that doesn't happen."

As the days passed, Daniel threw himself into his work and Julie did her best to give the outward appearance that everything was fine. With Daniel not around much, Julie spent more and more of her free time with her mother-in-law.

The two women worked at getting Clara's beloved yard into shape. Julie tried to disguise her unhappiness, but she was convinced that her mother-in-law knew something wasn't right.

"I was pleased to see that old engagement photo of you and Daniel on the television," Clara remarked, working the border of the flower bed. Clara had recently visited the condo for the first time since Julie had moved in.

"We both look so young," Julie said.

"It's strange to remember you like that."

Julie got the impression Clara wasn't referring to looks. "We've all changed."

"Something's bothering Daniel," Clara commented, studying her daughter-in-law closely.

"Oh?"

"I saw him briefly the other day and was shocked by how worn-out he looked."

"He's been working a lot of extra hours lately."

"Is that necessary?"

"I...I don't know." Julie moved on to the next section of the flower bed.

"You look a bit weary yourself," Clara continued. "Is everything all right with you two?"

Settling back on her heels, Julie sighed. "Clara, Daniel and I agreed—"

"I know. Daniel told me. But I can't help worrying. You love each other and yet you seem miserable. Whatever the problem is, it can't be worth all this torment. Believe me, I know how stubborn my son can be. Just be patient with him."

"I'm trying," Julie whispered.

Back at the condo, Julie soaked in a warm bubble bath. She had no idea where Daniel was. Although it was Saturday, he'd left early that morning, before she was awake.

Julie had hoped the bath would raise her spirits. She'd been so tired lately. It was ridiculous. It seemed she was going to bed earlier and earlier and often had trouble getting up in the morning. Her appointment with the doctor was coming up; she'd mention it to him. It was probably a reaction to all the stress. She'd had enough of that to last a lifetime.

Abruptly, Julie sat up in the tub, causing water to slosh over the sides. It seemed so clear. She was pregnant. So much had been happening that she'd completely lost track of time. Julie leaned back and placed a hand on her flat stomach. Daniel would be pleased, and despite her misgivings, Julie was, too. Tears flooded her eyes. She cried so easily these days and now she understood why.

Julie climbed out of the tub and wrapped a towel around her body.

Sitting on top of their bed, she reached for the phone and dialed Daniel's cell. The phone rang twice before she hung up. What would she say?

Julie dialed a different number and waited several long rings. "Sherry," she said. "Congratulate me—we're both pregnant." With that she burst into sobs.

Eleven

"Here," Sherry said, handing Julie another tissue. "You're going to need this."

Julie glanced at the tissue, then back at her friend. "I'm through crying. It was a shock, that's all." Sherry had rushed over to the condo as soon as she'd hung up the phone.

"Discovering I was pregnant was a shock for me, too," Sherry said. "At first I was ecstatic, then I had so many doubts."

"A baby is exactly what Daniel wants."

"But for all the wrong reasons," Sherry assumed. "If Andy knew about me, I suspect he'd be thrilled. But again, for all the wrong reasons."

Julie nodded, feeling slightly ill. She hadn't eaten since breakfast, but the thought of food nauseated her.

"What did Daniel say?"

Julie winced. "He doesn't know yet."

"What are you going to do?"

"I don't know." Julie sighed. "He has to be told, but I don't know when. He's…hardly around these days."

"So he's pulling that trick again," Sherry huffed.

"He's working himself to death."

"That's what I thought about Andy. You aren't going to sit here and sulk. I won't let you."

"I'm not sulking."

"No, you're crying." She gave Julie another tissue. "Come on, I'm taking you out."

"Sherry, honestly, I appreciate your efforts, but the last thing in the world I want is to be seen in public looking like this."

Sherry giggled. "I'm going to let you in on one of life's important secrets."

"And what's that?" Julie asked.

"When the going gets tough, the tough go shopping."

"Sherry," Julie groaned. "I don't feel up to anything like—"

"Trust me, you'll feel a hundred percent better. And afterward, I'll treat you to dinner."

"But Daniel—"

"Did he bother to tell you he wouldn't be home for dinner the past three nights?"

"No."

"Then it's time you quit moping around and do something positive for yourself."

Julie realized her friend was right. "All right," Julie agreed, "I'll go."

It took the better part of an hour to make herself presentable, but Sherry was right, she felt better. Before they left, Julie wrote Daniel a short note, telling him her plans.

Sherry seemed intent on having a good time. First they hit the outlet mall, scouting out baby items and trying on maternity clothes.

Next they took in a movie, followed by dinner at an Italian restaurant. On the way home, Sherry insisted they stop off at her house so Julie could see the baby blanket she was knitting.

"I think I'd better call Daniel," Julie said, sipping a cup of tea. The evening had passed so quickly. Already it was after eleven and although she'd left a note, he might be worried.

"Don't," Sherry chastised. "He hasn't called you lately, has he?"

"No," Julie admitted. They were like strangers who just happened to live together.

"I think I'll put on some music." Sherry reached for the stereo's remote.

The next thing Julie knew, she was lying on the sofa, wrapped in a thick comforter. Struggling to sit upright, she glanced at the clock. How was it light out?

"I was wondering what time you'd wake up," Sherry called from the kitchen. "How do you want your eggs?"

Julie was incredulous. "It's morning?"

"Right, and almost ten. You were tired, my friend."

"But…"

"I turned on the radio and within minutes you were fast asleep."

"Oh, no." Untangling the comforter from around her legs, she reached for her cell. "I'd better call Daniel."

As Julie dialed, Sherry handed her a small glass of milk and two soda crackers. Julie smiled her appreciation. Her stomach was queasy as it had been for several mornings. Julie had attributed it to nerves.

Several rings later, she hung up.

"No answer?" Sherry asked.

"No." Julie shrugged. "Maybe he was in the shower."

"Maybe," Sherry echoed. "Try again in five minutes."

"At least he knows I'm with you. If he was worried he would have called."

Sherry turned back to the stove. "He didn't know."

"I left a note."

"I stuck it in my pocket before we left. I'm sorry. I didn't know you were going to fall asleep. I thought if Daniel worried a little, it would be good for him."

"Oh, Sherry."

"It was a stupid thing to do. Are you mad?"

Julie shook her head. Sherry had no way of knowing that she'd walked out on Daniel once before or that he was worried she'd do it again.

"No," Julie said. "He doesn't appear to be concerned at any rate." For all she knew, he could've come home late, crawled into bed and not even noticed she was missing.

Fifteen minutes later, Julie was back home. The condo was dark so she walked across the living room to open the drapes.

"Julie?"

She swiveled around to find Daniel sitting on the edge of the chair, leaning forward, his elbows braced against his knees.

"Hello, Daniel." He looked as though he hadn't slept.

He stood, jamming his hands into his pockets. "I suppose you came back for your things."

"No." Somehow she managed to let the lone word escape. His clothes were badly wrinkled and his hair was askew. The dark stubble on his face was so unlike the neatly groomed man she'd lived with all these months.

"Well go ahead and get them," he said. "Don't let me stop you."

"You want me to leave?" she asked, her voice shaking in disbelief.

"I won't stop you."

"I see." Not knowing what to say, Julie took a step toward the hallway.

Daniel jerked his head up as she moved. His face was deathly pale.

"Julie," he called out.

She turned back expectantly. Tears filled her eyes and she wiped them aside with the back of her hand.

"I don't blame you for walking out on me," he spoke at last. "I drove you to it. I pushed you out of my life the first time and blamed you for it. I can't do that again." He took a tentative step toward her. "I lived for three long years without you and I won't go back to that. Julie—please—don't leave me. Let me make up for all the unhappiness I've caused you."

Julie flew into his arms and Daniel buried his face into her hair, taking in deep breaths as he refused to let her go.

"It doesn't matter why you saw Jim or any other man. I was a fool to think everything would be solved by having you quit your job."

"Daniel, listen—"

"Moving into the country was just as ridiculous," he interrupted. "I love you, Julie. You're the most important person in my life."

"Would you please listen for one minute? I'm not leaving and never was. I was with Sherry. And as for my job, I plan to work for another six months or so and then I'll think about quitting."

"Why six months?"

"Because by then the baby—"

"The baby?" Daniel repeated, completely stunned. "Julie, are you telling me you're pregnant? How? When?"

Julie laughed and lovingly ran her hand along his jaw. "You don't honestly need an answer to that, do you?"

"No," he said sheepishly. "All these weeks I'd hoped you would be. I wanted a child to bind you to me. I realize how wrong that was. You've always been with me."

When his mouth sought hers, Julie responded enthusiastically.

The doorbell chimed and Daniel glared at it irritably. "I'll get rid of them," he promised, kissing the corner of her mouth.

He opened the door to find a man Julie didn't recognize. "I'm looking for Julie Van Deen," the man said.

Julie looked at Daniel and shrugged. "That's me," she said, joining them in the front hall.

"Excuse me for intruding on you like this," the man continued. "I'm Andy Adams. Sherry's husband."

"Of course." Julie smiled. "I've heard a lot about you."

"Yes." He cleared his throat. "I'm sure you have. Sherry has mentioned you on several occasions, as well."

"Please come in. Can I get you something to drink?"

"No, thanks. If you don't mind, I'd like to ask you a few questions." He stepped inside, closing the door behind him.

"Is this about Sherry?" Julie didn't want to get caught in the middle of her friend's marital problems. That could get messy.

"Yes, it is," Andy said. "I hope that's okay."

"I know that she's decided to stop seeing you and—"

"But why?" he asked. "I don't understand. I love my wife. I always have. It wasn't me who wanted that stupid divorce. Sherry seemed to need space and I figured the best thing I could do was give it to her."

"But then you decided to taste a little of that freedom yourself," Julie supplied.

"It was all a game. I knew Sherry was going to be there that night. By that point, I was desperate. I thought a taste of her own medicine would help."

"It did," Julie confirmed, recalling her friend's reaction.

"A little too well," Andy admitted. "We were to the point of moving back in together when—whammo—Sherry announces it's over and she doesn't want to see me again."

"I thought you were the one who—"

"No," he said forcefully. "It's true I thought we should take things slow. I wanted Sherry to be sure of her feelings."

"Andy, I want you to think about something. When you and Sherry separated, she went off her birth control pills. Does that mean anything to you?"

Silence hung between them. "I'm going to be a father?"

Julie nodded happily.

"I'm going to be a father," he repeated as a smile lit up his face. "Why didn't she tell me?"

"I think that's something you're going to have to ask Sherry."

"I will."

"Good." Julie felt relieved.

"Thank you, thank you." Andy shook her hand then Daniel's. "I've got to talk to Sherry. I can't thank you enough." He opened the door and left, nearly tripping in his rush.

"I know exactly how he feels," Daniel said, taking his wife in his arms. "Like a fool who's been given a second chance at happiness. Believe me, this time I'm not going to blow it."

"We're home," Julie announced as her mother-in-law rocked her three-month-old son. Daniel had bought the house of her dreams and made extensive repairs. Most of the work they'd done together during Julie's pregnancy.

Clara had spent the evening with little Ted while Julie and Daniel attended a banquet at the Country Club.

"Was Jim surprised to be Man of the Year?" Clara asked, passing the baby to Julie.

"No more than I was last year," Daniel answered with a chuckle. "But then last year was a very good year."

"It was indeed." Clara smiled. "I was given a new lease on life."

"So was I." Daniel slipped an arm around his wife and leaned over to kiss his sleeping son.

"Was he good?" Julie asked.

"Not a peep. He's so sweet. So small. Theodore August Van Deen seems such a big name for such a tiny baby."

"He'll grow," Daniel said confidently. "And be joined by several more if his mother agrees."

"Oh, I'm in full agreement."

The baby let out a small cry.

"It isn't feeding time, is it?" Clara looked to Julie.

"Not yet," Julie assured her. "Don't worry, Grandma. Babies sometimes cry for no reason."

"Teddy-boy, Grandma's joy." Clara took the baby from Julie and placed him over her shoulder. Gently, she patted his tiny back.

Daniel wrapped Julie in his arms. "I love you, Julie Van Deen."

"And I love you," Julie said. She lifted her face to kiss him, perfectly happy to finally have the family she'd always hoped for.

* * * * *